THE TREASURE OF SOLOMON

THE
TREASURE
OF
SOLOMON

David Britton Peel

This Edition: 2021

ISBN: 978-1-7359491-7-8

Design and Typesetting by Great Writing Publications
www.greatwriting.org
Taylors, SC, USA

Dedication

To my Bride, Tricia;
God blessed me with the love of my life.

To my beloved children,
You are each a gift from God;
Britton, Collin & Megan;
L.U.P.O.U.

Arlington, Tennessee, July 2021

The Treasure of Solomon is a unique combination of *Raiders of the Lost Ark* and *The Da Vinci Code* with a delicious mix of hometown Memphis flavor—Bellevue, Blues, and BBQ. David Peel takes the reader on a journey around the world with God at his hero's side to find the treasure. Faced with insurmountable odds, will Sam Cohen prevail against the forces of evil bent on stealing the Ark of the Covenant from the world? Open up and find out. Perfect for believer and non-believer alike, this book is a must-have for Christians and non-Christians, and a perfect gift to share the gospel.
John Rountree, Strategist and Business Executive

The Treasure of Solomon moves at a great pace, while at the same time, through crack research, injects fascinating information on the world's most sought-after archeological treasure. Author David Peel also adroitly develops real and compelling characters that you cannot help pulling for. . . and against. At the same time, he adds the "Chef's kiss" of well-placed humor and comic relief. It is a timeless tale told through a fresh and modern lens. This terrific first novel causes me to eagerly await what Sam Cohen will search for next.
Bill Walk, Jr.,. Author of *Holes in the Soles of his Gucci Loafers*

Acknowledgments

This story is very important to me. It has grabbed me and never set me loose. But, a novel does not just happen. In 2008, these ideas took root. By 2010, a jealous injury law practice and a busy church and family life had pushed this to the back burner. (Well, really, somewhere behind the stove.)

In 2017, the light of day again reached the disjointed manuscript. I had completed my first non-fiction book, and I knew what kind of help I required to see it through.

I sought a talented editor to help me bring it all together, and everyone said I needed Jim Holmes. In Jim, I have found a brother, friend, and encourager, one who has patiently challenged, prompted, improved, and enhanced this story.

I am deeply indebted to Jim for his expertise and finesse in helping my first attempt at fiction be better than it could have ever been otherwise.

My staff are my friends. Few people can say that, let alone many attorneys. But Elena and Alice are some of my favorite people in the world. Together, with God's grace, we have been able to change many lives for the better. They have supported me at every step.

Our many friends from Bellevue and Love Worth Finding Ministries have been there for us through thick and thin, and life would be barren without their love and support.

Sam Cohen is on top of the world as the star of the unexpectedly successful Archaeology Channel, and the next ancient artifact he has tracked down and is unveiling, live on TV, promises to eclipse all others in all of human history.

However, Sam and his bodyguard, Kishor, are unaware that the priceless value of the find is known to Brisbane and his high-tech band of mercenaries. And, they now know the secret location of the fabled "Treasure of Solomon" sought for years by the Muslims, the Jews, and the American Christians. And they intend to take the sacred Lost Ark of the Covenant, all while the world watches, live.

-Prologue-

The American flag snapped crisply in the stiff breeze, as the four wary Marines gathered outside the chain link fence. With one of them watching circumspectly, the other three peered through the heavily tinted rear and side windows of the silver Audi that had been parked suspiciously overnight just outside the U.S. Embassy.

As the morning sun gleamed off the chrome trim, the blast's sudden concussion lifted the rear of the sedan up, as if a colossal spring had been released. Shards of glass, scraps of lead, shiny ball bearings, and galvanized nails tore through the clouds of pink mist that, only moments earlier, had been a squad of brave leathernecks.

Car alarms erupted into life along the street, headlights strobing wildly as the volcanic roar rolled through the quiet diplomatic district like an earthquake. The blast echoed down the empty streets.

Two additional squads of Marines promptly set a perimeter and secured the enormous iron gate. After the bungle of Benghazi,

Libya, back in 2012, American diplomatic security had been almost tripled on all subsequent anniversaries of 9/11.

Swedish fire engines and police responded in force, immediately closing down the district. Garbage trucks and dump trucks that had been on call, full of sand, were hastily positioned in front of each of the Western embassies, to help localize and dull the force of any additional explosions.

Earpieces crackled. Among the diplomatic institutions, some evacuation orders were given, while others were told to shelter in place. Outside, pandemonium ensued.

* * *

Just northeast of the Diplomatic District, an old Saab pulled up the secluded dead-end road, Kaknäsvägen 78, that ended at a secure back cyclone-fenced gate. Behind that gate lay a towering series of large white petroleum tanks of various sizes overseen by Petrolia Suisse. Each set of four-to-six was in a triangular pattern, with eighty-nine tanks in total. The long rows of the sets had been arranged years ago for ease of transport and maintenance between each set of tanks. No thought had been given back then to the advantage this gave an attacker.

Ahmad Al Rashadon, an aging, bearded Middle Eastern mercenary who hated all things Western, opened the trunk of the faded blue Saab, revealing that the rear seats had been removed. A large olive-green wooden box was partially removed and unshackled by his strong, dark hands—hands that moved skillfully and purposefully. He heard the echoing roar from the Embassy area and could see smoke rising in that direction.

The long box had white spray-painted letters that had faded over time. The barely legible imprint, in Russian, translated as "High Explosive—Armor-Piercing." Patiently, he pried the box open, revealing three rocket propelled grenades launchers (RPGs) packed in tan straw. As a former member of the elite Iraqi Republican Guard, these were familiar to him as they were the same kind he had used against coalition forces years ago in Operation Desert Storm.

While Sweden had only operated a battlefield hospital for the coalition, they had still sided with the crusading Americans in murdering most of his unit. He justified his embarrassing surrender to the coalition only with the solemnly sworn knowledge that he would spend the rest of his days carrying out revenge attacks against the American Infidels and their cohorts.

The largest fuel tank nearby was freshly painted white, and stood gleaming in the morning sun, like a sentinel. He comfortably aimed his dark, cold right eye at the top 10 percent, where the explosive vapors gather.

The RPG spat its deadly rocket with a whoosh of fire, wind, and smoke. Dust flew for twenty feet behind him as the missile blasted away in a gentle arc. Seconds later, a gushing explosion rocked the ground. Almost as soon as the initial fireball rose, a series of sirens and warning buzzers echoed. Yellow flashing lights lit up along each fence.

Just as expected, the panicked workers quickly closed inflow valves to Tank Set 1, and diverted their contents of the nearby tanks to the next set up the line, to Set 2, dramatically increasing their pressure.

The fireball and smoke obscured his location exactly as he had anticipated. He calmly reflected that, with proper planning, battles could be won without even breaking a sweat.

After waiting exactly four minutes, the second RPG was aimed over the initial tank, which was by now belching black smoke. He set it at a seventy-degree trajectory that would create a parabolic arc. This was to drop it in the large second triangular set of tanks, just as they were under maximum pressure. If it worked as intended, it would begin a chain reaction.

The rocket, however, missed, and only served to rupture a raised pipeline between two tanks and ignite an employee who had been running away.

The third and final rocket was aimed in a flatter trajectory in an effort to hit the more distant third set of tanks. It fell short, but it hit the very top of last tank in the second set.

As the tip impacted the heavy-gauge steel, the rocket acted exactly as the others had done. The tip's impact ignited high explosives that opened a hole in the metal. A millisecond later, a second set of explosives in the rear of the rocket fired, squeezing the copper core and instantly turning it to a molten state. Then the liquified, lava-like copper shot through the damaged first layer of the double-hulled tank and pierced it like a hot knife through butter.

Initially, he was disappointed that there were no further immediate explosions as he had hoped.

But then there was a hissing sound. It grew in intensity until he was sure a jet engine was nearby. The unmistakable sound of ignition roared. Then a series of fireballs began.

It was the chain reaction.

Ahmad turned and ran toward the nearby water as the heat at once scorched and blew the faded blue paint from the car. Both front tires caught fire and then popped. Ahmad swam to the boat waiting for him just offshore.

* * *

Every emergency vehicle in the city that had not already been assigned to locking down the diplomatic district made its way east to the Apocalyptic sight on the Eastern waterfront. Mushroom-shaped clouds and black boiling smoke were visible for miles. It looked to many as if there had been a series of nuclear explosions.

At that very moment, three men stood outside the just-opened Swedish National Museum, a building with open water on two sides.

They gazed toward the smoke in the distance.

One had the characteristics of an Eastern European and was wearing an olive surplus coat with military boots. He had a diamond stud in his left ear and he wore small, round sunglasses. He was fidgeting with his earring as he scanned the scene.

Next to him stood a large man with a square chin and an impressive dark moustache, who bore a striking resemblance to a young Tom Selleck. A well-worn brown leather bomber jacket hung off his broad shoulders. His stylish jeans, his Ray-Bans, and his custom ostrich-skin boots gave him the appearance of someone at a Texas barbecue rather than a Swedish museum visitor.

Tall and thinner, the third man ran his right hand through his intensely blond hair, sweeping it back. It was so blond it seemed almost as white, like an albino's hair. Dressed all in black, with black leather boots with silver accents, he checked his black chronograph and spoke in an Australian accent: "Ready, mates?"

* * *

They entered the museum, and the first man produced an Uzi 9mm submachine gun from his olive drab coat. He fired it wildly, spraying several bursts across the ceiling, the brass shells tinkling as they bounced, and as the members of the tour groups fell to the floor screaming.

The second man leveled a sawed-off double barrel shotgun at the two stunned guards. Squeezing each trigger, he simply blew them away, one after the other.

The third of the thieves was much smoother, and very deliberate in his manner. He went upstairs and selected the self-portrait by Rembrandt as well as two paintings by Renoir—*Conversation with the Gardener* and *Young Parisian*. They were smaller and the albino-like mastermind expertly cut them from their frames with a razorblade.

As the calm thief rolled up the three paintings and placed them into a tube he wore strapped across his back under his coat, he looked toward the nearest tour group.

In the obviously American tour group, he observed that one of the younger girls was clumsily trying to video the robbery from her prone position. He produced a pearl-handled, stainless steel 45 pistol, and executed each member of the small tour group with shots applied with deadly accuracy to their heads.

After they quickly excited the museum, they clambered into to a motorboat waiting nearby acting as their getaway vehicle.

The local news anchors would breathlessly report that terrorists had attacked the U.S. Embassy, killing four Marines, and blown up much of the petrol storage facility, initially killing nearly three dozen victims. Five Swedish firefighters died in explosions following or from smoke inhalation, they would say. The environmental damage would be mentioned, but always with the admission that the human lives lost were more tragic.

It was only much later that the brazen daylight robbery would even make the news at all. It would be stated that the stolen art was worth somewhere between $30-36 million. "The rare Rembrandt dated to 1630, 146 years earlier than the American Revolution began," they would explain. However, experts were also quick to report that the stolen paintings would be far too distinctive to be re-sold. When the stories of the cold-blooded executions began to leak out, despite authorities' best efforts to contact relatives first, viewers began to see a relationship between the events.

Later, the shaky cell phone video would be leaked. News-types would wring their hands about the newsworthiness of the shaky footage, versus the cold-blooded carnage it revealed; nevertheless, it was circulating on YouTube not many minutes later.

The tearful cries of terrified young American girls could be heard over the shaky video—cries of the "man with the white hair" as he would become known. The footage showed him cutting a painting out of the frame and rolling it up. The image jiggled slightly, and then a thumb apparently covered the lens for a moment. The image then changed to portrait format and showed a close-up view of black leather boots, with silver tips. The loud shots sounded like pops—more like fireworks than lethal head shots. An adult female chaperone could be seen being executed, as was a crying girl she had been clutching. And then, with a last pop, the phone was cast spinning across the floor. He had saved for last the girl who was videoing him. The now-still video simply showed a beautiful, ornate ceiling.

Shortly after the paintings disappeared, the museum received a ransom note for $3 million. No arrests were made for actual involvement in the heist. Two lawyers who had tried to act as middle men with the ransom demand were arrested. They were expected to be charged with conspiracy, attempted extortion, aggravated robbery, and multiple counts of murder, but both men died in jail under suspicious circumstances before they could even be interviewed.

Later, the body of one Boris Cyrek, still in an olive military surplus coat, was found floating in the sea near the port where the getaway boat was eventually located. The injury to his forehead was a hole, determined to have been from a .45 caliber bullet, in his left temple.

The white-haired man and his accomplice were never identified or apprehended.

-1-

"Thanks Mom. Yes, I am going on just a minute," Sam Cohen spoke in hushed tones into his cell phone. He stared into the celebrity mirror, surrounded by light bulbs, and observed his reflection, one revealing his rather Grecian appearance: a well-tanned skin, dark, closely cropped wavy hair, dark brown eyes behind rich lashes, and a tall, lean frame.

"Son, I am so proud of you. Your father would have been so proud today. . .so proud to see this." Sounds of sniffling slightly interrupted her voice. "I just wish he could be here," the elderly Mrs. Cohen managed over the line.

"I know. . .I wish he could see this, too," Sam confided, blinking back a tear. "They are coming in the green room now, so I have to go. . .I love you."

* * *

"Okay, Dr. Cohen," began Rebecca, the earnest young staff member, "Tamara is very glad that you are here, and will honor your request not to bring up what happened to your father. Is there anything else, sir?" the fashionable hostess inquired.

"Uh, no, uh thank you," Sam responded.

"You are on in thirty seconds, sir," she informed him.

As the applause signs went dark, the famous TV talk show host now known only as "Tamara" turned to Camera A. "Thank you for joining us on the Tamara Show on my new network! Today, we have the guy we all like to dig—or watch him dig anyway," she gushed. "He's so cute!" The audience roared and whistles sounded out. "No, really, he's my new fave. . .talented, cute and so very smart. Help me welcome A-Channel's new superstar, Sam Cohen!"

Amid fanfare that clearly embarrassed Sam, he strode out and gave Tamara the customary embrace and double kiss.

"Welcome to my new show on my own newest network. So, how are you?" the hostess inquired.

"I'm good. And I'm more than a little blown away by your great audience." The fans erupted once more.

"Now, your show on the Archaeology Channel—what we in the business call the 'A-Channel'—is the surprise hit of the year," Tamara continued. "Did you see all this coming?"

"Not at all," Sam confided. "I never thought that a channel devoted to live archaeological digs would be so successful. After all, even for me as an archeologist, the dig is actually the most boring part. Figuring out *where* to dig, there is excitement in that."

"Well, I have seen your show, and I and some of my producers are big fans," Tamara explained. "Sometimes I have seen you reading old scrolls, or trying to piece together old maps."

"Yeah, that was the stuff I dreamed of doing when I was a kid," Cohen mentioned, looking a little self-conscious. "But the actual excavation itself is usually just very hot and time-consuming."

"Always hot, huh?" Tamara laughed.

"Ancient civilizations had no regard for the temperatures we would endure while studying them," Sam quipped to the sound of polite laughter. "But it's not just the heat. It is always so hard to arrange permission to excavate with the local authorities, many of which want bribes—what we refer to as 'blessings.' You have to 'bless' the army, the fire department, the local inspector, and the equivalent of their local council men or whatever they call the leaders of their particular tribal factions."

"And all while you are stuck in whatever corner of a God-forsaken desert, right?" Tamara stated, smiling widely. Her TV manner was an engaging one, and it was no wonder that her audience hung on to her every word. "Now, you became famous by finding the actual remains of the biblical cities of Sodom and Gomorrah—is that correct?"

"Yes, finding the actual location of the doomed cities mentioned in the Bible, as you say, seemed to be the point we kind of took off. However, I had simply proven that Sodom and Gomorrah existed and that they were destroyed just as described in the Bible," Sam explained, his tone modest.

"Okay, if I understand, almost every old city has been burned at some point. But the fires are often after a year-long siege and are clearly set at ground level. But you showed us the evidence that the doomed cities were actually burned from fires that began on the roofs, which was consistent with, I suppose, raining fiery hail from heaven," Tamara recounted. "That got a lot of attention, even from the mainstream press that has usually ignored archaeology, right?"

"Exactly," Sam confirmed. "But that set the stage, giving me funding and credibility for the expansion of that dig, and that's when I found the tablets."

"Now, the tablets that you discovered, known ever since as the 'Cohen tablets,' made you quite famous, at age, what twenty-eight?" Tamara asked. "Explain why they are so important."

"Well, they were apparently recorded by Eastern travelers passing nearby the doomed cities, and they were not Hebrews," Sam explained, his voice now taking on the tones of a lecturer, as he engaged with the audience. "They describe almost on a play-by-play basis exactly what had happened as the raining hail of fire fell down upon Sodom and Gomorrah, just as described in the Old Testament of the Holy Bible."

"It was the Cohen tablets that made you famous, but naturally, they have been controversial," Tamara interjected.

"True. But everything connected with the Bible these days is getting more and more controversial, especially things that experts now have to acknowledge as true history. This has been especially irritating to those who have always disputed the Bible's validity," Cohen explained to the audience. The cameras clearly caught the excitement in Sam's gestures, as he continued: "The tablets described events and used the type of language common at the time that the cities would have been destroyed. The tablets themselves have been dated at the expected time of the judgments they described, and they featured specific details about the hellish scenes. There was no basis to dispute that it happened."

"But, it is controversial that a loving God would destroy people for their sexual orientation. I mean, that is a hard pill to swallow in our modern, more tolerant society," Tamara said, her face etched with some concern.

"God's standards are set, not changing just because society changes," Sam responded. "I am not God's salesman—I am a satisfied customer," he quipped. The audience seemed to like this comment, as the cameras cut to a commercial break.

Some minutes later, Tamara returned, and as she faced the camera once more, she said, "Now, the discovery of the Cohen tablets propelled Sam Cohen on an incredibly successful book tour, and he has become the most famous archeologist living. His show on the Archaeology Channel, *The Truth Behind the Bible,* has become a legitimate sensation, even with non-believers, and those—like me, you know—who had never really fancied archaeology." Turning to Sam, as large sliding images of his adventures sequenced on screens behind them, she said, "So, do you have a woman in your life?"

"Uh," Sam blushed, a small smile playing around the edges of his lips. "I guess I should have been ready for that question on Tamara's show, huh?"

"You don't have to tell everybody there, Sam, just us girls," the interviewer quipped.

"There is a special lady, down in Memphis, and I guess I never really stop thinking about her." A resounding "Awww" rose from the audience.

"Lucky girl. Details?"

Sam demurred.

"Okay, so, what is next for you? I hear you have quite a surprise for us—so much so that your producers won't even tell my people."

"Well, as you know we are pre-recording this show some weeks ahead of the broadcast schedule, but by the time this episode is on air, I will be in a secret location getting ready for our first live broadcast!" Sam said, clearly excited.

"So, what are you going to look for, live on television?" Tamara asked, her smile now etched widely across her face.

"Well, I am not looking for it; I am going to reveal it!" Sam responded in coy way. "But, at this stage it is a secret, so you will have to tune in live to see it."

"Are you turning into a little Geraldo Rivera?" Tamara asked, going along with Sam's manner, one that suggested he was on the verge of revealing something new and important.

"This is much bigger than an empty tomb, I can tell you that," Sam teased.

"Well, honey, we'll be watching. . .won't we, audience?" The crowd roared in approval.

"This sounds big, Sam," Tamara leaned over and touched his hand.

"It's big," he confirmed. "It's the biggest."

-2-

Upper Manhattan, New York City
The Archaeology Channel Headquarters

The money that he had made, and the sponsors that he had attracted to his TV archaeology show, allowed him to plot this new course and record every step of it. He was going after the greatest religious relic the world has ever known. Just like it had been with the discovery of Sodom and Gomorrah, he was sure that this time he knew exactly where it was. His search had taken him through the deserts of Israel, the plains of northern Africa, some of the ancient churches of Europe, and the Temple Mount in Jerusalem. But this time he was sure, and his sponsors were more than happy to bet big on his hunch.

The problem was how to get to it.

Sam's personal journey was much like his professional one. He had been raised in a household that called itself Jewish. However, his family was not Orthodox by any means. As a matter of fact, Sam was a young man by the time he realized what the word "Orthodox" actually meant. He had not even had his own Bar Mitzvah, a fact that he had often regretted since some of his friends had enjoyed theirs. He openly wondered why Western civilizations did not have a meaningful ceremony for young boys to become men like that. They were common in Africa, and knighthood had served that purpose in Europe. The violent murder of his father when he was just a teenager had sent him on a search for truth. Along the way, he became a self-taught expert on world religions. Eventually, much to the concern and horror of his extended family, he became a Christian, believing that the long-promised Messiah really was Jesus. He turned in repentance toward God and trusted in Jesus as the true and only redeemer of people, now understanding that through the Messiah, irrespective of their culture and background, God accepted people.

As a Christian, frequently visiting relatives in Israel, where most of the extended Cohen clan still resided, he became very interested in genealogy and archaeology. He studied in Israel in a Master's-level program that afforded him the opportunity to go on archaeological digs that were usually closed to other people. He was also able to make friends with many of the local Muslim leaders, and found them to be very helpful in his quest to find the truth of the ancient Scriptures. His study of world religions had given him a greater understanding of the varied faiths near his homeland. He came to understand that Muslims do not reject the Old Testament and, in fact, embrace much of it. Since his work centered on ancient history rather than New Testament history, they were not overtly threatened. In fact, they often proved to be helpful to him in his research. That is why he was eventually able, after a lot of coercion and even a good measure of ingratiation with some key officials, to actually privately explore the Temple Mount the year after the book tour that followed the successful release of his first publication regarding the Cohen tablets.

His conversion experience at age fifteen continued to be part of what he sometimes shared whenever he spoke with appropriate groups. That part met with mixed reviews, but he was such a likeable fellow, and so sincere, that people found it easy to be tolerant of his views—even if they found him somewhat controversial at times. After all, he was a renowned expert in his field, which is what he often referred to as nothing "but digging up bones."

He was fond of making the joke that if you go to the local cemetery to dig up skeletons and take the rings off of a dead person's fingers, you are considered a grave robber—among the lowest of the low in civilization. However, if you wait 2,000 years, and dig up that grave, you can become a famous archeologist, be on TV, and have your own show and possibly publish a very successful book, and that would always bring a laugh. He sometimes felt guilty about how much better he was doing than most of his bearded, mussed, Birkenstock sandal-wearing grad student friends who had gone into the same field but who had met with little or no commercial success. Most of them had wound up taking part-time teaching jobs and digging during the summer when they had a little time off. Sam, on the other hand, felt guided by the hand of Providence, and had been blessed to dig all he wanted, and to do so on national TV—with a $20,000 a month personal salary and a big expense account from the Archaeology Channel. They told him often that he was building this channel from the ground up, but he often liked to quip, "I am starting at ground level and going down."

But, he had created a hard act even for himself to maintain. And this particular discovery was going to be like no other in all history. Moreover, it was going to be digitally relayed in high definition video and broadcast worldwide. It was going to be the most famous and most valuable historical and religious artifact in the history of the world. He was going to show the world the truth: not only did this item once exist, but today, in fact, it still exists. The producers thought mostly about the ratings for that. He was focused on how close he was to reaching his dream.

His assistant at the Archaeology Channel, Marjorie, a thin-lipped woman with hair slightly graying at the temples, strode into his office and handed him a printout. She explained in her rather clipped tones, "Mr. Cohen your private flight to Ethiopia will be on schedule per the details here." Marjorie was a divorcee and forty-three years of age. As his assistant, she was efficient, professional, and kept his working world in good order—in her own somewhat clinical way. With no husband and without children, her life had little to offer her after hours, so she was inclined to over-expend her energies on her professional career. If only she had a life outside of work, Sam had sometimes thought to himself—something to warm her up. He thanked her. She knew he hated all of the flights before he got to dig. Running his fingers through his curly hair as he unplugged his phone from where it had been charging, he remembered how all of his archaeology tools would sometimes not actually make it to a dig. This time he had a crew flying in ahead of him to set things up and he figured they would have everything he needed. He would just fly in and do the discovery. And, this time, he would not be flying on a commercial airline.

He pictured where his discovery would be awaiting him: in a temple in a town in Ethiopia. But for the people there to show it to him, he understood that they had been forced to make a very special deal. One of the big issues that they had was that of the security of the relic. Although this was going to be broadcast live on TV, the actual location was going to be kept secret till after the broadcast so that the relic could be moved to another safe location after it had been unveiled. That was okay with Sam, since the important thing for him was showing that this item did indeed exist—not so much where it was located at the time. The Ethiopians had reason to be suspicious of Sam and his motives, but even in Ethiopia there are well-trained lawyers. There were agreements signed, and there was money placed in an escrow fund. Over the last year and a half, there were bonds executed, and there were more papers than Sam had ever seen at one time. There were documents changing hands with all kinds of Ethiopian seals and so forth, so he was thankful that these details could be handled by the company's legal firm and thankful for the ease with which Marjorie had kept him abreast with the key details.

Sam had every intent to keep each one of those secrets and promises.

Unfortunately, someone close to him at the Archaeology Channel did not.

-3-

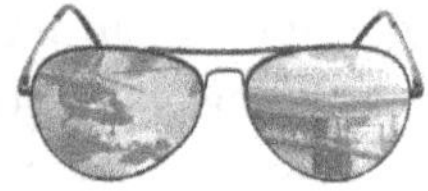

THE WEYNESBUROUGH LUXURY HOTEL
NORTH LONDON, ENGLAND

It was an unlikely cast of characters by anybody's standards. Brisbane, the unofficial leader of the group, hailed from Australia but lacked all of the laid-back charm that so many others of his countrymen had. He had hair that was so blond it seemed almost as white as an albino's. His frame was lean and strong, covered by a richly tanned skin. His eyes seemed restless and never stopped darting around. When he talked, the strong twang of his accent immediately gave it away that he was an Australian.

He was talking to T.J., a thickset man who bore a striking resemblance to the Magnum P.I. character made famous years previously by Tom Selleck. Unfortunately, he was just about as lazy as the part-time private investigator in that well-known prime time serial from the 1980s.

Also there, seated on the small couch, were two men, quite obviously Italians, Louie and Vince. They were mobsters whose boss had been killed in a violent incident about two years previously. They had apparently been wandering around the edges of the Mafia, mostly involved in smaller crimes until they had been recruited by Brisbane.

This was the first formal meeting of this group, and it marked the beginning of what Brisbane knew was going to be a much larger operation. The small conference room in the hotel that Brisbane had rented was getting warm.

As Brisbane hit the play button on the video player, a collection of stories about the recent botched robbery at the Louvre Museum in Paris filled the screen. With no editing, one recorded story butted right up against the next one as they played out the saga of a team of criminals that were supposed to have been the best of the best. The news clips and documentary cuts gave an interesting perspective on a team of criminals that had attempted to go into the most famous art museum, and steal the most valuable painting ever created—and this from one of the most complex and secured fortresses in the history of civilization.

That much was clear. And it was no wonder that it had not succeeded. Brisbane, himself a successful art thief who had specialized in seizing Renaissance paintings and statues, seemed to take great delight in pointing out the obvious failures of this supposed "crack" team of intruders. They had managed to screw it up so badly, he pointed out, that they had come off "like a bunch of little joeys hopping around in a field with a dingo chasing after them." After taking a few moments to explain to Louie and Vince that a joey was a baby kangaroo and that a dingo was a wild dog, both native to Australia, Brisbane continued, although clearly frustrated by the fact that they could not easily understand or appreciate his wit.

"Don't you see, guys, we could pull it off," Brisbane almost pleaded.

T. J. said, "Man, they just tried and they did not get anywhere; and why do you want to steal the Mona Lisa, anyway?"

Brisbane responded indignantly, "You numbskull, I don't want to steal the Mona Lisa; I am not settling for that. There's something *much* more valuable for the taking!"

Vince, anxious to appear smart after not knowing anything about native Australian wildlife, said, "What have you got in mind, Boss, that you want to go even bigger?"

Brisbane responded, "I want to go much, much bigger, but we are going to need a much larger team. I have a shortlist of the kind of men for the project, but we need the best. So, the first order of business in today's meeting is to determine who else we know that we can trust and, frankly, if we can't trust them, who we know that can help us, and we wouldn't mind eliminating when it is all over with." His lips were drawn and his eyes were narrow and steely as he spoke these words.

It appeared that the three criminals gathered with him really wouldn't mind shooting any particular person if it would further their own wealth, so plenty of names were proposed. The first order of business was for Brisbane to talk over the name of each individual proposed until they reached the magic number which, he said, would need to be twenty-one.

"Twenty-one!" Louie interrupted. "Man, what are you thinking about having with twenty-one people?"

Brisbane responded with a glare that seemed to have been saved for just a moment like this as he drove his fist down heavily on the conference table. "Louis Ricardo Paparesta," Brisbane started by calling Louie by his formal name, "do you even know what we are after? Do you even understand a scintilla, of a piece, of a scrap, of a minutia, of a detail of the plan that is now coming together?" With barely a pause, he resumed: "I didn't think so." Casting his eyes over them, he continued his speech: "Gentlemen, let me try to shed a little light on this and make it so even Louie here can understand. The Mona Lisa is *not* the most valuable thing ever created by man. Does anybody even know what the most valuable item that we could steal is?"

"The Venus de something," said Vince, wincing as he could not complete the name of the famous statute by Alexandros of Antioch

"What about that painting with the scream, that awful one with her mouth wide open or was it a he—do you know if it was he or a she?" Louie asked blankly.

"Shut up," Brisbane said directly to Louie.

T. J. waded in, "Hey, bud, I don't know what you are getting in such a snit about. There is a lot of famous artwork all around; there are famous diamonds, paintings and sculptures but I think if we are going to look for something kind of on the artsy side, what about like King Tut's coffin. You know, that coffin within a coffin within a coffin deal?"

Brisbane, now clearly unable to hide his impatience, said, "It's a sarcophagus."

T.J. replied, "Yeah that's it, the sarcophagus thing that's like gold, and it's real heavy, but with twenty-one of us it shouldn't be any trouble."

Vince looked at T.J. "Yeah, you wouldn't want to get your hands dirty, would you there?"

T.J. glared at Vince, saying, "Look, punk, I don't care who you think you are; I know you are just a two-bit, washed-out Chicago mobster."

"You had better watch it," Vince said in his most menacing tone.

"Yeah, I am *real* scared of you," T.J. replied sarcastically.

Brisbane interrupted coldly, "Men, I am serious now. You guys were on the right track, but you are still missing it by a mile. You are missing something of, let's just say, of greater proportions, maybe even *Biblical* proportions. . . ."

-4-

Sam Cohen arrived in Ethiopia after much more time than Marjo-rie, his assistant, had told him he would have to be in flight; apparently there had been some confusion, some mix up. He thought it would have gone faster using the new company jet. Nevertheless, it was still a very long flight. Sam felt he had spent way too much time in planes and airports, and they held him back from what he really enjoyed doing—tracking and digging. If his hands weren't dirty, he wasn't really happy. The rest of the crew had already used one of the jets for the Archaeology Channel to fly over the equipment and the paraphernalia that the producers would use. They would be waiting and refreshed. He needed to stretch his cramped legs.

As Sam walked down the side street near the temporary trailer compound where he was staying in Aksum in Ethiopia, no one seemed to notice him. He found this odd. Back in the United States, he was now just famous enough to have people come up and talk to him quite spontaneously. Fortunately, the fans of the Archaeology

Channel were not generally nutty people—in fact, they were mostly pretty intellectual types. He wondered what it would take to propel him to rock star status, so that girls would go crazy for him like they used to for Michael Jackson or some other such celebrity. It had not happened up till now, which, to be honest, was for him a little un-flattering. At any rate, it was good to be anonymous for a while in Ethiopia. For the last year, whenever people had seen him and asked him about his next project, he had been very vague. He usually gave an unclear answer about where he would be working next. In fact, the flight plan out of the USA had been filed almost at the last min-ute and was processed in a confidential fashion, according to Mar-jorie, so that no one—at least in theory—would know his location. The Archaeology Learjet had taken a fairly long course to get there and had not even filed a flight plan for the last leg of the journey, so as to leave some doubt about where they were going after they refu-eled on the Cape Verde Coast. From that extreme western portion of Africa, they could have reached anywhere in Europe, Africa or the Middle East. This was important to keep the operation quiet.

Secrecy seemed less important now that he was on the streets of Aksum, and as the dry wind blew lightly through his hair. He regarded the sights of the town through the tinted lenses of his sunglasses, brown buildings made visually mute as the brightness of the East African sun bore down on him. The sound of traffic and the wafting of smells from a nearby market pressed subliminally against his consciousness giving him the same sense he so often had when he was away from home—that this was a different place altogether. It certainly smelled different. He had been around the world several times with his travels, and had seen some strange places. More than one person had compared him to a real-life Indiana Jones. He would joke that he was not Indy because he detested wearing old hats. He was tall for a Jew, looking more Greek in appearance, his wavy hair almost black in the bright light. His skin tone and clear eyes suggested he led a healthy lifestyle. His height was enhanced by his erect posture. When he smiled, which was quite often, small crease lines appeared around his eyes and at the corners of his mouth. His teeth were even, and when he smiled it was an engaging sight. This had proved so helpful to him when he signed books or ap-peared on TV. He adjusted his sunglasses and glanced at his watch. It felt like time for some refreshment.

A little further down the sidewalk, he found a street side café that served what looked like American coffee. As he wondered if his change was correct, he realized that this was probably the last time he would be alone for long time. Soon, he would have the constant badgering of a producer, a director, the lighting people, and what seemed like a hundred other voices shouting at him at any moment. They had to get all of the shots just right. Slowly but surely, with his new-found fame, he was having a little more input on the day-to-day aspects of his shows, but he was still only an employee. As he sat on the creaking metal chair in the open-air café, he thought a lot about what the next few days would hold. He anticipated several days involving meetings with all of the different people who had signed on with his channel, and also with the production team to help guide him through this process. There would be another few days of getting everything set up and then, fourteen days from today, they would actually pull the trigger. This would be the first ever live shot prime time television in the States at 11:00 p.m. Eastern US time, and it would be at 10:00 p.m. Central in Memphis, Tennessee. This would make it prime time all the way to California. He was over seven thousand miles from Memphis and eight hours ahead of it.

As he drank his coffee—it didn't have the body to it that he would have liked and it tasted pretty lousy—he noticed the taste of the dust in the back of his throat. In this part of Africa, the dust had a light reddish tint and was powdery in texture; not gritty like beach sand. No one who had ever experienced the sands of a desert would compare them with the sugary white sands of beaches of Florida in the States. He had noticed that every time he had been in Africa, whether it had been in the northern, southern or central parts, there was some type of dust that just seemed to find its way everywhere. It got into his clothes, the back of his throat, his ears, his nose; and a few times he had lost his voice working outside in the blowing, dusty sand storms that occurred in the open areas of the desert regions.

As he sat there reflecting on why in the world he had ordered a hot drink on a hot day, he thought about Angela. It was not exactly the classic "love left behind" story, but it had most of the hallmarks. They had been sweethearts since college days when he was a freshman at the University of Memphis, and she a junior. She was a couple years older than him and had delayed her studies as she had wanted to take a few years traveling before settling into the rigors of a medical career. She was far from a lover of all things archaeological; in fact, she did not truly appreciate what she called "his study of things that once were."

Instead, she was fascinated with what could be, at least from a biological standpoint. He was sure that she was one of those visionary folks who could be destined to actually find a cure for cancer. He thought back about how, as she neared the completion of her degree, that there was only one place she wanted to go: St. Jude Children's Research Hospital in Memphis. Many years previously, Danny Thomas had nurtured a vision for a hospital that would treat all sick children, regardless of the ability of their parents to pay. It had morphed into a colossal research facility in which the cancer survival rate for children dramatically soared under the watchful hands and eyes of the country's best doctors, and it benefited from some of the world's most highly regarded researchers. Angela was born to be one such researcher, Sam knew.

There was no doubt in Sam's mind, even toward the end of his freshman year, there would be a future with her. Slight in build and rather short in stature, her head reached his shoulder when they stood side by side. Her honey-blonde hair was shoulder length, and often tied back to keep it from her face as she conducted her research in the laboratories. Her eyes, blue to gray in color, looked out from between light lashes. She did not wear a lot of makeup; her natural skin tones directed her only to use a little mascara and sometimes a little blush—but never much. Her gentle spirit was complemented with a soft smile—though she was often serious, and most of the time preoccupied with the details of her work. Intelligent, witty when she wanted to be, and articulate, she seemed a good match for Sam, but it had to be said that their relationship had never moved forward at a very great pace. She had always assumed that he would be off to parts of the world unknown. After all, Memphis was no archaeological Mecca. People dug through some Indian mounds for arrowheads and Indian bones and, beyond that, there wasn't much else to dig for. Only once was there any archaeology news there that she had noticed. She had sent him the newspaper clipping of the time city workers were replacing the old cobblestone landing down at the Mississippi River. It was at the foot of the street famous for blues and rock-n-roll, Beale Street. City workers had inadvertently excavated the location of a very old landfill. They found hundreds of bottles, trash, and paraphernalia from the 1880s. She had trouble locating him to even send that clipping. As he thought about her, he felt a twinge of guilt for being away from her so often.

The slow speed with which their friendship had developed was, in part, intentional and self-imposed. Angela and Sam had tried hard not to progress their relationship further than they knew their careers would give it sufficient space to flourish. After almost two years, but a very good two years, Angela graduated and, predictably, committed herself to the work of St. Jude Children's Research Hospital in Memphis. Sam stuck out his studies and was accepted into the exclusive Master's Program in Israel that he had coveted for years. As an ethnic Jew who embraced the Christian faith, he had begun to be active in an organization known as Jews for Jesus. There, his associates referred to those Jews who believe that Jesus came and died for the sins of the world as the predicted Messiah as "Messianic Jews" and to Jesus as "Jeshua Homeshea." But Sam's initial excitement in getting involved in that organization waned. It didn't involve digging somewhere, or piecing together clues, which were stronger passions in his life. But, he still supported the operation and put up with the occasional question about it at a press conference, or at a book signing.

It had now been more than a decade since he and Angela had hit it off in college. While they had seen each other since for short trips together or visits, it never seemed possible to fully recapture the earlier spark they had felt. Maybe this was because it was so temporary and known to be so; maybe because there could no real future in it, given the careers they had chosen. If their relationship were to develop, Angela would have to be very understanding about his travel schedule. In the event of marriage, it was unspoken but understood that any children they might one day have would suffer from his absence if they tried to make a real go of it.

He looked at his watch once more, and noticed the date. He was going to turn thirty-one years old this very week. He couldn't imagine a better present from his network than getting to reveal, live on television, the existence of the most celebrated relic of all history.

He was aware of how careful the network folks had been not to let the location be known, especially since Ethiopia had always been one of the main five or six locations where it was thought be housed.

However, he had called Angela just before he left and told her something about it. He didn't have to tell her, she said, as she kept up with his news. She was a frequent visitor to his blog on the Archaeology Channel website. A sweet-natured person who would put herself out for others, she really went out of her way to try and be interested in what he was interested in. He wondered to himself how well he did that for her. Of course, he was interested in how a cure for cancer might be found, and in helping children, but the day-to-day details of what she did seemed to him to be pretty boring. On one particular research project, she had spent sixty consecutive days just investigating something to do with whether a cell membrane could be penetrated by something in certain temperatures. He never really understood why that mattered but figured he probably could if he really tried. He just didn't really try. Life seemed too full of other things.

Shifting his weight on the squeaking chair, and taking one more sip of his coffee, now tepid, he made a commitment to himself to get his mind straight for these next two weeks. He would have to be at the top of his game, because this was going to culminate in the most record-breaking rating of any show, probably in the history of television. Already, people were comparing this to July 1969, when the public watched Neil Armstrong set foot on the moon. They were making comments that reminded him of what he knew of the Kennedy Assassination from 1963, or 9/11, because everyone would remember where they were when they saw it for the first time. That gilded box with the cherubim facing each other with their wings outspread held a world full of mystery and history. Then, of course, there were the legends of the curse of the Ark, that couldn't help but to assist the ratings. The nation of Ethiopia would finally have credibility and respect that only he, Sam Cohen, could offer. He would reveal the most sought-after item in history. His career would redline, as they say. But these people trusted him to securely validate their claims. The pressure felt suddenly much greater.

Rising from his chair, and pushing it back, he hurried off to his meeting with a sense of the intensity and significance of the matter.

-5-

The motley crew of suspects was looking all the more odd by the minute. Earlier that day, Brisbane had brought in Slim and Speck, the two computer and communication guys. Both wore spectacles, and Speck's pair, large and round in shape—glinting in the muted light of the room—gave him something of the look of an owl. If it is a rule that all computer and communication guys should look nerdy and be small or skinny, they qualified. That made the party six, including Brisbane, T.J., Vince, and Louie.

Brisbane had told everyone that other team members would be arriving as the evening progressed. Two giants of men did arrive. "Oslo and Gundy, welcome," said Brisbane as he greeted them. It was obvious at a glance they were the members of the operation who would do the heavy lifting. With both stature and strength, each of these men would easily fill the doorframe whenever they would move from one room to another. Oslo's nose bore the tell-tale shape of one who had been in more than one skirmish. His hair, closely cropped, gave way above his temple to a skin surface badly pockmarked from teenage acne. According to notes handed out by Brisbane, Oslo had been a weight lifter from Norway. He had washed out of the Olympics on two separate tries, apparently because of his misuse of steroids. His neck was bigger than Slim's waist, or so it appeared to everyone seated there.

Gundy was a professional wrestler until he had beaten up the third manager that he had, and could no longer find anyone to manage him in the business. He eventually had to find some other way to make a living. He had tried to be a bodyguard on two occasions but had actually assaulted or threatened the man that he was supposed to be protecting. His head, often completely shaved but today showing a few days graying stubble, bore the scars of what looked to have been serious wounds. His closely set eyes made his appearance not a little menacing, especially the thin line of a scar that ran from his left eye to his ear. Everyone was pretty nice to Gundy. That brought the party to eight.

Next to arrive was the crew of four Europeans that Brisbane had called the "gunmen." They were very quiet and serious, and their Slavic features gave them an air of solemnity that communicated itself in a sense that they were individuals who were not to be trifled with. As much as the others talked, these fellows almost never spoke, and seemed to use hand signals with one another. No one was sure where exactly they were from, and the notes did not say, except that at one point they had been involved in some kind of crack unit of anti-terrorism in Eastern Europe. These men were every bit the part. They were dressed in black fatigues, the army outfits with more pockets than most can fill up. Later Louie would complain to Vince, "They are always talking to each other with these cursed hand signals. What's up with them?"

Brisbane was evidently enjoying himself as each new arrival was greeted. A call on Brisbane's cell phone seemed to be from someone needing directions. These he gave, his face animated, and his hands gesturing as they pointed to imaginary lines in the room demarcating the route he was expecting his listener to follow as he neared their location. His Australian accent took on an even greater twang as he spoke into his cell phone.

A few minutes later, more men walked in. They were in excellent shape and had cargo vests on. Brisbane explained that they were the three sniper teams of two each, a total of six men as they strode down the hall. "They've just walked right out of a bad country song," T.J. observed to no one in particular. "I guess we will hear them start talking about momma, trains, getting out of jail, drinking, cheating, and driving a pickup truck," he joked.

Two of the men from the sniper team chewed tobacco and spat pretty much anywhere they could find a spot. After a few questions from T.J., they made the point that they were not all snipers, technically speaking. Vince and Louie looked a little surprised. Vince asked them to explain further. One of them was happy to clarify by stating that a sniper is part of a team consisting of a sniper *and* a spotter. The spotter's job is to determine what and where to shoot, whereas the sniper's job is to hit that target. "One shot—one kill," they seemed especially fond of saying. T.J. could tell that it was going to be a long meeting.

These three teams of snipers, six men in all, brought the total up to eighteen. Sitting together, they made an impressive sight. As Speck surveyed them, he found himself thinking that they were not unlike characters from an Xbox who had come to life and stepped from out of a TV screen. They were hardly the kinds of people that one would want to meet in a dark alley in the twilight!

Just as Vince began to ask Brisbane who else was coming, the other three walked in. With their light brown skin—a few degrees lighter than that of most African-Americans in North America— they looked as if they were Ethiopians. They had rounded heads, long necks, and were thin and wiry in build. T.J. said quietly under his breath that they looked as if they might have walked right out of a *National Geographic* magazine. Two of them made conversation with Brisbane in well-spoken but heavily accented English; the other spoke barely a word, though he seemed to understand it fairly well. No one was sure of their names and since they were probably the hardest ones to learn, nobody really tried. After all, they were probably expendable.

For this meeting, Brisbane had picked out a rather nice, large old countryside inn north of London, England, in which to hatch this plan. He had leased several rooms for the men to sleep in, as well as arranging for the use of a large conference room and adjacent suite. For all of the English bravado about helping the Americans with the surveillance of international terrorists, the English were missing a lot—especially out in the gently rolling countryside near Hertfordshire. The old buildings that now housed an exclusive golf retreat had once actually been a convent and chapel. The look of this meeting had to give the gentle Londoners some pause, especially the sight of Oslo and Gundy the two monstrous-looking, muscular fellows.

With everyone seated, after a few preliminaries, Brisbane started the meeting with another video show. The first three who had seen it previously were quick to let everyone else know that they had been through this before, and so with sighs and deep breaths and rolling eyes, they appeared to endure hearing and seeing all of this again. No one was sure how much the Croatians—or wherever it was that the gun team was from—picked up, and it was pretty clear that two of the Ethiopians were not following all of this as clearly as they might have.

However, the original three noticed that Brisbane had included a long segment at the end of the video that hadn't been there when they had first seen it. This segment was about an archeologist and a show called *"The Truth Behind the Bible."* At this point Speck— well named because of the thickness of his glasses—appeared to want to go on record as being as macho as anybody else in the room. In his thin, somewhat high-pitched voice, he demanded Brisbane tell him why he was here, as he had flown all the way out to come to "Nowhere-shire" outside of London, England, to watch a show about Biblical Archaeology, "that I could have watched from the comfort of my home in high definition!"

Brisbane glared coldly at him. Speck shifted uncomfortably. There were no other comments offered after such a display. The sounds of the video continued with the promos of Sam Cohen and his exotic locations. He could be seen, first in a sequence that appeared as if he were repelling down the side of the walls in Petra, and next exploring the same caves in which the famed Dead Sea Scrolls had been discovered. It even showed Cohen climbing the Pyramids, and saying he was "uncovering every stone looking for the truth behind the Bible."

As there was not anyone who made any kind of religious profession in the room, they viewed this with a mix of boredom and incredulity. It was clear that everyone instantly resented having to sit through anything suggesting absolute truth, right and wrong, or good and evil. Oslo finally leaned forward, his large head tilted toward Brisbane, and snapped in his broken English, "You dumb Aussie, why you bring me here make me watch boring show about a myth and fairy tale?"

Gundy's voice joined in next, "Yeah, what is next—Mother Goose, the Little Old Woman in the Shoe?"

At that, Slim added, "How about Goldie Locks or Little Red Riding Hood, ha. . .?" His forced laugh was not returned by the other men. Indeed, most of the men looked at him as if they would cut his head off—if it were worthy of the effort.

It proved to be a dramatic and defining moment, one that would establish Brisbane as the undoubted leader, one who would not easily stand for anything less than complete respect for his judgment and wishes.

In an act swiftly executed that reminded everyone in the room of Crocodile Dundee, Brisbane reached into a piece of luggage near the TV. Seizing a huge Ghurka knife in one hand, he lifted it high above his head and, in a contorted whirl of energy, threw it dramatically into the center of the antique conference table where it quivered with the residual energy of the force that had driven it there. With every gaze fixed on him, his beady, darting eyes fixed on Speck for just a moment. He was locked in an eye-to-eye, man-to-man, courtroom-type stare. Brisbane simply put his finger to his lips and said, "Ssshh." Speck did not say anything further.

"No, you idiots!" Brisbane resumed through gritted teeth, "This man has become famous in finding religious relics of great significance. He has uncovered clay tablets and maps and even the locations of Sodom and Gomorrah." Vince looked at Louie curiously at the mention of such things. Brisbane continued, "I am talking about the highest value item ever carried in the hands of man that was believed to house the very presence of God."

Vince interrupted more hesitantly, "You're talking about God like He is real."

"I am not here to talk the details of religion with you, nor do I think some of you could carry on a conversation about it," Brisbane said in a condescending tone. He took a deep breath and resumed, "According to the ancient Hebrew Scriptures, there was one item that housed the very presence of God, and I will read it to you." Brisbane took out a Bible that looked like it had been laid out especially for this particular event. The crisp, new leaves of the gilded edges of the pages stuck together in places as he flipped to a reference with some difficulty. He had written it down on an index card, and turned to some verses in the book of Exodus. He described the Ten Commandments texts. He then turned to spots throughout the Old Testament and described the various items that were kept with the tablets of the Ten Commandments, which included a brass bowl of manna and Aaron's staff that had budded.

The room was not impressed. Two or three men began to speak at once, indicating that this was all a mistake and a waste of their time. The cacophony of voices made it difficult to understand any one particular person or sentence.

Commanding their attention once more, Brisbane spoke over the voices saying, "Gentlemen, this was all placed into a golden box, with supernatural, magical powers."

"Oh, I have read this; it is Raiders of the Lost Ark. You know, guys, Indiana Jones," T.J. quipped.

"So, who does that make you, Sweetheart, the screaming little girl who almost gets bitten by all those snakes?" snarled one of the snipers.

"Hey man, where is your whip?" asked one of the other snipers as they were feeling their way through this social situation.

"No, no, no!" roared Brisbane. "Indiana Jones was a fictional tale. But, Raiders of the Lost Ark was about a real historical thing. I am telling you a *real story*. . .about a *real item*. It is currently known as the Lost Ark of the Covenant. It was the holiest item in all Hebrew and Christian culture to ever exist—and priceless in value—and I know where it is! Or, more precisely, I know the man who knows exactly where it is."

"Correction," said T.J., anxious to appear in some control. "You know the person, who knows the man, who knows where it is."

"Touché" said Brisbane in a rare, approving glance toward T.J. Smiling, T.J. drank in the boss' approval.

"Each one of you have been brought here for a particular purpose," Brisbane announced in a manner that was, for him, bordering on the grandiose. "We have everyone that we need, here in this twenty-one-man team, to carry it off. Some people may call it the crime of the year, or the crime of the decade, or maybe even the crime of the century. But I am telling you, other so-called 'crimes of the century' have come and gone. Most of you could not talk about any of them, with any specificity." Brisbane now stood, pulling himself to his full height, and addressed the group: "Listen, I can tell you that if you join me, your reputations will go down in history, because this is not going to be the crime of the year, of the decade, or of the century." Brisbane pushed a button on his tiny, high-tech cell phone, which changed the image on the screen. There before them was a painting of the golden Ark, surrounded by angels and fire. "Gentlemen," he continued, "I mean to say that this is the greatest crime of all history."

"Aw yeah, right" John David, one of snipers said, now bolder, sighing loudly.

"Yeah man," said the first of the Ethiopians. They all pretty much sounded alike with their thick accents.

Vince looked at Louie for some direction.

T.J. piped up, "So, if this is the crime of all history, even bigger than the Mona Lisa, bigger than the Hope Diamond, bigger than the Brink's Train Robbery, bigger than D. B. Cooper, bigger than Al Capone, you are saying bigger than *all* of those things?"

Brisbane grinned, "I am now appreciative that you are a serious student of the criminal mind. It is worth more than all those combined!" He strode over to where T.J. was sitting and continued: "You see, it is not just the value of this item that makes it so special. It is really a trinity, an unholy trinity if you will, of attributes that makes this so special. Number one, it is historically priceless. This is a one-of-a-kind item—it is truly not reproducible." Brisbane backed away and held up numbers with his fingers as counted down his points. "Number two, it has immense religious significance— three major religions trace their way back to the contents of this box in one way or another. It would be exceedingly important for each one of those religions to obtain this item." Brisbane hit another button on his cell phone and then on the screen the image of the Ark faded out, and a photographic representation of Solomon's ancient temple brightened. "Gentlemen, thirdly, it is going to be available to us. You see, it is not protected by some unusually complex security system, as we understand it in the West."

"You mean they don't even guard this box?" Vince asked, now wide-eyed.

"No, there will be guards," Brisbane corrected. "Seriously motivated guards. But, the very secrecy of where it is hidden, combined with the doubt that it exists at all, compose the actual walls that has separated it from all potential intruders for all this time."

One of the spotters, Jim Bob, for the sniper team interjected, "Well, this sounds a lot like some kind of search for Noah's Ark. I once watched a show on that. I would assume that people found it years ago, and they would have just cut it up over the years and sold little crosses made out of the wood—that is what I would have done. Assuming what you say is right, how do we know this Ark box deal is even still around?"

Brisbane said, "Well, you are not as dumb as you look there, Bubba."

"My name ain't Bubba, it is Jim Bob."

"Jim Bob. . .are two first names a requirement in the Southern United States?"

"Hey, watch it there," responded one of the other snipers, Bubba warned, his tone menacing.

John David looked at the sniper who had helped him, and said, "Thanks, Bubba." Brisbane smiled, and paused. His point was made.

T.J. asked, "If its location is such a secret, how are we gonna find it, and get to the darn thing?"

Brisbane pointed silently to the image of the temple on the screen. "The secrecy of where this has been hidden for hundreds of years is about to be destroyed, because of this video you saw earlier. Sam Cohen, who has prospered himself on TV, is going to lead us right to it. He just doesn't know it yet."

-6-

31 Days to Broadcast
Abandoned Indoor Rifle Range
Somewhere North of London, England

All at once eight machine guns opened fire, sending copper-jacketed bullets ripping through the air at a rate of almost a dozen rounds per second down each white-hot barrel. Their targets were completely destroyed in a matter of three seconds of fully automatic fire from these deadly assault weapons. This time their targets were made of thick paper cut in simple black silhouettes. The next time these guns were fired, the targets would not be cardboard silhouettes. T.J. wondered aloud how Brisbane had arranged to have this whole military indoor shooting range rented out without arousing any concern on the part of the UK authorities. He hadn't even been aware that there was an indoor shooting range anywhere in England. Brisbane seemed pleased that his connections had enabled him to make use of a facility that was ordinarily used by military personnel associated with the Royal Air Force.

The snipers seemed somewhat displeased at having to even be around this, since the .50 caliber sniper rifles that they used could not even be fired inside any building. So they stood around while some of the men who were less familiar with weapons were briefed in the various different kinds of automatic and semi-automatic hardware that was available. They had Sigs, Uzis, HKs and a whole box of Glock handguns.

After a little fun with the paper targets they went back to the inn where the conference room had been readied for their meeting As they settled in around the table with the easy chairs lining the edges of the room, a pretty English waitress brought in fresh pastries and small glasses of orange juice for everyone. As she set the items down on the small tables, one of the spotters, Colton, his eyes watchful under his heavy brows and lips pursed in mimicking the sound of a kiss, made a comment about liking the way she talked and hinted that maybe she would like to come to his room and talk a little more that night. Averting her eyes and furrowing her brow, the waitress made a comment not quite under her breath using the words "bloody bloke" before quickly leaving the room.

This meeting had a completely different feel to it than the earlier meetings in which Brisbane had had to rule with an iron fist. As the primary mover, he had been set on convincing everybody what the situation was and why they should be involved. This time, the meeting took on a tone of greater earnestness since the team now had a much stronger sense of the outline of the basic plan. This had been helped by that fact that on an ITV newscast they had seen during dinner, there had been a short news feature that had made a reference to worldwide previews of the Ark of the Covenant. They now appreciated, for the first time, the significance of this particular artifact and how much it would mean to so many different people. That made Brisbane's job, at least in this meeting, so much easier.

Brisbane handed out a sheaf of papers, describing the printouts as the basic itinerary of one Sam Cohen.

"What is this about?" Louie asked, his dark eyes squinting at the pages.

"Yeah," Vince said, as if that added anything to the conversation.

Brisbane responded tersely: "Gentlemen, this is the bloke that is going to lead us to the greatest discovery and the greatest crime in the history of the world. We have someone on the inside of his organization there and she has faxed us this information. As you can see, they will be doing a prep in Ethiopia."

"Where?" John David asked.

"Ethiopia, you dope," one of the spotters responded to him. "You know, it is like in Africa or somewhere."

"Correct," Brisbane said, "and it has long been said to be the last resting place of the Ark of the Covenant. Given the fact that Cohen is there, it must be where the temple is that houses it. And, as you can see," he continued as he began to pass out satellite images, "from our photos this building is not particularly large."

"Wow, it is amazing what you can do with the Internet and a Google map, huh?" Speck said, peering at the sheet through his thick lenses.

Brisbane continued, unmoved by the observation. "As you can see the building is encircled by fences—a fence inside a fence, inside a fence, inside a wall if you will. They may appear to be decorative, but I assure you they are real fences. Two of our nationals on the ground there have actually visited the place and stood outside the fence. They are here because of their inside knowledge of the language, the customs, the traditions, and their ability to get us in and out more cleanly. Those fences go four feet down in the rocky ground. Everything is made of very strong iron and, as far as we know, there is only one way in and out. Further, it is guarded twenty-four hours a day, seven days a week and there is a temple priest, it is rumored, that never leaves the building."

"Well, how does he go to the doctor and stuff?" asked one of the Bubbas.

"I am quite sure I don't know the answer to that question," Brisbane said in a condescending manner. "At any rate, this is our target, gentlemen."

"Well, how do you want us to get in?" asked Louie and Vince almost simultaneously.

"The simple answer to that," Brisbane replied, "is that everyone in the building dies except possibly for Mr. Cohen, as he may prove valuable. Think of it. . . ." Brisbane looked out to nowhere, his blond hair reflecting the gleam of the inn's concealed lighting. "This entire soap opera on television regarding this relic is just like a commercial for us to raise money from." Brisbane lowered his gaze to the men again. "For this to work we must execute a strike plan upon the building just a few moments after this is found and being broadcast live for the world to see. The staff of the archaeology channel that is sponsoring this whole adventure is actually putting out false information for any potential espionage operation to throw people off as to the real location. I have it on very good authority from our inside source that we are the only other people in the world that know about this. Further, they do not know that we know, so their security will be at a, let's say, manageable level."

Sniper Jake Johnston interjected, "Manageable, huh? You give me a clear line of sight to anything within one mile, and you will have to sift for the fingerprints."

"You bet!" said one of his spotters, Colton, as the palms of his hand met with his colleague in an impromptu high-five. It immediately reminded the others of a macho locker room scene; however, no one doubted the ability of these men to do exactly what they said they could do.

Now Brisbane continued, "I have taken the liberty of chartering an aircraft for us that will fly there in an inconspicuous manner. It is a cargo aircraft and, as such, there are only six passenger seats, so most of you will be doing what you can, sitting on your gear. I will let you gentlemen decide who gets the seats and who doesn't. I will be sitting up front with our pilot." Immediately, Oslo and Gundy, in almost perfect unison, said, "One of the seats is mine." No one was heard to argue with them.

Brisbane took the opportunity to add, "Oslo, Gundy, since you are talking, would you mind please explaining to everyone what will happen if they call their wife, their girlfriend, their mother or anyone and even so much as hint as to where they are going—if they even mention what continent they are headed to?"

Oslo responded in his broken English, "Is this part where I talk about what I will do to them?"

Brisbane said, "Yes, that is so."

Oslo, with a gleaming grin, continued, "Part of this deal was I am the sergeant-at-arms in group; Gundy and I are in charge of making sure everybody stays straight. You got some idea of writing or calling anybody out this room, telling anybody about this, even making comment where somebody could figure it out and you mess the deal up, Gundy gets one side of you and I gonna get other and we are gonna pull you into two pieces, like in old country."

At that point, Gundy leaned in, saying menacingly, "We have done it before."

At that moment, Brisbane took a coconut from the fruit bowl and rolled it across the table where he had embedded his knife. Oslo threw his fist down on the surface with such force that it shattered the coconut, making a crack in the table top and splashing the liquid from the coconut in all directions. No one was heard to complain. Gundy, who though huge may have been the smarter of the two, was quick to point out that it "took 1,300 pounds per square inch to shatter a coconut and it only takes 1,200 pounds per square inch to shatter a human skull." No one would forget that demonstration. Brisbane smiled a smile of quiet satisfaction.

Opening a cardboard carton, Brisbane handed out new secure international cell phones to several the men. He also handed out earphones and watches, all synchronized. "This is just like in the movies," T.J. said, clearly impressed.

"Yeah, except in the movies nobody dies for real. Some of us got a good chance of not making it through this one," Vince, the Chicago small-time mob player, said.

"Are you chicken there?" one of the Bubbas openly challenged him.

"No, I ain't chicken there, John-boy," he responded.

"John-boy, I got your John." Bubba, who actually went by the name Bubba, stood up, wearing a green army sniper shirt with the sleeves cut off, emblazoned with a skull and crossbones. His biceps bulged. He had a tattoo that read, "One shot, One kill." He rose and began approaching the place Vince was seated.

"Gentlemen, that is enough," Brisbane announced. "We will be meeting at the number seven cargo hangar in the morning at 8:15 sharp; do not say anything to anyone outside of this mission that can give away your target. It is important that you just disappear. When you exit this hotel in the morning, make sure that you leave nothing that would cause any suspicion. When you are tempted to chat, brag or visit—remember the coconut. The stakes are so high that there is no one in this deal that I won't personally kill or have killed. This is your only warning; there are no second chances. We only get one chance to do this. This is the right time in history. I don't mean to sound philosophical, but with all the advertising on television and the new interest in all things religious, it is like all of the parts are falling into place, all of the stars are in line, if you will, for this to happen. I am destined to succeed. We all are. But we must preserve the element of surprise. I am not going to let any of you screw it up."

Producing a worn folder, he began, "This is the deal for tomorrow morning: we move from here to a cargo hangar at Luton airport. I have tickets for the train to get you there, but you must come in stages so as not to attract attention to yourselves being in a large group. Work out between yourselves who will catch which train; they depart every fifteen minutes in the early part of the morning, and I don't want any more than six in each party. Be sure to split up, and to ride in different parts of the train. So as not to attract too much attention, be sure that you look as much as possible like oil rig workers, as there are a lot of them who have to catch flights from Luton to other parts of the world, especially the Middle East, where the oil rigs are.

"At Luton Airport, be sure to exit and to go off the far end of the platform where it is marked 'Commercial and Cargo.' I'll be waiting for you there so that we can get through the security division without any questions. I've arranged for the weapons to be concealed in cartons and they are being loaded just after midnight tonight. T.J. arranged that, right?" His eyes were momentarily cast in the direction of T.J. as he sought confirmation that the stash had been taken care of. His glance was met with an affirmative nod.

"Our plane is a relatively old, propeller-driven one. It won't be too comfortable, and you will prefer using ear muffs. Be sure you dress comfortably for when you no longer have to act as oil rig workers. Good night and sweet dreams!"

-7-

This time, in Sam's mind the producers' meeting had a different feel to it. More than ever before, people hushed to listen to what he had to say. He felt, if not equal to the producers, certainly that they were rather enamored with his success as well. He found himself thinking that even though he was not yet thirty-one years old, his career was showing signs of an excellent trajectory. He had a worldwide, live archaeology special show, and here he was, thousands of miles away from home, making history that not even *he* could fully put into perspective.

The basic idea was to spend several days shooting the promo footage that would be used as a build up to the actual discovery. The special had initially been slated to be a one-hour feature program but there was talk now of extending it to two hours. They were going to need more footage than they had originally planned.

The location certainly lent itself to video recording. The pale East African sky, sometimes studded with cumulus clouds, provided a backdrop that contrasted with the browns and sandstone colors of some of the buildings. Exotic-looking trees dotted around offered limited shade, and the bright clothing of the children, their smiling faces and rich, sallow skin tones added a sense of mystique to the faraway setting. Not far from the town itself, goats and sheep were to be seen against a dusty background of scrub and brush. Taking these and other matters in mind, the producers knew that they had good context for some rich film-making.

Bill, a senior producer, also announced it was confirmed that CNN and Fox News were both going to carry a significant portion of it live. Things just seemed to keep getting better for Sam.

The initial shooting would be of the grounds to the temple and near the entrance of the complex maze of tunnels that secretly underlie most of that area where the temple had stood, in one form or another, for well over a thousand years. Then, on the day of the big discovery, they would be scheduled to walk through many of those tunnels and make it appear that they were on a very long journey by a secret route through various gates—perhaps even having to get through some booby traps—to reach the Ark itself. There was some talk, when this plan was initially hatched, that making the route seem long, difficult, and secret wouldn't serve much purpose because, according to the local sources on which they had relied, the Ark actually sat relatively near the surface and might even be located really only in a deeper part of the basement of the temple. Sam wanted to keep an open mind about this and sense the right thing to do at the time; in his mind, the Ark was probably at least a five- or ten-minute walk underground, and would not be easily removed from such a secure location.

Immediately after the broadcast, the plan was for it to be moved to a new secret location—not even leaving it in its place of discovery overnight—and without making public where the actual discovery had taken place. The thinking of the producers was that the Ark would actually be taken out through one of the tunnels under the cover of darkness—everyone liked the tunnel idea and thought it would make good television. Someone suggested that if one or two of the cameramen made some of the rocks fall in front of their own cameras, this would give extra dramatic effect to enthrall the viewing audience.

Everyone agreed that, with the recent success of reality television shows, this would be hugely successful. Reality television had become especially popular in recent months with shows documenting the deadly world of crab fishermen, the precarious nature of ice road truckers, and the ever-popular saga of police known as COPS. But if the reality in "Reality TV" was not already real and exciting enough, surely there would be no harm in adding a little more by the producers? It actually caused Sam somewhat of a sense of concern. While admittedly not perfect, and still struggling in areas of his life to reconcile his desires with his faith, he was troubled by it. He had spoken out about these concerns and his opinions were met with respect by other team members. However, the best arrangement he was able to negotiate was that the recording would be scientifically accurate about the actual relic and its history. With that, he decided the theatrics of how they gained entrance into the area really didn't need to concern him. Not one to fight over non-essential matters, he would go with the consensus view.

One of the younger associate producers, Everett (a name that Sam thought was a very strange for any child ever to be given), seemed very concerned about the so-called "curse of the Ark." It appeared that he had been to Sunday School more than a few times, and he seemed to remember a story in the Bible. He explained, "Okay I know that The Ark of the Covenant was like God's throne on earth. It was kept in the Holy of Holies in the Temple. But if they moved the Ark, it had long poles and if you touched it, you'd die on the spot.

Sam interrupted, "Yes, and I imagine you are going to ask about God striking Uzzah dead when he tried to steady it, right?"

"Yeah," Everett answered, "Why'd He do that?"

"The story is in 2 Samuel, chapter 6. But, you already know— if you touched it, you would die," Sam explained. "But it's much deeper. The Ark of the Covenant was only to be carried on poles, up high, like the Egyptian royal palanquins."

"Uh, royal penguins?" the producer asked, quizzically.

"Royal palanquins. You know, those raised chairs that you carry kings and royalty on, supported by poles. You did not have the king bounce around in some old ox cart! So, when Uzzah grabbed it to steady he was struck dead on the spot. Since then, either in myth, legend or in a movie, the curse of the Ark of the Covenant had become widespread and well-known."

"People died for just looking in it, too, right?" Everett confirmed.

Two or three of the people at the producers' meeting looked to Sam as the person best able to give guidance, since he was the only expert in such things in the room. Sam looked at everyone and wanted so badly to give a more correct, biblically accurate and archaeologically significant answer. But, he had none to offer. Their knowledge of the story was fundamentally right and he felt in a way as if he had been shown to be impotent at a critical moment.

Struggling for something to say, he simply responded, "I am a little nervous about taking the lid off of it, honestly." Two of the younger associate producers immediately agreed and said that they were nervous, too. The older, more battle-hardened men were blasé and did not seem too concerned. Then, again, they wouldn't be lifting any lids anyway.

Nevertheless, Sam took the opportunity to remind everyone at the table of the religious significance of these things, and the long mysterious route that the Ark had apparently taken to get to Ethiopia. "How many men had probably sacrificed their lives to save it?" he wondered aloud. "How significant this would be in Christian circles, Jewish circles, and Muslim circles?" he asked openly. Once more, Sam underscored just how valuable this item was, and what a great a risk the Ethiopians were taking by allowing it to be photographed and video-recorded before it was spirited out of the area to a place secretly prepared for it.

This led Everett to the inevitable question: "Where is it headed after the broadcast?"

Sam explained, "One of the conditions of the numerous contracts that our attorneys had to sign back in the States regarding this matter was that each member of this crew would not be able to ask anyone, in any language, where it was to go. That was partly for your own protection."

There was a lengthy silence, a little uncomfortable, as the men thought of the implications of this. Everett cleared his throat and said, "OK, understood; but it would be helpful if we could know a bit more of the picture of what is meant to happen after we've gone live on this. There's gonna be such a surge of excitement on the part of some of our audiences, especially in the southern states of the USA.”

In his heart, Sam was enamored with the idea of opening up the Ark of the Covenant. He explained with passion, “This is something that contained the tablets upon which the finger of God actually engraved words; that contained a brass bowl full of some of the manna He miraculously provided that sustained the Hebrews for forty years in the wilderness wanderings; Aaron’s staff that actually budded, showing Moses’ mantle of authority being passed on to Aaron as they approached the Holy Land. The box itself was overlaid with gold, and by now is thousands of years old.”

One thing was for sure, Sam thought—he knew that he would be forever linked with the Ark of the Covenant. It was going to change his life.

He could not have known just how true that thought was.

-8-

Six of the men were late, even though there was precious little else for them to do. Brisbane paced, the emotions showing on his tanned face a mixture of anxiety and anger as he waited for them. The others had gone through the security checkpoint with the false documents he had passed out to them, and so far everything had gone according to plan. With the stragglers now present, matters moved quickly and soon everyone was positioned in whatever level of comfort or discomfort the old cargo plane afforded them. Its weathered aluminum skin rattled as the props turned and the engines roared to life. Smoke billowed out of one of the engines at one point, but eventually dissipated.

The murmuring of the men under Brisbane's command had reached a fever pitch as everyone found a place, but now its four loud propeller engines vibrated at a different pitch as they began to ascend. It would be necessary to keep the plane below 10,000 feet due to the lack of oxygen masks, and the lack of pressurization of the plane. They would be slower than most other planes, so a trip such as this would involve flying time of well over twelve hours. Given their later-than-planned start, and then a delay because of some complications in the air traffic control system, it was only in the early afternoon that they were finally aloft over the crisscross patterns of the fields of the English countryside.

After several refueling stops, they arrived at dawn the following morning in a very different setting. The old air strip looked like it had not been repaved since the Second World War, and a mixture of dust and grit caused the plane a strange series of vibrations as it taxied to a rough stop.

First to deplane were the local Ethiopian men who made their way into a low-roofed building to make arrangements to get the vehicles that Brisbane had ordered. At a prompt from the blond Australian, who had had his cell phone glued to his ear since they had landed, two white vans that resembled smaller UPS trucks in the USA backed up to the plane next to the hangar. Another local army troop carrier arrived. Some distance away from behind a fence, some local townsfolk stood by, idly looking on. Under the watchful eye of Oslo and Gundy, the other men loaded bags and cartons concealing their weapons, along with various other supplies and equipment, and it was not many minutes before these were soon stashed in the back of the two vans. This type of scene would have heated up the phone lines in England or America, but barely raised an eyebrow on the outskirts of Aksum in Ethiopia. The last item to be loaded was the large, empty wooden crate built to specifications laid out by Brisbane according to his newfound biblical knowledge of such things.

As the vehicles pulled away, Speck looked out toward the runway. As he watched, the old cargo plane started to taxi on the perimeter strip toward the end of the runway from where it would soon lift off on its return flight. As it disappeared from his vision, he wondered what it would be like on this operation in such a remote location as Ethiopia.

-9-

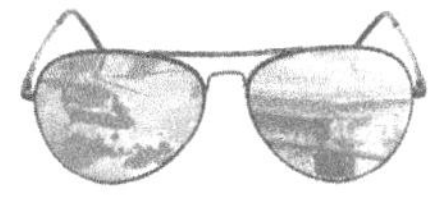

After a few days of downtime while the initial background shooting was taking place, Sam's attention was somewhat engaged with thoughts of Angela. He was surprised at how much he seemed to miss her when he was halfway around the world from her, in comparison with when he was stateside only a short distance away.

She had settled in Memphis for her job at St. Jude Children's Research Hospital, whereas Sam had not actually settled in at all. He preferred the great West with its heritage of large dinosaur digs in Montana, South Dakota, North Dakota, and Idaho, to the humid and lazy South, or the uptight and cold Northeast.

When he had visited her in Memphis to see her the last time, he had only been able to stay for three days. They always made sure they did a couple of tourist-like things every time he came to town. During that time, it would break the ice that might have formed between them and things like this would help reconnect them. "It is us against the world," Angela would often say, her eyes smiling, when they got together.

"Yes, we are sane and they are all crazy," he would laugh in agreement.

This most recent trip had included a favorite for tourists and locals alike—the famous Rendezvous Barbecue Restaurant. "Only in Memphis would a world-famous barbeque restaurant be in an alley," reflected Sam. Angela, who only worked a few blocks away and could ride the trolley down for lunch whenever she had a long enough break, told him that dry barbeque (as opposed to wet barbeque) was very unusual.

"You don't have to tell me," Sam said. "Everywhere I have been, barbeque has sauce all over it."

Angela explained, "There is sauce on this, but without the liquid, so your mouth makes the sauce." She brushed back her honey-blonde hair as she regarded him from over the table, taking a drink from her ice water. They split a full rack of ribs, and, toward the end of the meal, Sam had become a believer in this very unusual type of barbeque. Angela informed him, "If you do put sauce on it, and mix it with the spices, that is called getting it muddy." Of course, Sam had to try it. That and the endless supply of sweet tea, and extra-sweet Red Beans and Rice made him not want to leave, even when he was done.

He looked around at all of the waiters. Angela explained that almost all of the waiters in this restaurant had been there for decades. They were mostly dignified looking black men who had a soft touch with people. They might scream at the cook and tease the customer in the same breath. It gave Sam just a moment's sadness that some two hundred years ago, the ancestors of some of these waiters had come from some of the regions not too far from where he was going. He was looking forward to spending what promised to be the most significant point of his life doing the live televised find.

After the barbeque, Sam, not exactly the most romantic of men, figured out at least one thing correctly—that women love carriage rides. They walked over to the famous Peabody Hotel and took a carriage ride around the edge of Beale Street and through Confederate Park, Court Square, and arrived back in time to go see the ducks parade out of the fountain in the Peabody lobby.

9

"That is a fascinating tradition," Angela explained, an expert now in all things to do with Memphis. "Back in the '30s, I think, well-to-do duck hunters would sometimes stay here on their way back and forth to Arkansas' famed duck hunting areas. Back then," she explained, "they did not have plastic decoys; you actually had to use live ducks with a weight tied around their legs and they would just place them around in the water to bring in other ducks to shoot them. Turns out some of the hunters, probably after a beer or two, had left their live decoys down here in the fountain, and the guests loved it. Let me take you up on the roof; they actually have a mansion up there for the ducks."

Sam looked at her blankly and then said, "You are kidding; I guess I have to see a mansion made for ducks." They rode the elevator to the roof of the Peabody and stepped out. It was not a huge building but it was certainly tall for the Memphis skyline, and it afforded a wonderful view. The exterior part of the roof was surrounded by an ornate, wrought-iron fence rail along the edge that allowed one to look almost straight down to the bottom of the building. The back of the bright red, electrically lit letters on the "The Peabody" sign shone down onto Angela's face and highlighted her blonde hair as they walked around to the little mansion built for the ducks.

"Well I'll be doggone," Sam said. "You are right."

In the evening stillness, the sounds of the street seemingly a long way below them, Angela looked up at Sam and said coyly, "So are you gonna stand there or kiss me?"

Sam said, "Hmm," and feigned having trouble deciding between the two. Then he took her in his arms and kissed her tenderly.

But, she got tickled and just could not stop giggling.

Moments like these made for good reminiscences. When Sam's thoughts came back to his present situation, he was sitting in a trailer on the outskirts of Aksum in Ethiopia looking at a mirror across from him and smiling stupidly. Seeing his reflection, he said, "Would you stop grinning like that!" but he mused upon the fact that it had always been Angela, her face lit up with her gentle smile and infectious laugh, who had been there for his happiest moments—and those moments that were not defined by his archaeological work.

He wondered if his life could be split between the two. Could he have a wonderful career all around the world and yet still have a happy home life with Angela? He suspected it would not work out, that, even selfless as she was, she might demand more than he had to give, and that she would be very jealous of his long travel schedule. But there was so much more to discover, and Sam had proven that he had a knack for putting information from the Scriptures together, using ancient clues, maps, and other writings to locate things that other people had searched for their entire lives. He still couldn't get over that he was turning thirty-one. Being thirty didn't bother him and yet he thought it should have; but being thirty-one, well, you see, he wasn't thirty anymore. Thirty is a sole number; you are either thirty or you are not thirty, but once he had turned thirty-one, he was into his "thirties." That was a different category. He wondered if the same thing would happen to him at forty-one.

As he surfed through the channels, he was amazed to find that there was actually some cable television there. However, they were not carrying the Archaeology Channel. "Not yet anyway," he said out loud.

-10-

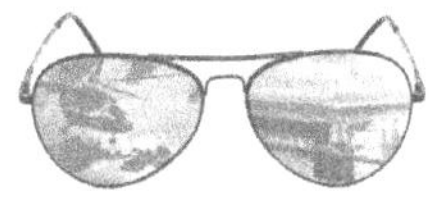

As the trucks arrived in the old school parking lot, a large gate was unlocked. It occurred to several of the men that so many things in Africa, so far, had big chain link fences around them—even places like schools—including those that had been long-abandoned.

Brisbane explained, as they entered, that this was going to be their temporary home for the next eleven days. After their heist, they all could live wherever in the world they wanted, he boasted. There had been some talk about what the take would be on this deal. Every time somebody had talked about the gross total being in the millions, Brisbane would look at them as if he were a priest they had committed a cardinal sin. "Not millions; Billions with a big B," he would chide.

Louie and Vince were talking amongst themselves as they heaved their bags from the vehicle. "Why would he pay the gross national product of a small country for a box full of rock or whatever else was in this thing?"

When he overheard this, T.J. explained briefly, "You guys don't understand; Brisbane has something here, and not only is this thing the most valuable thing, it is not that well protected. On top of that, it is in a country that has virtually zero security. We just unloaded assault weapons out of an aircraft into trucks and nobody even looked sideways at us. Furthermore—and I don't want to go too fast for you boys—but everybody will want this thing; the Jews will want it because they want to rebuild their temple. Brisbane showed me some of the stuff that he had been reading about that. The Christians in America and around the world will want it because it is evidence of the existence of God and their whole way of thinking. It is like Noah's Ark, or even better. Heck, the Muslims are going to want it because they accept a lot of the Old Testament and they just simply don't want the Jews to get it."

Louie asked, "Why do the Muslims hate the Jews so much?"

"We don't have time for that story today," T.J. answered.

Brisbane came through the school house and directed everyone to their various rooms which had apparently been pre-assigned. Nobody could fault the Australian for not being a good planner. Everything so far had been handed to them. When they needed communication equipment, Brisbane handed them headsets. When they needed a specific kind of watch, Brisbane handed them watches. It became interesting to a few of the participants just to wonder what Brisbane was going to walk by with next.

"So what do we do now, Boss?" Vince asked him as he walked by very hurriedly.

"You just stay here and stay out of sight and you will have your instructions soon," he replied in an emotionless tone.

The following morning, Brisbane had somehow arranged with two of the Ethiopians, the ones he called Popeye and Garfield, for a real breakfast to be brought in. The whole team had survived for over twenty-four hours on granola bars, beef jerky and protein shakes, and whatever else they had bought with them. Now they had an actual breakfast—scrambled eggs, biscuits, gravy, and something that looked a lot like ham or Canadian bacon, but not exactly. It tasted wonderful and these men put down a lot of food.

Bubba, the biggest of the snipers, quipped, "What's for dinner now that I am finished with breakfast?" Brisbane ignored him.

10

Missing from all of the action at breakfast were Speck and Slim, the men who had been assigned to work on communications and computers. Brisbane explained that they were in the process of turning one of those white vans into a mobile communication center. Several moments later, Speck appeared and asked if Mr. Oslo or Mr. Gundy would please come out and help them unfold the satellite antennae. With a grunt, Gundy got up, leaving the remains of what looked like the rinds from over four pounds of bacon on his plate. Some of the other team members looked around, one wondering aloud if Gundy would eat them if they were just late feeding him one day.

At the truck, Gundy took the satellite antennae that had handles for four men to pick up, and seized it up in a bear hug, lifting it into position, high in the truck. "Do you want me to put on top?" he asked.

"No sir," Slim said. "We feel like that would be kind of obvious so we cut a hole in the top of the truck and covered it in a smoky but still transparent type of glass that allows the signal to pass through but does not allow the antenna to stick out. That is why we just need it lifted up to that shelf, sir." Slim was careful to say "sir" to a man like this who looked as if he could throw him into space using just one arm.

Gundy grunted, "Anything else?" in a way that made Speck think about the character made of the stone called "Thing" in the *Fantastic Four* comic books.

"No sir, thank you, sir." They were both quick to respond.

Gundy stepped off the van. They felt the vehicle lift on its suspension as his feet touched the ground and the suspension returned to its normal position now that his massive form no longer weighed it down.

Walking back in, Gundy helped himself to another plate of food. Brisbane was glad that he had not underestimated the amount necessary. Gundy spoke to Brisbane and asked why they needed a satellite. Brisbane did not seem to mind the intrusion and appeared to regard Gundy as smarter than most people considered a man of his size and raw strength. He explained in the hearing of a few that that satellite feed was actually designed to pick up the feed coming out of the television truck that would be broadcasting for the

Archaeology Channel from the temple. Brisbane further went on to explain to Gundy: "Live television does not mean actually in real time, as there is still a delay that is mandated, sometimes as little as seven seconds, just to censor unwanted language. Also, with a satellite drop feed all the way from Africa there is often a delay to make sure that there is a seamless transmission and so that static does not mess up the whole thing. I believe the delay here will be about twenty minutes. But we are going to have access to it in real time because our satellite feed is going to pick up the actual broadcast from the Archaeology Channel." At that point, Brisbane called one of the Ethiopian nationals to come and join him at the table.

As they discussed the plan, it became clear to those who were close enough to hear that this man—they called Raphael—was an explosives expert as well. Through either the broken English of Raphael or Brisbane's explicit instructions, it was clear that Raphael would be in charge of wiring the Archaeology Channel's production trucks all to explode simultaneously the day of the strike, but only after their digital signal had been fed to the whole world—everyone that would be tuning in. It was clear why no one roomed with Raphael since he had all of the explosives. It was not a room in which to stumble around in the dark.

The snipers and the spotters had found an old soccer ball in one of the empty classrooms, and had somehow arranged the top lid of an old garbage can temporarily mounted from a window as a makeshift basketball goal. Brisbane looked out the window as the snipers took the spotters on for a little three-on-three after breakfast. Brisbane hoped they were as good as they were supposed to be. For this to work, every part of the plan would have to come together at the right moment. Even so, Brisbane had built in certain "contingencies" in case of a problem. He grinned to himself as he thought of this.

-11-

There were going to be a lot of hands to shake. After a long chartered van ride, Sam's first day of meeting the various people began early the following day. Given what seemed to be the incremental nature of the importance of each person he met, it was almost like a stairway. The first people that he met were some local folks that he felt must have ranked in terms equivalent to members of a chamber of commerce in any town in the United States. It included local business executives, smalltime businessmen, key religious leaders, and some of the governmental leaders that existed in the lower level in this part of Ethiopia, known as the Tigray region.

At lunch, he was able to sit down and eat with the people that he had actually made contact with a year ago this month to arrange for this very project to take place. They were essentially associate staff of the particular temple and also included some officials linked with local government. Every church that had emerged from under the jurisdiction of the temple up in Aksum, as well as the ones scattered throughout the regions beyond, all had one thing in common: they all had a scale model of the Ark of the Covenant, built exactly as Scripture described it. Even the one in Memphis, at the Ethiopian Orthodox Church, had one. If anything happened to one of these models, the church ceased to exist. This had been one factor that years ago had pointed Sam's thoughts to Ethiopia—in contrast with Jerusalem or one of the other locations many people more popularly believed that the Ark had landed. In his thinking, it was likely that the Ark would have been taken far away from the Jerusalem Temple, which was destroyed at the end of the early New Testament era.

These men seemed to understand the uniqueness of what was in their possession. They had come to believe that an object such as this being locked away in the secret recesses of an underground location was not doing much good, and it certainly did not serve well the God that they all claimed to worship. That was another thing that they held in common. Sam, being ethnically Jewish, was more immediately accepted by the Ethiopian temple officials who themselves referred to themselves as Jewish. His being a Christian did not threaten them, because of the presence of evangelical Christians in the area and the fine work their missionaries were doing.

"In a sense," Sam had once written in his private journal, "it is a perfect storm." His words continued, "I am young and bold enough to come and ask these people to let out the biggest secret known to history, and they have seen the need in the world, like never before, for the evidence of the one true God to be shown—to have some role internationally. This is indeed a profound and holy thing that I have gotten myself into."

Sam tried to enjoy a dinner that involved some foods that he was not exactly sure of, but he thought he would have probably eaten live worms had they been put in front of him. "If these people change their minds, my career is instantly over," he mused.

His mind sprang back the famous Geraldo Rivera live shoot where Geraldo, who had as much archaeological training as a bowling ball, sensationalized a historical find that was supposed to be earth shattering. It turned out to be some empty mummy's tomb that had been robbed eons before. That kind of thing was not going to happen here! This was either going forward in full quality, with full disclosure (with the exception of the exact location, of course), or it was not going to happen at all. He could live with the associate producers, whom he called "APs," making the journey down underground look a little more dangerous than it probably was, because the lasting archaeological value of this find was going to be so huge that nothing could diminish it.

The one thing that he had been unable to convince these people in more than a year of trying (and had since given up on this point) was putting this in some type of museum. They were just too wary of security issues. What had protected them, they had explained, was the power of God and the power of silence. And really, walls of doubt. The power of neither confirming nor denying the existence of the Ark, its location or its existence at all, while openly celebrating it, was, to them, a strength. In their words, "Secrets are given away one word at a time." Sam could see the wisdom in that, as he sat there lost in thought over his meal, that this unspeakable treasure had been in this place undisturbed by outsiders for maybe a thousand years.

His mind turned to how, at that very moment, other archaeologists had spent lifetimes searching through the temple mount in Jerusalem looking for this lost Ark there. A sense of pride filled him, and he felt a little like a modern-day Indiana Jones, he had to admit. But, his better judgment told him that it wasn't a whip, pistol or snake-jumping skills that got him here. It was, in essence, his ability to relate to people in a warm and natural manner. His mother had taught him early in life to be able to talk to anyone at any level. He had refined this skill ever since. He connected at a heart level with these people, and they trusted him. It was almost like in the United States when celebrities want to get the story out about their lives, they might only talk to a person such as Barbara Walters or Larry King, or whoever it is that they trust. This was a lot like that; there was a greater good that these people sought, and they felt his sincerity.

Apparently, there was also some reason that they were going to have to move the Ark. He could not understand if it was a construction issue with the temple, or if it was just a mandate that was coming down from the head of their temple to move it. He also wondered if it had been moved many times in the past. If that was part of the whole secrecy plan, maybe people were brought through from time to time so that they could see that nothing was there, and then it would be returned. A shell game? It is an ancient concept. They certainly did not seem to have any trouble saying that they could move this out within a half hour after the show aired. Maybe that was the plan. Maybe there was a whole set of interconnecting tunnels and maybe they moved it all the time. Maybe that was why they had been so successful, he wondered. He wanted to ask—yet he did not feel this was the right time. Maybe back at the temple? But he resolved that this was a time of looking forward, not asking a lot of questions. His belly was tight at the thought of the fragility of this whole plan. He thought about all the meetings yet to come at the temple.

Just then, he was jarred back to reality as he was asked a question in broken English. He struggled to understand exactly what the questioner was asking. "Oh, this is better than McDonald's, without a question," he stammered. "Thank you very much." The young Ethiopian waiter seemed pleased. Sam smiled to himself. "Some things from America are known worldwide," he found himself thinking. He was about to be known here, too.

-12-

After another long day of traveling back to Aksum, the sight of the modest temple took his breath away.

It was finally time to meet the Chief Priest and Minister. Some referred to him as "The Monk." Sam and the senior members of the production team were escorted under heavy guard from the hospitality chamber through the multiple fences and walls into the temple courtyard. The ancient iron gates creaked eerily as they turned on their hinges.

With some subdued fanfare, but with very much respect in evidence, the Chief Priest and Minister emerged from a room in the basement. A large-boned man, he carried himself with an air of gravitas. Lines etched the edges of his eyes, and closely cropped gray hair could be seen emerging from under the miter that adorned his head, his robes giving him a sense of dignity and majesty. Notwithstanding his evident importance, and the respect that others around showed him, he seemed to have a warm and friendly spirit. As his hand clasped Sam's, the grip was firm and steady and conveyed a sense of sincere warmth and welcome.

It was hard for Sam to believe he was this close to the prize. He was attending a private banquet in the main hall, knowing that somewhere down below was the lost Ark of the Covenant. But it was not "lost" at all. The Chief Priest stood before them, and everyone ceremonially bowed. His dress was not particularly ornate, but it was clear by his bearing and demeanor that he was the Chief Priest, and everyone knew it. Sam was given a seat that he had actually not noticed that had been left empty for him. With a start, he realized that he had been seated almost directly across from the Chief Priest.

The table was decked with an array of good food; Ethiopian hospitality was being well demonstrated. Watermelon slices gleamed invitingly on a large platter, and bread rolls, freshly baked, were piled up. A selection of cold meats stood next to tall pitchers of water sweating with condensation from the ice inside them. The silverware added a sense of ornate beauty and dignity to the occasion. Servants attended at each end of the chamber, ready to wait on the needs of the distinguished guests.

Sam was the first person that the Chief Priest and Minister addressed. In surprisingly good English he asked how Sam's flight had gone, and they wound up engaging in so much small talk that Sam almost forgot the importance of the situation he was in. As he glanced back and forth at the A-Channel's producers and associate producers, however, it was clear that the importance of the moment was not lost upon them. They knew their careers would be made or broken by how this went, and a careless comment by Sam—something that sounded sacrilegious, disrespectful or too much like an "arrogant American"—could be wrongly construed very quickly, and end this entire effort.

Moreover, the associate producers knew that some of the temple staff had come around to them, hinting that they knew there was much money to be made in this, and they would be glad to have a little cut. Before their arrival, the associate producers had referred matters such as those to their superiors in New York who had negotiated the deal. Without question, there would be significant financial implications for the temple and all of the churches and its dioceses all over the region. There was going to be a major cash infusion, but it would not happen immediately—that would look a little too suspicious. Shell corporations had been set up offshore, and they would be the ones somehow funneling money in under different names to the relevant parties. Significant sums of money had also already been deposited in an escrow fund. Sam was not aware of all of the particulars, but knew that it would not be easily traceable. As a journalist he knew the values calling for one to stay objective and fair, and actually paying for stories like this would kill the deal with CNN and Fox News.

Sam was not entirely surprised to learn that the Ark of the Covenant was apparently not the only relic that had been preserved in being rescued from the temple in Jerusalem. The Chief Priest explained, with an occasional broken English word, about the linen ephods that hung from the special breastplates that the priests wore, and about how small they were. In fact, he continued, only the smallest young man in the church could wear what was designed for some fully grown Jewish men 3,000 years ago. He also said he had a portion of the original veil which measured around seven inches in thickness. "Not length, but thickness," the Chief Priest and Minister emphasized. "It had to mask the actual glory of the LORD."

The Chief Priest explained that some other elements from the temple mount included a bronze laver, a large bowl that was used for ceremonial washing, and a candlestick that was made of gold, ceremonial goblets, and so forth. "These are still at Lake Tana," the Chief Priest mentioned, referring to a place the Ark had previously been located.

Sam recalled his previous visit to Lake Tana, and the things he knew were to be found in the monastery on the island there. His mind went back to what an august island it looked like, and how it could only be reached by either boat or by helicopter.

So many things hurried their way through Sam's mind all at once that he could not form the proper questions. The veil was seven inches thick. Okay, that was to hide the glorious light of God, because God came and dwelt in the Holy of Holies in the temple, Sam reasoned. He recalled some details from his studies: the temple was divided into three sections—boxes within boxes, as it were—the Outer Court and then the smaller Inner Court and then finally toward the rear and inside, the inner court was known as the "Holy of Holies." It was bordered by the thick veil, and only the chief priest could go in, and then that was only for special sacrifices—blood sacrifices. It was a grisly thought, the idea of slitting the throats of innocent animals, and having their life blood run all over the mercy seat, but it was an important symbolic gesture.

Sam knew the Bible taught him that in the Garden of Eden, when Adam and Eve sinned, an innocent animal died. This was inferred from the passage in Genesis 3 where Adam and Eve were hiding with those well-known fig leaf coverings. Due to their sin, God struck an animal down and made "tunics of skin" for them. That was the first shedding of innocent blood for the sin of man, and was mentioned in the book of Genesis.

That practice—the shedding of blood—was carried on in the well-known story of Cain and Abel, two of the many sons of Adam and Eve, and two of only three that are mentioned in Scripture by name. Sam thought back to how Cain had offered the first fruits of his field. However, God's requirement was that innocent blood had to be shed in the sacrifice. Abel was the keeper of the flock, so he had a spotless new lamb to offer. Cain would have had to go and trade to get a sheep to do an offering with, and was likely too prideful to do that. Abel offered his firstborn lamb in sacrifice to God, and God showed His approval of it. But when Cain offered the first fruits of his grain and garden, God was not pleased. Cain's jealousy led to the very first murder ever recorded in history when Cain slew Abel. Pride was man being his own god. And, pride led to murder in short order.

"Didn't he say something about goblets, too?" Sam thought. "A goblet? Is he talking about the Holy Grail?" The idea exploded in Sam's mind. But no, the goblets of the temple would have pre-dated the coming of Christ. Still, that was another mystery that he hoped to solve one day. He really would seem like Indiana Jones then, he thought. Maybe he could even solve that one on Pay-Per-View TV where the profits were even higher than those of cable television.

Sam's thoughts were interrupted again, this time by the Priest who had asked him a question. He was so deep in thought that he had not realized what he had been asked. With a quick smile and ready apology, Sam explained to him that he was still overcome with excitement that this was all happening, and he was feeling so much a sense of anticipation for what this could mean for the world that he had missed the question that he had been asked. "Please forgive me and be kind enough to repeat your question," Sam requested.

With a hearty laugh, the Chief Priest asked, "Was your meal better than what you get in your McDonald's in America?"

"Yes, your Honor, it is." Sam wondered if that was on some kind of list of suggested talking points to speak to the Americans about, and especially to compare sumptuous food like this with the food served at McDonalds! It was so true—American culture had reached everywhere he had ever traveled. In a few more short days Americans, Europeans, Australians, Asians, Africans and South Americans would all see Sam's larger-than-life persona live on TV, unlocking the greatest mystery of the greatest treasure the world had ever known.

-13-

For a few days now, the explosives expert—the Ethiopian they called Raphael—had been exceptionally busy, tasked, as he was, by Brisbane. The stash of explosives in his room included everything a bomb-maker could ever need. Also, the communications men had hardly come out of their van since they had arrived at the school house. Each day, they had spent hours running tests and making adjustments to the complex circuitry they had installed in the vehicle. Speck, his light form hunched over a laptop or bending over an exposed circuit board, screwdriver in hand, was constantly preoccupied with the small but significant improvements he was able to make to the equipment.

While they were working on these matters, there was only one inquisitive visitor, an elderly lady asking what was going on, and Brisbane speedily sent out Raphael's assistant, one of the other Ethiopian nationals, with a trumped-up story about making a documentary—and this seemed to satisfy her.

The school house was Spartan. In the sleeping quarters, the cots were made of metal, with flat mattresses and one sheet and a blanket—quite sufficient for the men in the warm Ethiopian summer climate. Everything was kept in order as directed by Brisbane, but it was not particularly clean. Brisbane felt it a little ironic that big macho guys in his crew were constantly asking about bugs and spiders native to Africa that they had heard about. Apparently, other than the Ethiopian nationals on the team, none of them had been to Africa for any length of time and certainly not to Ethiopia. Brisbane thought it was a little funny that these man-eating, skull-busting mercenaries, to call them by such a term, would be afraid of a few creeping or flying insects. "If it were poisonous snakes, it would be more understandable," he found himself thinking.

It did not take long for the hot and somewhat squalid conditions inside the old school complex to erupt into a brawl between one of the cocky southern snipers, named Jake, and Fabijan, a member of the gunmen's squad that had come from Croatia. While Jake was strong and had a good right hook, he wasn't ready for the smaller man's speed and training in Krav Maga and Brazilian Jujitsu. After a mighty swing by the sniper, Fabijan quickly swept his legs with one giant kick and sent the sniper to the ground, causing him to fall flat on his back and with a sound like a giant bag of flour hitting the floor. The air rushed from his lungs on impact. Within a second, Fabijan had mounted Jake's belly in the way a man sits on a horse, grabbed one of his arms, and begun twisting it. The Eastern European leaned back in such a way as to leave the arm cradled between the Croat's legs, being held against his chest, palm up, as the sniper began to panic. The Croatian then threw his hips into the air and began to bend the elbow of the sniper backward in a move known in Jujitsu as an "arm bar."

Alerted by the sounds of the scuffle, Brisbane strode in and, his voice piercing in its commanding tone, and broke up the skirmish before the capsule in the elbow of the sniper snapped and allowed the entire arm to break backward at the elbow. With his eyes flashing menacingly, the Australian slapped the Croatian across the face and said, "He is on our team! We are together, you blimey idiot. How is he going to shoot with that right arm if you break it? His shot could save your life, you stupid soldier. *Think!*" Brisbane stomped out of the room, obviously disgusted.

The Croatian helped the sniper up, and the sniper, now somewhat humbled, was really fascinated by how he had been beaten. He shook the Croat's hand and asked him to show him a few of those moves. What followed was about a succession of martial arts lessons between some members of the Croats and of the three snipers' teams.

Meanwhile, Speck and Slim were still spending hour after hour cocooned in the van, unraveling what appeared to be miles of wiring inside it, resequencing some circuitry, and busy soldering several connections. Speck's face was permanently shiny with a light film of perspiration, and his glasses kept sliding forward down his nose, leading to an irritating habit in which he had to readjust them, sometimes as many as three or four times a minute. For his part, Slim seemed to be constantly cross-referencing data from a hand-held device before disappearing once more into each of the vans to recalibrate one of the system-linked circuits. "It's vital that we eliminate any potential static interference," Brisbane had told him, and he was anxious to ensure that no electrical discharge could take place that might cause even a small surge in the current.

In the back room, the remainder of the Croatian hit team numbering three, and the couple of snipers and spotters, who were not currently involved in the martial arts lessons, were talking. As they found common ground, they discussed what they thought the total take of money would be. One of the Croatians, Jusuf, brought up something that the snipers had never thought about. A souvenir or just a small piece of the Ark would be valuable. Even ground into powder and sold in little souvenir key chains, it could still bring millions of dollars. "There will probably be other relics there, too," volunteered one of the spotters. The other Croatian, Tadej, a burly man with broad features, offered the comment that, "The less of us that is on the team, the fewer portions it must be split into."

"Aw you noticed that, too," said one of the snipers.

"I'd like to know what that Vince and Louie have to do with all of this," Tadej offered in surprisingly good English. "I mean Brisbane is putting together a pretty good little plan. He has put research into it, done a regular multimedia presentation for us, and all I can see Vince and Louie doing is sitting over there looking confused."

"I noticed the same thing" sneered Jusuf.

"Well, they must have a purpose," said the spotter, Jim Bob. "Brisbane didn't bring anyone in here without a purpose. I understand why the three nationals are involved. One of those guys, Raphael, is a crack bomb guy—anyone can see that. He was showing me some pretty cool stuff," he went on. "He has got enough C4 to blow this whole place away."

"Two of them, the ones Brisbane calls Popeye and Garfield, are very well connected and can get us in and get us what we need while we are here. I understand that," Jim Bob continued his thought. "I sometimes wonder whether their connections here in town are always being used to everyone's best advantage here in our group."

Jusuf added wryly, "I also understand the place for you sniper guys, assuming that there is some type of outside positioning for you. I certainly understand why we, as a gunman hit team, are involved. The two geeks out in the van make sense, and I understand Oslo and Gundy—you need some weight lifting because all of this stuff is going to be heavy, and if there is a security breach, I wouldn't want to face either one of them with just a knife."

"Man, you can say that again," said John David. "One of those guys looks like three of me, and I am no small guy."

"That's so true," said one of the spotters.

"You don't snore like a small guy either," Jim Bob joshed.

"Aw hush, I'll give ya a kiss tonight when we lay down, darlin'," John David laughed.

"So that brings us back around to Louie and Vince. Did they finance some of this operation or something?" asked Jim Bob.

"Beats me," said Jusuf, shaking his head slowly, "but I would like to find out."

"Well, can't we just agree," said Jim Bob, "that all of us shooters will hang in it together to make sure each other gets taken care of. I am not really worried about the rest of those boys."

"Done," said Jusuf.

"Done," said Tadej, who had remained silent for some minutes.

* * *

In another room down a passage, Brisbane was sitting with Raphael, the Ethiopian national. His dreadlocks hung heavily around his neck, and the opening of his tee-shirt displayed small outcrops of hair covering his rippling chest. "Raphael, how many remote detonators did you bring?" he asked.

Raphael responded, "Well, sir, I brought five large ones for the production trucks as we thought they may have at least four, and I wanted a spare."

"What about the small ones?" Brisbane asked.

"I brought twenty of them, just as you asked, but you never did tell me what those were for."

Brisbane responded, "I will get to that later. In the meantime, take your C4. I need it as thin, small, and as light as you can get it—and no bigger than this," he continued, holding up a small smartphone.

Raphael looked quizzically. "That would be the right size to kill a man sitting at a desk, or to kill a man opening a locker. The large sections are to blow up the truck. I also have some other manual detonation C4 in the event there are vault doors or walls, as you said. But, I still don't understand the twenty remote detonators and these small amounts of C4 that you wish for me to aggregate."

"You just get them ready and keep it to yourself," Brisbane said tersely, his eyes steely blue in the dim office.

"Yes, sir," Raphael responded dutifully.

-14-

Sam felt as if he had done about all of the bowing and hand-shaking and mouthing the words "Your Honor" and "Your Highness" that he could possibly do for one day. It was as if he had been to a dinner with celebrities such as Prince William and Kate or perhaps a cluster of film stars after an Oscar awards presentation. Everyone was really nice, and he did not screw anything up, much to the relief of the associate producers who were to be seen everywhere. But he was now feeling tired of this whole formal ordeal, and he was ready to lay his jet-lagged body down.

Before he did, he checked to see what time it was back in the USA. "She will be up by now," he thought, as he took out his cell phone to call Angela. He caught her on the way out the door of her apartment. He could hear the sound of keys in her hand as she answered.

There was a breathless "Hello," as Angela spoke.

"Hey, hon," Sam said, smiling.

"Where are you?" Angela asked.

"You know where I am—I cannot tell you," Sam said in a confidential-sounding tone.

"Oh, that is right, I am sorry; I almost forgot about the top secret cloak-and-dagger guy that I am in love with."

"Well this cloak-and-dagger guy is in love with you, too," he replied, "although I am not sure where I go to get my cloak and dagger. I have not been issued anything close to that, and it is way too hot over here for a cloak, but that is more information than I should really give you. Now I think I have to have you killed," he quipped.

"Yeah, yeah, I got it," she said.

"Are you heading off to work?" he asked.

"We are making some breakthroughs!" she said excitedly.

"Angela, I don't want to cool your jets or anything, but you say that every single time," he responded with a smile in his voice.

"No, I know, I know! And I know that a lot of the breakthroughs are just like Lego pieces; they are one little tiny bit at a time, but they are bringing us to a greater point," she explained. "We have now found what seems to be a genetic mapping protein that might rearrange the sequencing on one kind of cancer gene. It literally makes it not reproduce, or we think so anyway—we are still testing." Sam paused for a minute; he was interested this time, so he did not have to fake it, but he didn't want to seem too uninformed.

"Angela, I thought all cancer did is reproduce," he said.

"Well, right, that is true," Angela said. "But it is the sequencing that codes the cells to do that; we figured out if we reorder the sequencing, at least in laboratory rats, the cancer may not die but at least it doesn't grow. And if it doesn't grow, and we can kill what is already there."

"Let me get this right. . .are you saying that you might have cured cancer?" he asked, truly surprised.

"Well, no, but I am saying that it is a great possibility. At least for this type of cancer anyway," Angela answered, "but you have got to keep this on the hush-hush, too. We need a lot more funding to carry out more tests."

"Aw, I understand, now I have a cloak-and-dagger girl, huh," he joked.

She laughed; he could hear the smile in her voice as she continued: "I guess so, but hey, I really have to get to work. There are some people coming downstairs to see what we are talking about today, and I really want to be prepared."

"Hon, I am very proud of you," he said, very sincerely.

"Well I am very proud of you, too, Mr. Sam Cohen, you big-time globe-trotting archeologist."

"Don't call me that," he said shyly.

"I love you," she replied.

"I love you, too," he said.

"I will try to talk to you soon. Hey, don't forget to watch!" Sam reminded her.

"I wouldn't miss it for the world. Everyone will be watching. It is all over the television already," Angela said. "I've arranged to record it on Tivo, too, so you can watch it with me when you get back," she said.

"Love ya!"

* * *

In Sam's office back in New York, the whole studio complex was abuzz with activity. But Marjorie, his personal assistant, was standing at a lone fax machine in the executive suite, her thin lips pursed as she keyed in some numbers. She brushed back a graying wisp of hair from her temple as she did so.

An updated itinerary, complete with all of the broadcasting times and feeds including when CNN and FOX News would pick up the broadcast, passed through the facsimile machine.

At that moment, in Aksum, the fax machine located on an up-turned box in Brisbane's makeshift office in the old school house rang; within moments, several sheets of paper emerged. Brisbane reached over, paged through the information, and, with a look of strong contentment, assured himself that he had the best mole for this job that he could possibly have.

Some moments later, there was the sound of feet at Brisbane's office door.

"Hey, Brisbane," the usually quiet spotter, Tex, asked, with a knock on the door. "How long are we going to sit around this school house waiting on some action? We have only a few days left, and you have still not gone over the whole plan with us."

"We'll talk tonight at dinner," Brisbane replied calmly, still perusing the printed facsimile sheets.

"I heard that the Ethiopian guys are supposed to be getting us some American style pizza; I sure could use it."

"Seven p.m.," Brisbane said without looking up from the sheaf of papers in his hands.

In the back of the school house, the martial arts lessons had concluded. The men were talking excitedly about their favorite Ultimate Fighting stars and all about arm bars, triangles, and other jujitsu holds. The evening meal would be welcome when it came.

-15-

Sam was awakened by a call. As strong as his constitution was and as much as he was accustomed to trying new cuisine in the different countries he traveled to, the variety of foods from the previous day had not mixed very well, and he was feeling groggy in the pre-dawn darkness. It was too early. Drake, one of the producers, was on the phone. Drake had always sounded a lot like a soap opera name to Sam, and he couldn't help but think of this every time he heard it.

"Sam, I have been going over the security implications with each individual crew member once again here, and we have had some additional concerns expressed by our liability carrier."

"Are you talking about the insurance company?" Sam asked, thinking that that sounded like a mighty strange subject to discuss.

"Yes, we have been contacted by the liability carrier and the underwriter, or actually the re-insurer for them, which is a large consortium in London," Drake said. "This is a fairly dangerous mission in their eyes. It was not easy to get it insured in the first place.

I am sorry to call so early, but I have been on the phone with New York all morning. The time difference is a killer."

"Well, I don't see what is so dangerous about it—other than the heartburn, of course," he groaned as he rubbed his stomach. "I mean all we are really doing is going into a room and taking pictures of something, for goodness' sake. It is a lot less dangerous than when I had to be guided into the caves where the Dead Sea Scrolls were found!" Sam exclaimed.

"I knew you would feel that way," Drake said, "but you are so close to this that you don't see the greater picture, Sam. Maybe it is because I have got a lot more gray hair than you have. I have just sensed from the very beginning of this project that maybe you don't understand how big the risk really is."

"Okay, so what is the risk? Why don't you just spit it out and stop talking in code?" Sam asked, irritated at being awoken with this issue.

"Sam, if somebody finds out *why* we are here and *what* we are doing, this place is really very vulnerable," Drake related. "Have you seen just how lax everything is from a security point of view, at least outside the temple grounds?"

"Well, they have kept the Ark here or near here for probably a thousand years or so—and you well know that, anyway," Sam pointed out.

"I know, I know," Drake said. "They have kept the Ark here for maybe a thousand years because they have moved it around, they have kept it guarded, and they have never really memorialized it. They have never shown it. Heck, they have never even officially acknowledged its existence!" Drake exclaimed. "God knows all of the different steps they have taken to keep this place secure—or at least to keep everybody off balance long enough that nobody has seriously attacked them," he observed. "You are aware that there have been attempts in the Temple Mount in Jerusalem, aren't you?"

"I know. I have seen the evidence of those. All of that digging and blasting, and all of the unauthorized excavation that ruins objects," Sam said, sickened by the memories.

"Right, right," Drake agreed. "You know, if here in Aksum wasn't about the fifth or sixth most likely site that people thought the Ark was, it would have already been stolen. The only thing that may have saved them here is that this is probably the least likely of all of the suggested Ark sites, based on the evidence that is out there on the Internet and everywhere else. Plus, this temple looks so innocuous sitting out here, no one has made anything like a serious attempt to break into it," Drake concluded. "Everybody looks at Mt. Nebo, or the Dead Sea Scroll caves, or under the Temple Mount, or even in Petra."

"I have been to those places, too," Sam reminded Drake.

"But what I am talking about is *risk*," Drake said emphatically. "If somebody smells what we are doing here, we are all sitting ducks. We are going to pinpoint this thing on worldwide, not just national, but worldwide television."

"But these folks tell me that they can move it at a moment's notice and that they have done it several times, though they won't tell me about the stories behind that. But, I trust them," Sam responded.

"I know that they said in negotiations that there are tunnels that go in loops for miles that are purposely designed that way. As a matter of fact, Sam, they actually said they find old skeletons down below sometimes from people checking out the Ark stories," Drake mentioned.

"Good to know," Sam said. "Maybe we could include a video of them because that would be great teaser right before the show—to add the skeletons." Sam began to get excited as he imagined this being brought into the plan of shooting.

Drake interrupted him. "The purpose of this call, if I could interrupt your youthful enthusiasm for just a moment. . . ."

"Okay what is it?" Sam relented.

Drake continued, ". . .this call is to remind you of risk. You *cannot* let anyone know why we are here, or even that we *are* here. You have to be vague, and you have to act noncommittal. If you go out and do anything in this town, you could be recognized," Drake continued.

"Well they don't have our channel here; I was walking around here all day yesterday and nobody has ever seen me," Sam confided. "I just look like some kind of Jewish or Greek tourist."

"I hear you. I am just telling you to please watch your back, please realize the value of what we are dealing with here, and just how far wrong this *could* go," Drake responded. He cleared his throat and continued: "Just consider how fast this thing could go *horribly* wrong. I think I have got the liability insurance guys calmed down, but they want me to bring at least one armed guard."

"For what?" Sam exclaimed.

"I guess just to babysit us, and hold our hands. Maybe to discourage people, even the locals. I personally think it could bring more attention, so I have tried to talk them out of it. Plus, the more guns that we have around," Drake said gravely, "the more likely someone is going to get shot. Besides, how do we even know which ones of these locals to trust? We could get set up by one of them."

"None of the locals are even allowed to come in this temple, at least not the part where the Ark is supposed to be," Sam said.

"I know," Drake said. "But I think these are just knee-jerk reactions from the insurance company because they claimed that we did not brief them clearly enough on this trip right from the start, and they wanted a lot more safeguards than we have. Now they are craw fishing, you know, going backward, on the coverage. No coverage, no shoot, Sam. Heck, they are even peeved because not everyone has a satellite-phone."

"But Drake, we've got giant satellite trucks out in front, for the love of Pete!" argued Sam incredulously.

"I know," Drake said, "but they are concerned about a hostage situation. When I talked to them, it sounds like they are concerned about a kind of situation around the Ark where everybody will be held hostage or killed when we try to get to it."

Sam said, "You know, they have been watching too much Spike TV."

"That may be true," Drake said. "But I think I have got their jets cooled. I talked to a vice president who sold us the first policy a long time ago when we were a smaller operation, and explained to him that we have been in a lot more dangerous places. Heck, we've been digging bones over there with shells and rockets going right over us out of Palestine and Gaza," Drake said.

"Tell me!" Sam rejoined. "Remember the mortar shell in Gaza that flipped our truck, so we had to walk?"

"Exactly, that's what I am talking about with them," Drake said.

"They didn't seem to be worried about that and there was an

actual war going on then," Sam said.

"But, you are worth a lot more now, Sam. We *do* have you insured for much more now, though," Drake informed him.

"Well I wouldn't worry too much about it," Sam said. "It sounds like you cooled them off," Sam assured him as he upturned a bottle of antacid tablets and chewed them noisily.

"All right, well I will give some thought to whether or not we need an armed guard or whatever. I don't really see us finding somebody that we can check the background on this week."

"Well," Sam said, "that is why you are a producer and I am just a pretty boy on TV, just a talking head. I am glad that you have your job, and not me."

"Aw, go back to sleep!" Drake said.

"All right. Look, it will all be fine. Nothing will happen! Take care," Sam said, and he hung up and settled back in bed as the dawn began to lighten the cracks around the window blinds.

-16-

"**H**ow is it coming on in here, gentlemen?" Brisbane asked as he stuck his head inside the van. It was bristling with wires, gadgets, gizmos, readouts, radar displays, and various screens. Brisbane was genuinely impressed—and he was certainly not a man easily impressed. Slim answered, "Sir, we are doing fine. Give me another day, and I will be able to tell you when the president of Zambia goes to the bathroom."

"Well that will be quite valuable information, I'm sure," Brisbane remarked in an expressionless voice.

Speck added, his eyes magnified behind thick lenses, blinking, "Uh, sir, we are looking good on everything, and I am actually already picking up the routine communication from their production vans. Mostly it's cell phone traffic, but we have a couple feeds where they are doing video recording of the countryside around the area. I think it is for later broadcasts after everything is done, you know, 'B-roll' stuff, but I think they are taking pictures before everything gets trampled down, and so forth."

"Okay. Digitize and store everything just in case it comes in handy later," Brisbane ordered.

"Got it, Boss. Already on it," Speck responded. He turned the dial on one of the recording devices near the back of the vehicle.

"By the way, there is no way that they can tell that we are intercepting their signal, is there?" Brisbane asked.

"Not with what they have got," Slim said. "Those guys are the equivalent of eight-track tapes over there, but they think they are cutting edge. With the power that we have here, I could overload their satellite feed and just burn it up if I wanted to."

"Well, I don't think that will be necessary," Brisbane said.

"Yes sir, but it would be really cool," Slim interjected.

Brisbane smiled, patted the side of the truck with echoing thuds as he exited, and walked back into his school building office.

As he entered his office, the fax machine was spitting out sheets listing account numbers—ones that had been issued in the last seventy-two hours in offshore accounts in the Caymans and Switzerland. There was also one account that had no apparent origin as it was purely Internet-based. "I hope these come in handy," Brisbane said quietly to himself as he shuffled them into separate stacks, neatly labeling each one.

-17-

The bright light through the window told Sam it was later in the morning when the phone rang again in his trailer. "Hello, you had better be beautiful," he grunted.

"Sam, good morning, ahem, it's Drake again."

"Um, what time is it? Weren't we talking when I went to sleep earlier?" Sam asked.

"Uh, we probably were. I have already spoken to people at the home office earlier this morning or at least this morning *our* time. I hate the time difference. Anyway, this is what I need to tell you: they are definitely going to send a guy over to keep an eye on you."

"What do you mean to 'keep an eye' on me?" Sam asked, trying to mask a yawn. "What do they think I am going to do?"

"No, I mean keep an eye on you to keep you safe," Drake said.

"Oh, that's right! Safe from the boogeyman!" Sam said in a mock scary voice. "I forgot about the bogeyman," he continued, his tone a little sarcastic. "They are going to come and what. . .fly planes into the building? They did not stop that in New York. They hit that same insurance company's own corporate office on 9/11. I feel safer here than I do in Manhattan."

"Now, I don't have any time for that," Drake said sternly. "I am just doing my job, and watching out after you at the same time."

"I haven't done anything, and nothing is going to happen. These people you are talking with are nutty. I have been in a lot more dangerous situations than whatever they have conjured up in their dreams," Sam said, his tone reassuring.

"I can see the wisdom of this," Drake said. "You know, whether you like it or not, Sam, you are star, or at least a rising star. You are probably going to need some security from here onward, wherever you go."

"Really?" Sam asked. He had not given this any thought until now.

"Yeah, I am not just saying this to blow up your already overly inflated TV-star head." This time it was Drake who spoke in something of a sarcastic tone.

"Oh, thank you, and a good morning to you, sir," Sam quipped. "Drake, you really think it is like that, that it is going to be that way from here onward?" he asked, genuinely concerned. "I won't be able to have a normal life?"

"Normal life?" Drake asked. "What is normal about your life? You fly off to all kinds of weird exotic locations, dig in the sand finding bones, and figure out maps, treasures, and obscure Scripture verses. It would make more sense to me if you got to keep it all, but it goes into some museum some place, and then all of the commercial people make money on you," Drake complained.

"Like you?" Sam rejoined.

"Sam, you have just now got yourself a fairly decent contract, which you know is going to get a lot better if this thing goes well here. That is the point. If this thing goes well, the channel will wind up providing security for you from now on. You don't think Tamara just walks around without anybody, do you?" Drake asked rhetorically. Sam thought back to the beautiful Tamara, his primetime interview with her on the A-Channel, and how the audience had been almost eating out of his hand.

"Are you are comparing me to Tamara?" Sam rejoined.

"Well, you understand, I mean you are going to wind up a very rich and famous man, and you really need to start thinking that way, probably sooner rather than later," Drake underscored. "So anyway, they are sending this guy, some kind of bodyguard, over. I have not met him," Drake clarified. "They tell me that he is really good and he will just be with you and make sure that nobody bothers you." His tone was reassuring.

"Great, I get a chaperone," Sam said with a sigh. "Can I get a hall pass because I am going to have to go wee-wee in a while and I will need to go to the little boys' room?" His voice intoned that of a little boy.

"Ha ha," Drake replied in mock humor. "You really may not understand the security aspect of being a prima donna, but you are definitely understanding the behavioral aspect of it. Maybe we should move you to Hollywood, where you can get arrested for 'driving under the influence' about nine times, go through rehab, wreck a few Ferraris, and complain loudly that your mocha cappuccino is not just right," Drake said, launching into a full belly laugh.

"You crack yourself up, huh! I don't like where this is going at all," Sam said. "You know I still have not had any darn coffee!"

"Have you already tried the coffee around here?" Drake asked.

"Yeah, it tastes kind of burnt and warmed over, I know," Sam said.

"Look, I'll tell you what, I smuggled some Starbucks coffee into my trailer to brew. I have got a coffee maker with one of those awful adapters that took me thirty minutes to get plugged in right, and I think I almost caused a fire. But I have got good coffee and the trailer is set up pretty well. Come on over to my trailer, and I will tell you more about this bodyguard," Drake said.

"All right, sounds good. I will be there. But I really need a shower first," Sam said. "You think I will be safe enough by myself, or do you want to join me, Drake?"

Laughing, Drake hung up.

-18-

"It looks like we have got just about everybody here," Brisbane said, as the boxes of pizza were brought in by one of the locals. His vehicle, a rather beaten up van, stood outside, its engine occasionally misfiring. The smell of hot pizzas wafted invitingly through the building complex. "Most of you have figured out much of what is happening in this situation. In short, gentlemen this is a historic moment."

John David turned to Jim Bob and said in a hushed tone, "Aw, great; more of the 'historic moment' speech."

"Haven't we heard this before?" Oslo asked loudly. This was what everyone was thinking, but was too afraid to say.

"Yes, and I will not belabor it," Brisbane said, "but don't lose sight of how big a deal this really is. It is the biggest." He pulled down on a string, unrolling a map that had been mounted on the wall. "Now New York and Aksum has a seven-hour time difference. At 11 p.m. in New York, it is 6 a.m. here. Our computer guys, Slim and Speck, have confirmed from their live program feeds that they are going live with the shoot at 11:00 p.m. New York time, or Eastern Standard Time, so viewers from all over North and South America will all be watching at or near prime time live. It will also be fed live through the Internet on CNN, and on Fox News, in addition to the Archaeology Channel."

"Excuse me," Vince said, "just so I understand this point, do you mean there is an entire channel about guys digging up rocks? That is real? Who would watch that?"

"Pretty good stuff," T.J. said, "I watch a lot of TV. I can tell you about TV."

Brisbane interrupted them, "Thank you, gentlemen, for the mutual enlightenment, but let's get back on point. We need to be poised to strike within moments of the broadcasting of the discovery of the Ark. Whatever happens, we have to wait for the broadcast trucks to get the signal out and are broadcasting it before the people in New York know there is anything wrong. This is vital because, at the critical moment when we seize the target, we want to be live, and then allow the signal to continue for the few seconds of satellite lag time. Raphael will detonate the production trucks, but only after we are out with our prize and we are in transit. Everything else that will happen will happen basically underground. Whether or not there are any survivors in the temple doesn't make any difference as far as I am concerned—main thing is that we get away with the Ark and all the other treasures down there." There was a colder, more deliberate tone in Brisbane's voice than anyone had ever heard before.

"Okay, but how are we going to know all of this is going on underground?" asked Jim Bob.

"That is not a bad question there, Billy-Joe-Jim-Bob," Brisbane said mockingly.

"Very funny," responded the spotter.

"Remember, my friend, that we are reading the feeds coming out of the tunnels in real time, courtesy of Slim and Speck's monitoring," Brisbane reminded him. "Now we will cut all of the electronic communications equipment and satellite feeds only *after* the attack. It is vital that the attack be seen by viewers. Let me just get to the point where you three sniper teams with spotters come in. Because of the kind of work that will be going on, there is going to be a lot of coming and going of the satellite trucks with lighting, sound, and so forth. When I give you the command, I want you to take everybody out that you can see.

"Well, that is fine, but if we use the .50 Cals, we could take the trucks out too," John David advised.

"I know that, and I am sorry to tell you that we are not going to use your .50 Cals. We are not trying to shoot somebody a mile away, and we are not trying to blow up an armored car," said Brisbane. "This should *not* be over-kill. A good deer rifle with a silencer on it will do fine, and tomorrow there will be a truck here that will take you out far into the country for you to get practiced up with a .223 round. I assume that you are familiar with that caliber—at least that is so according to your dossier?" Brisbane queried.

"Heck, yeah, we are familiar with a .223, that's what an M16 shoots, you little. . . ." Jake checked himself and trailed off.

"I am a little. . .what?" Brisbane said, looking at him with an expression reserved for people who have challenged his manhood.

"Uh, we know all about them," the sniper quickly recovered.

"Good. These have the newest silencers on them," Brisbane said with quite evident pride. "I have heard them myself. When they shoot, they make a sound no louder than flicking a match. They are the best that money can buy."

One of the Croatian gunmen asked, "So when do we come in?"

"Okay, I am getting to that," Brisbane said, "Snipers, you will take everybody outside when I give the command. The strike team will then descend within seconds. The feeds, I am assured, will continue to broadcast. We will seize the target, while still live on television. Once we are topside, we blow up a portion of the building itself which will make the tunnel system cave in, and we will then torch the trucks. You did you bring enough C4 for all of that, Raphael?" Brisbane asked, sounding like a teacher asking for homework from a lazy student.

"Yes, sir, and I can always get more from one of my contacts in town," Raphael responded dutifully.

"Go ahead, and get more," Brisbane advised. "This part of the job has to be done thoroughly."

"Daddy want a big boom!" said one of the spotters in his southern drawl. Several men laughed.

Brisbane continued, unmoved: "The four-man strike team will go in to eliminate all resistance and our own Ethiopian nationals will be out front to conjure up whatever story we need, and also to deal with the locals if necessary. They will be well financed. The snipers will also have you gentlemen's backs in the event any authorities show up to give you any trouble. I think that most of the police and military have all been invited to attend a gathering we have sponsored far away from here, right Popeye?" He turned inquiringly to Popeye. In turn Popeye nodded to confirm that the decoy event was in place. "Yes, sir," he confirmed. "You've thought of everything, Boss."

"Does that mean we get to keep our .50 Cals nearby?" John David asked. "Because if the local police come out there in one of their trucks, or something, I am going to take the whole thing down."

"That is agreeable," Brisbane said. "Good thinking."

John David pulled out a huge .50 Caliber Sniper round that measured about six inches in length.

Someone whistled at the sheer size of the shell.

"So, on this old box, you know, that we are lifting, where are we going to take it once we got it?" Vince asked, referring to the Ark.

"You remember that cargo plane you came here in?" Brisbane asked.

"Man, do I? I have still got a headache from that thing," Vince said, rubbing his receding hairline and acne-pocked forehead.

"Well, that is just going to be the distraction," Brisbane continued. "One of our big white vans will be loaded up with a crate and taken to the airport. But, the Ark—the real ark, not the decoy—will actually be removed by an ordinary civilian car parked nearby that will draw no attention to itself. Raphael's friend has arranged for this vehicle—it's the white Chevy we saw for sale at the dealers' yesterday, and the deposit has been paid for it to be picked up tomorrow. The back seat will be removed, so it can hold the Ark."

"All right, I understand that, Boss," Louie said, again trying to establish himself as the brains of the operation. "It is in the car, but where do we take it from there?"

"You will be told that at a later time," Brisbane answered in a dismissive tone. "The plane is presently in Nairobi, and is scheduled to arrive here in the morning on a routine charter flight. Most of you will load the crate on the plane and fly with it out to a rendez-vous at a later point that will be told to you. All of you—you have to all be on the plane, so the getaway from the temple has to be executed flawlessly and quickly."

"Naw, naw, naw. . .I don't like the way this is going," Gundy said, breaking his normal silence. "I am staying with that box because that box is where the money is going to be!"

"When we blow up the production trucks after a live theft on national TV, it might get us a little attention," Brisbane said reassuringly, "regardless of our efforts to suppress outsiders' involvement in our little operation."

Gundy grunted impatiently.

"We *have* to split up, and it is critical that the Ark make it out okay," Brisbane explained. "But, Gundy, you and Oslo will be escorting the Ark personally, and I will be directing you in this matter."

"Good!" grunted Gundy, seeming satisfied.

"For the rest of you, everything will be told to you at the appropriate time," Brisbane assured them. "Remember, gentlemen, we are still five days out. In the morning, you sniper teams will be going out to practice a little shooting with your new rifles. You will be leaving at 8:00 a.m. sharp."

-19-

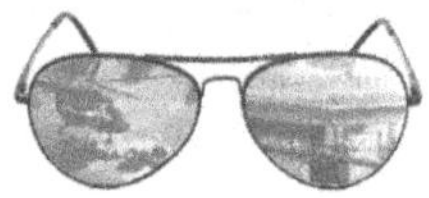

Sam went about his day feeling as if he had already met everyone with a title in Ethiopia the day before, but apparently there were a few stragglers that had been left out. He wondered if the dignitaries that he was to be meeting today were the equivalent of the Miss Cotton Bowl festival or the National Potato Queen or some such event. That is not to say they weren't nice—they *were* nice and their dress was certainly colorful enough; even the men had particularly gaudy robes on.

Sam slipped away before the afternoon meetings began for what might be his last stroll without some giant, dumb, hulking bodyguard.

As he walked along the gritty sidewalks in the warmth of the late morning sunshine, he found himself taken by the women's long necks and to the way they could carry things on their heads. They were not just things that you might expect, such as small baskets, but they actually carried large jugs of water. He remembered from his days as a student when he studied physics, that water weighs 8.3 lbs per gallon. Some of the jugs they were carrying looked to be three to five gallons. He began to notice things about the town—the kinds of things that one just would not see in the United States. There were small stone walls, such as those seen around planting beds, that were designed to add touches of beauty to the semi-urban setting. But there were also sharp spikes sticking up from the concrete. This seemed dangerous, and as he reflected on this, he realized that they were designed to be dangerous. "Loitering," he thought out loud. "Even though I can't read the language well, they don't have any signs up that say 'Don't loiter,' but those spikes pretty much say it for them." He reached down and touched one gently. "If I sat on one, I guess I would be in one of their God-forsaken hospitals here." He mouthed his words quietly. He had already heard nightmare stories about the local hospital. He made a mental note to himself: "Don't get hurt, and if you do get hurt, think twice about even seeking medical help."

With that decision made, he strolled back to the site and went in to see Hal, one of the younger associate producers working in one of their new trailers. "Hal, I can't believe they let you park these cans all over this place," Sam said.

"Well, that was, you know, page 474, paragraph A, sub-paragraph 9, section 1 in this mass of papers that our lawyers all sat around and negotiated for, like, a year," Hal said. "Do you have any idea what the channel paid just for legal fees to have them figure out every possible contingency?"

"I have no idea," Sam said, as he checked out the trailer's accommodations. "Remember, that is why I am just a talking head and let you APs handle all that stuff. Hey, have you heard about me getting some bodyguard?" he inquired.

"Yeah, they made us do it," Hal replied routinely.

"So, when is my special, private bodyguard getting here?" Sam asked, just as Drake entered the trailer with some paperwork for Hal.

"The fellow should be here this evening, and is probably going to be pretty jet-lagged," Drake advised.

"Oh, and I suppose we aren't?" Sam said. "I am just now figuring out when it is daylight! I know, because I get ugly calls from abusive producers, and then have to go shake hands all day with

National Potato Queen Contestants!"

"National *what*?" Hal asked, obviously confused.

"Never mind; it is an inside joke," Sam smiled.

"Thanks for sparing me," Hal said.

"Hey, is that coffee made?" Sam asked.

"Check my trailer; I think there is still some, but if not you will have to grind more," Drake said. Sam excused himself, and stepped down from the trailer, slamming the door.

Hal turned to face Drake and asked, "So, is this bodyguard guy for real? I mean, what do they think is going to happen?"

"Well, I will spare you the whole song and dance, but Sam argued with me at every point like he usually does," Drake said.

"Yeah, I remember when I was thirty or thirty-one years old, too," Hal said.

Drake walked back over to his trailer to find Sam using a large stapler as a hammer. "Hey, what are you doing, Sam?"

"I am grinding coffee the old-fashioned way. I could not find your stupid grinder, so I just put it in two plastic bags and beat it with this thing," Sam said as he held up the bag of now mostly crushed coffee beans.

"You are so impetuous. I have a grinder up there in the cabinet," Drake said in an irritated tone.

"No, I am fine. It is ready to brew," Sam said, seeing no point in Drake's irritation.

"You are turning my hairs gray, Sam," Drake said smiling slightly.

"Your problem is not that your hairs are turning *gray*," Sam quipped. "It is that they are turning *loose*!"

-20-

The Croatians, snipers, and spotters were outside talking in the courtyard sitting on what was left of an old playground. "I just don't understand this," Tex said. "How come we get split up from the Ark if we go to all of the trouble of getting Brisbane there? I mean, what if we don't get a good 'evac' on this, we could get left behind to deal with who knows what from the Ethiopian forces?"

"Yeah, but we are okay as long as nobody spots us," said Bubba.

Another of the Croats added, "Well I should be riding with the Ark, but the plan sounds like a civilian car, and only two people would be able to ride in it: Oslo and Gundy."

"I don't believe Brisbane wants to tell them no," added John David.

"But we are a lot more deadly than those muscle-heads are when you come right down to it," said Jake.

"However they move it, they definitely can't keep the Ark here, man; this place will be swarming. Can you imagine the nation of Israel—how fired up their guys are gonna get?" John David asked.

"You are going to have the Muslim nations coming, the Americans all beside themselves, and some of the Western Europeans, too. Having that Ark could be like a validation of whatever church and country owns it. Brisbane is right, it is huge! For us, though, I'll tell you what, you talk about being most wanted on the Post Office wall—we are going to be on the Post Office wall even in, like, Uzbekistan or someplace!"

"Watch it," said Fabijan, "my uncle is from Uzbekistan."

"Hey man, no offense, I don't even know where that is. Heck, I am surprised I even said it right," he said laughing.

"You sure can't spell it," his spotter quipped.

"Well, we need to think more about this," said Tadej. They signaled to each other, and all got up together and left.

"Man, why do they do all that signaling?" Jim Bob asked.

"Got me; I heard that they have been on a lot of operations together. I heard that they were brought in on that big school hostage thing in Russia and that just those four took out twelve terrorists and none of them even got a scratch," Bubba related. "But their signaling is driving me nuts. I mean they could use words in this dorm facility. It is not as if anybody is listening to them or anyone cares what we think or say."

* * *

Inside the van parked outside, that conversation was downloaded to a CD and brought promptly by Speck to Brisbane. "Here you go, Boss. This was all of the gunners and snipers talking."

Brisbane stacked it with the other CDs that cataloged every conversation that had been going on among everyone at the school. "You never know who you can trust, huh Boss?" Slim said.

"Right," Brisbane replied, his thin lips barely moving, without even looking up.

Brisbane had always been adroit at planning and anticipating "the human factor" as he called it. He could sense just when his team was at risk of going stark-raving crazy sitting in this school house, while the communication and tech guys worked on the specifics of the operation; he knew just the moment to walk in. "Gentlemen, here is something for a little fun!" He pushed in a cart that the tech guys had assembled the night before during another of their relatively sleepless nights. On it were three small flat-screen televisions and three of the newest X-Boxes, along with every shoot-'em-up game there was.

"All right, you might be all right after all, Brisbane," said John David with a thick Southern drawl.

"Yep, you are all right with me," said his spotter, Jim Bob.

With a smug expression Brisbane turned to leave the room. "Boys, boys, boys. . . . Boys and their toys," he said, a light smile playing around his normally tense lips.

Brisbane stuck his head in the room where the Ethiopian nationals were. "Popeye, Garfield, are you going to be ready for our meeting this afternoon?"

"Yes, sir, Boss," Garfield said. They had real names—real names that did not derive from cartoon characters. Brisbane had trouble with those names, and had dubbed them "Garfield and Popeye." Garfield had long dreadlocks and was also a Rastafarian like Raphael. Rastafarians followed the teachings of an African leader named Rastafari, and they tended to look somewhat like a famous guitarist, Jimi Hendrix, but they were a lot less peaceful.

Popeye, on the other hand, had large forearms. It had something to do with the fact that he had once worked in a gold mine, Lega Dembi, in the southern area of the country. Apparently, he had been involved in earth-moving of some kind, and as a result his well-toned physique still made an impressive sight.

Brisbane had told Popeye how much more profitable this little excursion was going to be when compared to the value of all of the gold in the world.

*　*　*

Entering his makeshift office, Brisbane logged on to the Internet through his secure encrypted satellite connection—one of the first projects that Slim and Speck had managed for him on the day of their arrival. While he was a fairly studied individual, and had certainly poured himself heart and soul into this project, he still wanted to understand more about this so-called lost tribe of black Jews that, it was believed, had housed and guarded the Ark for so long.

Their names started with the letter "F" but the actual term escaped him at the moment, so he called up the Wikipedia site and began to search.

At that moment, Speck stuck his head in, knocking first very respectfully, "Uh, Boss, I just want to let you know that even though we are a couple miles away from the site, we are picking up their satellite transmission feeds very well, so we know exactly what is going on. They are having some equipment problems with the cable they are thinking of running down into these tunnels, which is affecting how they want to shoot some of what appears to be the pre-cast. We are picking up even their conversations in their vans."

"Excellent," Brisbane exclaimed. "I am glad that our equipment has held up to its the manufacturers' promises."

"Oh, yes sir, it is great equipment, and truly, sir," Speck went on, "it is an honor to use it, and I'm just so thankful. . . ."

"That is enough sucking up—there is no need to ingratiate!" Brisbane said sharply. He liked showing his power and eloquence in using longer words.

"Uh, yes sir, thank you. . . .sir," Speck sputtered, as he quickly dismissed himself from the room.

Brisbane then keyed in the terms "Lost tribe, black Jews, Ethiopia." When he had the meeting with Popeye and Garfield later that day, he would wish to appear informed.

Outside Brisbane's open office window, the snipers noisily clambered into one of the trucks. As the motor cranked and doors slammed, their rowdy conversation could be heard from inside the vehicle. Brisbane said to himself, "Guess every country has its rednecks, but these American rednecks are the loudest."

"Roll tide!" one of the men exclaimed at the top of his voice as the truck began to accelerate out of the yard. Brisbane had no idea what it meant. Since anything he didn't understand bothered him greatly, he quickly opened another web browser and, in the Google search field, typed in "roll tide." He was somewhat disappointed to learn that it was only about American college football in a state called Alabama, and a team made famous by a coach named after a bear, who always wore a checkered hat. He closed that browser tab and, turning his attention back to the earlier matter, began to read about the "Falashas" that the search engine had called up for him.

He paused a moment and thought how ironic that he was essentially studying for a final exam, that would be his last test, his last job, the last effort he would ever have to make for the rest of his life. He, and anyone else that he deemed worthy, would be set for life. Actually, not just for life, but set for multiple lifetimes. The prospect of making so much money from this one event was thrilling.

He scrolled through his notebook computer information, and pulled up the contacts that included Israeli leaders, the PLO's successors, Jews for Jesus, the United Nations, the White House, the Smithsonian Institution, and contact people in the Kremlin, Saudi Arabia, Jordan, Libya, Iran, what is left of Iraq, and even little Kuwait—they were all there. He wondered aloud why he hadn't included Morocco (given that there were so many Islamic leaders there), but there was still time, he thought. This contact list was going to fill the coffers of those three accounts if everything went according to plan. Brisbane loved plans. Brisbane hated complications.

-21-

ABANDONED MINE AREA

Out near an old, abandoned opencast mine, the white truck with the three sniper teams and all their equipment wound down the bumpy roads, guided by Garfield and Popeye. The sun bore down heavily on them as they turned from the main road. Squinting through his sunglasses, Garfield remembered the sign he was to place at the entrance and reached into a door compartment to take it out. As they prepared to drive into the mine, he got out and placed it securely next to the gate. It was an official looking barricade sign inscribed with a text in the local language, its Amharic characters odd looking to the Americans in the vehicle. Everyone assumed that it read that construction was going on or that blasting was happening so that no one would be concerned about the gunshots in the event anyone fired without his silencer. There had been some talk of firing the .50 Cal sniper rifles just to stay in practice, according to Hank who was quickly becoming a spokesman for the group. As they wound down a switchback gravel road into the bottom of the opencast mine, they were amazed to look back up and realize that it looked as if they were in the bottom of what appeared to be a meteor crater or a volcano. The sides had been dug so smoothly they were slick in appearance. One of the spotters, Hawk, looked around and almost immediately said this mine had to have been dug by hand. "No heavy equipment dug this hole," he said. Although classified as a red neck, he was apparently part American Indian, though he preferred the term "Native American." His given name was William, but nobody dared call him William. He preferred the name Hawk, which he explained had belonged to either his grandfather or great grandfather, though nobody followed the story that well.

"All hand tools," Hawk continued.

"You are kidding me!" said Jim Bob, as he lifted the equipment out of the van. "This thing is huge. It would have taken them forever!"

"He is correct," Garfield said, in somewhat stilted English. "Many men die digging this hole. Ethiopians good at digging the ground, making tunnels, and so on"

"What was in the bottom of it—gold?" Bubba asked.

"Uh, turns out, not very much," Popeye added. "Many men die anyway."

"Man!" exclaimed Hawk, as a whistle came from John David.

"Let's get to it," said Jim Bob, as he was already lining up a makeshift firing line. Popeye walked down range. He carried small, white cylinders the size of a half-gallon milk jug. "What has he got for us to shoot there, Garfield?" Jim Bob asked.

"Those cylinders filled with a white powder," Garfield explained. "It tells quickly whether you have a hit or not."

"Whether I have a hit?" Jim Bob asked excitedly, "Let me just tell ya there, my dark brother, there ain't no question about whether I get a hit. . .it's a matter of whether I put it in your eye, or between your eyes. Hell, I can pierce your ear at a mile's walk."

"Hey, man, that's just so!" Bubba exclaimed.

"He speaks the truth," said Hawk, laughing.

"Well, that is what we bring," said Garfield.

Popeye walked for what seemed like a really long time. The men had set up and even had a water break by the time Popeye walked back.

The targets were set up at 75 yards, 200 yards, and 400 yards—

which is roughly a quarter of a mile. "I can hit further there, if you want me to, Popeye, or are you just plain tired of walking?" joked Hawk.

Garfield spoke up, reading from a note, "Now, for this operation there will be no shots required over a quarter of a mile, so there is no point in wasting ammunition, time, and risking discovery here practicing something you will not be asked to do in this operation."

"Makes sense to me," said Hawk.

As soon as Popeye cleared the front of the barrels, the spotters had already dialed in the position of the first white cylinder and one of the snipers was heard to say, "Let's see what these little things can do."

As they lined up the .223 sniper rifles with the custom silencer, one of the spotters announced, "Range hot!" and then each sniper was given the direction from his individual spotter to fire at will. Three muted pops erupted in quick succession. Each sounded a lot like a pellet gun sounds like when one of its shots hits a tin can— just like a slight metallic tearing sound.

"Man, those things *are* quiet," Hawk said, taking his ear plugs out.

"Shoot, I've heard light bulbs pop louder than that!" a spotter said.

Hawk observed, "But, they are too long and shiny; they must be matte black."

"Good point there, Hawk," said Jim Bob.

Garfield, quick to realize the need, asked, "What you need, flat black paint?"

"Yeah, matte black paint, or some non-shiny tape, not electrician's tape, but like black cloth tape or matte black paint," Hawk clarified.

"I understand. Will this evening be okay?" Garfield asked.

"Yeah, sure, as long as we have it before the operation," Hawk said, turning back to the range. "Let's get cracking on this, boys." The spotters again called out coordinates and helped the snipers line up, as the snipers made mysterious clicking sounds on each of their scopes.

Three more shots, three more clouds of white dust. Now it was time for the quarter-mile shot. "I think we ought to use the .50 on this one," Jim Bob said.

"Man, we ain't out here to practice the .50," Hawk reminded him.

"Hey Garfield, have you got any more of those cylinders?" Jim Bob hollered out.

"Yes, sir!" Popeye rolled his eyes, knowing that meant that he would be walking again.

After Popeye returned, a thunderous boom rang out as the .50 caliber round ripped through the air. Dust flew up from all around the muzzle as the shock wave fanned out. The white flour had exploded and was suspended in the air, before the sound began to echo—and echo it certainly did. The cylinder was much further downrange and looked as if it had torn almost in two.

"Okay, that's enough, that's enough," Garfield said. "That's way too loud. You practice with those enough. You all hit your targets."

As they turned to leave, Popeye picked up every dispensed shell very carefully. They piled back into the van as Popeye and Garfield turned their attention to the drive back to the briefing they had promised Brisbane. He wanted to know everything they knew about the lost tribe.

-22-

Once again, Sam was awoken with what become the now-normal call, and again, he found it was still too early. "Sam, this is Mark Sims, one of your APs."

"I know who you are, Mark, but what on earth do you need?" Sam replied, rubbing his eyes with his free hand.

"Well, you know, the research staff was supposed to get us all some information, maybe before we left, so we could have read it on the plane, regarding the history of the Ark. You know, how it might have found its way around, and you were going to do teasers about all of the different places it could be?"

"Yes, Mark, I remember," Sam said stretching. "You are a morning person, aren't you?"

"Uh, well yes, I am." Mark then rattled off, "How did you know? Is it in my voice, my tone, how clear my eyes look in the morning?"

"Uh, okay, I surrender there, Mark," Sam grunted. "Where is the research? Is it here yet?"

"Well, it turns out," Mark said, "it is not an *it*, but a *he*."

"What?" Sam asked.

"It seems that the researcher himself is coming live and in person with that bodyguard type of person. Do you know anything about that?" Mark asked.

Sam said, "Yep, I have been briefed by Drake, the soap opera star."

"The what?" Mark asked.

"Inside joke," Sam said. "So, when is the bodyguard supposed to be here? I thought they were already overdue?"

"Well, they are actually coming in today around lunchtime. There will be a meeting when they get here at noon. This morning, we are doing equipment tests, so you kind of have the morning off," Mark said.

"Aw gee, thanks," Sam said. "So, let me clarify this. You called me on a morning that I don't have to work. You called me early and woke me up to tell me about things that would be happening later on in the afternoon when I did have to work? Do I have that correct?" Sam asked incredulously.

"Uh, yeah, though I wouldn't have put it that way," Mark stammered, "but yes, that is correct." He hung up.

Sam murmured to himself, looked at the clock, and flopped back down on the bed. He drifted off into a fitful sleep, his body clock still confused by the time difference between eastern Africa and the central regions of the USA, and eventually arose a little before lunch. Sam enjoyed the most leisurely lunch on the trip so far. He found himself procrastinating on the way to the meeting at Drake's trailer, especially seeing that he would then have to meet the bodyguard and the researcher. Upon his arrival, it was not difficult for him to determine which one was which.

The bodyguard, evidently of mixed ethnicity, had a shaven head, his skin was tanned a deep color from the sun, and he had cold, gray eyes with remote expressions that were always moving, never still for more than a moment. He stood tall, and his healthy-looking, muscular frame made an imposing picture as he stood in the doorway. At well over six feet tall, he had broad shoulders and a narrow waist. He was wearing black fatigue cargo pants and a similar matching smock, but one that fit only loosely. Sam wondered for a minute about how many weapons might be underneath it; he knew there would surely be some. He appeared to have on a black, tight-fitting athletic type shirt against his body on which numerous holsters probably hung—maybe even hand grenades, Sam wondered.

In contrast, the researcher wore glasses, sported a small goatee beard, and was actually wearing a tweed coat—in this part of Africa, of all places! He wondered almost out loud if tweed coats and corduroy pants were issued in all grad schools, and if they were mandatory, as they surely appeared to be. All of the grad students that he had known in archaeology and paleontology wore the Birkenstocks, the wrinkly pants, the un-tucked shirt or the nasty sweater, and had the scraggly beard. It was an emblem of academia, almost as if to say, "I am just too smart to take care of myself; I am too smart to pick out clothes that match or that might be cleaned or that could be pressed. I don't want to be mistaken for a marketing teacher or a businessman, so I will be sure that I stand out with this academic pinhead wardrobe."

"So, what do you think?" The question came out loud from Drake, and apparently it was a question that he was supposed to have heard and answered, but in fact it had not penetrated his consciousness. "I am sorry, please repeat what you said," Sam said.

"What do you think about the bodyguard's recommendation?" Drake asked.

"Uh, could you repeat that also, please?" Sam asked, very aware he had been daydreaming.

"Do you feel okay, Sam?" Drake asked, obviously concerned.

The bodyguard, in a much quieter voice than one would have expected from a man who is supposed to be so lethal, said, "From now on I am with you twenty-four hours a day, seven days a week. A cot has been provided for me to sleep near you, and at the appropriate time I will need for you to wear body armor."

"What?" Sam asked out loud. "Body armor in this heat? Are you kidding me? Even just wearing one of these white gauze shirts and these little khaki cargo pants is burning me alive. I am certainly not wearing any body armor, and that's for certain."

"You are in Ethiopia now," the bodyguard said as he moved a pace toward Sam.

"What are you going to do—beat me up if I don't listen to you and do everything that you say? You are not meant to boss me around; you were sent here to try to protect me."

The bodyguard looked at him through narrowed eyes as if to say, "Are you done yet?" He spoke aloud, his tone deadly serious: "Sir, my job is simple; I make sure that that even if everyone else dies, that you do not—do you understand?"

"Well, yeah, I mean I get the bit about you being a bodyguard and all," Sam said.

"Sir, it is not 'a bit'; it is a mission," the bodyguard continued. "It is a mission with one critical objective, and that is to keep you alive so that the people that care to hear you talk can listen; but I, sir, am not one of them." Turning to everyone else in the room, he said, "Thank you all; I will be outside."

As he excused himself, he bumped against Sam on his way out of the door as if to say, "I will keep you alive, but I might not keep you happy."

The researcher who had been sitting quietly, observing the events of the last several minutes from an armchair, was left quizzically looking at Sam. Sam looked blankly back at him. "Oh hello, sir, my name is Gordon. . .Gordon Duley III actually, and I am a specialist in studies that many people call the 'Lost Tribes of Israel' and the history specifically of the Lost Ark of the Covenant. Although I understand from my briefing that it is no longer 'lost' but found—is that correct?" His voice, rather reedy in its tone, was already grating on Sam's nerves as well as his ears, even though he had not even sat down in the room yet.

"Uh, yeah, that is right; may I excuse myself?" Sam asked, already moving to the door. "I would like to go speak to the bodyguard out there for a minute."

Sam stepped down onto the metal stairway, and felt it tilt and give a bit under his weight. "I guess we will be spending some time together," he said as he looked at the bodyguard, but the large man made no further eye contact, as he was scanning the horizon. Sam felt the sting of being totally ignored. But as he watched him for several moments, he was reminded of the way a deer looks when it is feeding. It will stop and look all the way around, and turn its ears all the way around, trying to sense danger.

"I didn't get your name," Sam said, extending his hand.

"Kishor," the bodyguard answered, looking at him and slowly grasping his hand with the firmest grip Sam had ever felt.

"Kishor? I am pleased to meet you. Of course, you know I am Sam," he said weakly. Kishor was scanning again. "Do you always do that?" Sam asked.

"Do what?" Kishor asked, as he continued to rotate his head.

"Look all around, like some lizard on a limb, or something?" Sam asked.

"Like a what?" Kishor asked, feigning that he had not heard him properly, even though Sam suspected that he heard every word and probably never missed anything.

"You know, like a lizard on a limb, you know, the kind that can turn their heads all the way around; that is kind of what it looks like you are looking, the way you are doing it," Sam explained somewhat clumsily.

"Oh, I hadn't noticed," Kishor said dismissively, as his gaze continued its traversing motion.

Sam felt as if he was a fly and had been flicked off of somebody's arm.

"Do you have any more questions?" Kishor said, with some impatience clearly perceptible in his voice.

"Yeah, that bit about being with me a lot—I mean not really all the time, right? I mean that you have got to do your job, and you have got to look like you are important," Sam said, pacing back and forth, his feet making light impressions in the dust, "but this idea of you being on a cot in my room is just not going to work."

"I was unaware that you had a choice in the matter," Kishor said quite matter of factly.

"Choice? Well sure, I have a choice," Sam stammered. "I am the guy that is doing all of this. I am the guy who put two and two together and figured out that the Ark was here, and that my efforts on prior work are what gave me the credibility to talk to these people in the first place. They knew I was a serious scientist and not just a TV personality. You see, I am the one who is really in charge of this whole thing and has put it all together."

"That is not what I understand," Kishor said, again in matter of fact tones. Pretty much everything Kishor said was in a matter-of-fact manner, now that Sam noticed.

"Why am I debating this with you anyway, Kishor?" Sam asked. "What kind of name is 'Kishor' anyway? Is it from India or something?"

"That is not my real name, but it will do for now," Kishor replied.

Sam began to speak, but stopped as Kishor looked him dead in the eye for the first time since this conversation had begun, saying, "I am here to protect you, not to listen to you prattle along endlessly about your accomplishments and your opinions. I am taking orders directly from the head of your network, and if you have a problem with me, you should take it up with them. My job is to keep you alive. Once again: my job is not to listen to you babble, and this will be the end of the conversation."

Sam stood there stunned for a moment. He had just been shut off. It was no different than if Kishor, or whatever his real name was, had taken out a remote control and had hit a giant mute button. He felt he had been muted. He didn't recall ever having been muted before. It was like the way he had felt when he had once asked a girl out and she said that she was going to wash her hair. It was not unlike somehow being jilted at the altar. He started to wander away, but at that moment Gordon Duley came to the doorway and called his name before retreating to the confines of the trailer.

He was waiting anxiously to share his research, he said. It was research that probably nobody had ever read, except maybe to give him a passing grade in some type of dissertation or Master's thesis or such an endeavor. But he did have a real interest in it, and the man that presumably knew it all was there in a trailer just a few feet away. Nevertheless, Sam found himself entirely dumbfounded by Kishor's snub—the sting of the absolute lack of need for him, and his lack of regard of him as a human being. "This is the man who is going to keep me safe," he thought. "This is the man who is going to save my life?" He stepped back up the metal stairs, rattling the trailer as he did, to find Gordon sitting exactly where he had been sitting before. He was there clutching a worn-looking, brown, expandable file on his lap. His goatee appeared especially scraggly in the muted light of the trailer, his hair was unkempt, and the frames of his thick-rimmed glasses were brown, but had turned a little green around the edges.

"Yes. . .Gordon, isn't it?" Sam asked, "Sorry to keep you waiting there."

"No problem, Mr. Cohen," Gordon said. "I have come a long way to talk with you."

"You can call me Sam," he assured Gordon.

"Okay, Mr. Sam," said Gordon dutifully.

"Please, just Sam will do," Sam continued.

"You can call me Gordy," he said.

"Really," Sam said flatly with a look on his face that looked as though he had just sniffed some bad milk. "Gordy, huh?" Sam echoed.

"Uh, yes. That is what my friends call me," Gordon assured him.

Sam wondered to himself just how many friends this bookworm actually had. "Uh. Okay, that is fine Gordy. So what did you fly half way around the world to talk to me about?"

"Well I am here on assignment at the request of your network, which I, by the way, respect very much and I am, like, your biggest fan, so I am very excited to be here with you," Gordon gushed.

"Thanks," Sam said. "But just kind of tell me what you are here for, Gordy." Sam had had a fan or two, but this one seemed a little too close. He kept his distance in the trailer and then collapsed into the chair.

Gordon eagerly began taking off rubber bands surrounding his expandable file. It was bursting with papers, post-it notes, and dog-eared, highlighted computer printouts.

Sam wondered to himself what people used to do for research before Al Gore supposedly invented the Internet. Sam was young, so the Internet had been a huge part of his Master's level dissertation, even when he had been conducting his research in Israel. He often had to explain to people that Israel is not backward, as some thought, but actually had all of the technology that he used in the West. After all, cell phones had even been invented in Israel. The other big surprise was that Israel even had pretty nice beaches. Some of the best years of his life, so far, had been spent in the Holy Land. Sam forced his attention away from the thoughts that were distracting him and regarded Gordon again from his position on the easy chair.

Gordon pulled out some information that he had marked with

a large blue highlighter. "Let's start at the beginning!" he stated earnestly. "Of course, the Ark of the Covenant first appears in the ancient Hebrew Scriptures known as the Torah, which is also the beginning of the Old Testament. . . ." Gordon had begun with the energy, and the single-mindedness of someone who always starts at the beginning, goes in order and exact sequence, and always completes his task.

Sam settled in to make himself comfortable. He felt that most of this lesson would just be a review, but he thought he may learn a few more things.

From outside the trailer, there were sounds of footsteps and cheerful whistling. One of the associate producers was approaching and wished to see Sam, but Kishor demanded to see his identification and intended to frisk him. People were wearing as little as possible to try to stay cool so the young AP, Mark Simms, was astonished that Kishor was concerned about weapons or anything menacing.

"If anybody should be asking for identification, it should be me," Mark Simms said resolutely. It might have been one of his first steps at trying to establish his own manhood.

Unfortunately for him, he had chosen the wrong person to do it with. Kishor stepped so close to him that Mark could smell the coffee on the bodyguard's breath. Kishor said coldly, "Everyone here must prove their reason to be here, or to see the client. Once you have done it once, you will not have to do it again, but you will have to do it once to begin with. Any questions?" Kishor's tone made it clear to Mark that there should be no questions.

Mark replied in a very respectful tone, "No, sir."

"Good," Kishor said emphatically.

Mark reached down underneath his tee-shirt, producing out a worn "all access pass" that was all the staff were required to keep on them at all times—all but Sam, who had refused so far to wear his at all.

"Thank you, Mr. Simms," Kishor said. "Please be sure to always have your identification badge with you and visible at all times."

"Uh, yes, sir," Mark responded. Mark felt juvenile and insignificant in the presence of a man who knew his mission, and would clearly carry it out with unhesitating resolve.

After being given clearance by Kishor, Mark knocked on the flimsy aluminum door, and it seemed to shake the entire trailer.

"Sam, Drake needs you," Mark said.

"Tell him to come here," Sam said. "I am actually enjoying this little lecture. Plus, the air conditioner is doing great."

"Uh, oh, okay," Mark stuttered, and removed himself from the step. He wondered to himself if anyone would ever take orders from him, since he felt that all he did was take orders from others. He excused himself, giving Kishor a fairly wide berth, and headed back through a white canvas tent that had been erected to shade some of the production equipment.

Moments later, Drake emerged from behind the tent, a little frustrated, and headed toward the trailer.

"Hi, Kishor," Drake said, having already made his acquaintance. He opened the door of the trailer and interrupted Gordon's breathless recitation of Old Testament Scriptures mentioning the Ark of the Covenant.

"Uh, Sam, they'll need you to do some audio checks in about one hour, and I won't bother you unless we really need you, but you will need to be on call in case we need you," Drake said. "Hey, you guys stay at it; it looks like you all are enjoying one another." He gave a little laugh as he stepped back out of the door and left.

"Thanks, Kishor," Drake said casually.

Kishor did not respond. As Drake passed, he noticed that Kishor's head was always moving, his eyes never ceasing scanning the horizon. His mirrored aviator sunglasses flashed in the sunlight. The lenses gave a distorted reflection of the setting of tents and trailers. The hum of the air conditioners filled Drake's ears as he retraced his steps to the makeshift studio where he and the other APs worked.

-23-

The two Ethiopians, Garfield and Popeye, freshened themselves up by taking showers in the dilapidated restrooms before presenting themselves to Brisbane in his office. "Take a seat on the cot, there," invited Brisbane, pointing to the bed that he used for the little rest that he took each night from after midnight to just before dawn. The overhead fan whirled slowly and the buzzing sound of a fly persisted in the stillness.

The men declined the offer to take a seat. That didn't surprise Brisbane. He had gotten to know the Aborigines in survival training in Australia. He realized that these men had some similarities to their distant Aborigine relatives.

He thought back to his exposure to the primitive way of life that Aborigines had once lived. "There, oral tradition is how everything is passed down," Brisbane thought. Brisbane had heard the Aborigines telling a story year after year, virtually word for word, and for generation after generation they had done this. His grandfather had taught him, as a young boy, that it was a feature of their culture.

It gave him great confidence in oral tradition and the ability of one generation after another to pass on their sacred stories, teaching and writings. That is why, though he rejected the moral principles of the Old Testament and the New Testament, he had little doubt about their actual accuracy. "I am more sure about it than most of these professing Jews and Christians around the world," he thought.

Garfield and Popeye stood waiting for Brisbane to acknowledge them. Looking up, he came to the point: "Which of you gentlemen would like to start?"

"I would, sir," Garfield said, "with your permission."

"Certainly," Brisbane responded.

"The Lost Ark of the Covenant appears often in Hebrew Old Testament, as you know, sir," Garfield began in his halting English, "However, at one point in Hebrew history, the Ark disappeared and is barely mentioned again. Only a few clues appear in the Hebrew Bible about its location or when it disappeared. Other clues are in the sacred writings that have been passed down to us here in Ethiopia. The journey of the lost Ark of the Covenant here to Aksum in our country has been long indeed," Garfield drew breath deeply. "There are some gaps and different theories in how it all occurred according to what one of my family's priests once told me, but one thing is for certain: we sit just a two short miles from the most significant find in the history of the world. It is widespread knowledge in Ethiopia that the Ark rests here. The rest of the world has just begun figuring it out."

"Well, we are about to discover it all over again," Brisbane interrupted.

"Correct, sir," Garfield agreed. "Are you familiar with the Falashas?"

Brisbane nodded. He wanted to appear familiar with everything, but not so familiar that he would not learn more from them. Brisbane fancied himself quite a student of history. "Please enlighten me on what you have been taught and have learned here," Brisbane asked.

"Our royal family here came from a lady ruler, Makeda. You may know her as the so-called 'Queen of Sheba.' If you study the ancient holy text that our Ethiopian people call the 'Kebra Negast,' which means 'the Glory of Kings,' you will find that King Solomon seduced the Queen of Sheba. Their son, Menelik I, became our first Emperor of Ethiopia. Do you wish me to tell the story?" he asked Brisbane.

"Sure," Brisbane replied.

"The Queen visited Solomon in Jerusalem long, long ago. That part is even in your Bible. But the story is not all there. You see, King Solomon tricked her because he wanted her for himself. And he was wise, and always got whatever he wanted. Even though he had many hundreds of wives and concubines, he threw a large feast for the Queen of Sheba. All they served that evening was spicy food. She was a guest in his palace that night. But Makeda was wise as well. She made him swear that he would not take advantage of her if she stayed in his palace. Solomon agreed, but only if she would also agree not to take anything from his palace. Makeda was offended, but agreed. However, because she was so thirsty from the spicy food, she woke near midnight. She found a jar of water in her room, and just grasped it, but as she did, King Solomon stepped out from the shadows. He questioned her as to what was the most valuable material possession. At that moment, it was agreed that water was, as it supported all life. Solomon gave her the choice, and she chose to quench her thirst with his water, thus freeing him from his oath. And so, in that way, it is told, he had his way with her."

-24-

Sam's Trailer

In the meantime, more explanations were going on in the trailer where Sam and Gordon were seated. Sam found himself enthralled; two hours had flown past as Gordon had given some in-depth insights into the history of the Ark. Indeed, he was an expert in all of this. Sam's network had certainly sent the right person. They may have let him down with Mr. Congeniality outside—a bully disguised as a bodyguard—but Gordon was surely coming through for him. While Sam found Gordon's voice somewhat grating, the subject matter was fascinating, and within minutes the reedy tones had ceased to irritate him.

Presently, there was a knock on the door. A voice from outside announced: "Sam, I need you out here; there are some sound checks and fittings that only you can do now." Drake was a dead ringer for the late Ted Knight from the Mary Tyler Moore show reruns.

"Sure, I will come. Gordy, can you wait here for a while?"

"Absolutely, sir," Gordon deliberately placed his finger on the page at the point his explanation had been interrupted.

Sam somehow knew that that was exactly where they would pick up in when he returned. As he stepped out of the trailer, he noticed Kishor start for the production tent just a step or two behind him, his head constantly swiveling.

"Isn't your head going to get sunburned there, buddy?" he asked Kishor.

Kishor did not even acknowledge him, but continued walking exactly two steps behind him, step for step, always looking. As Sam entered the production tent, he turned around to see Kishor stop outside and stand guard. Sam stood there looking for a moment and concluded that Kishor reminded him of the concrete lions to be found on either side of the driveways of rich and important people. Strangely, the thought crossed his mind as to whether he would ever have a house like that—perhaps he and Angela? He wondered for a just a moment, until Bart's voice calling his name broke the silence.

"Sam, Sam, we need you over here," called Bart, one of the associate producers. He was a conscientious, anal-retentive type man who probably had three haircuts a week back in the United States. He was neat and well-kept. He may have been the only one without sweat stains on his clothes. Sam wondered how he was able to do that.

"Just stand here for a moment, sir," Bart continued as his hand grasped some audio equipment. "We need you to stand here while we measure this cord for the earpiece."

"Aw, the glamour of being a TV star," he said sarcastically, as he stood like a manikin for a while.

Bart was joined by another technician, and for a half hour or so, they ran some microphone and recording tests. "Good thing we aren't asking you to sing a soprano piece!" joked Bart. "I'm very happy now that we've optimized the recording levels. Keep in mind the risk of echoes when you are in a confined space. This mike is very directional, but with it mounted quite high on your lapel, I think you should be good for as long as the recording goes on."

The measurements taken and data entered, Sam started walking back to the trailer to pick up the conversation once again with Gordon.

-25-

THE FORMER UNIVERSITY

The snipers, lying on their cots in the deserted school dorms, had enjoyed their morning exercise, even if it had been short-lived, as they had been given rather limited ammunition supplies.

"Those silencers are cool. When is that guy going to be back with the black matte paint?" Hawk asked.

"Aw, who knows? They have probably got to bribe a bunch of warlords or something to go get that stuff," John David pointed out. "Speaking of warlords, you remember that time in Bosnia?"

"Aw yeah," Hawk was quick to say. "John David iced a couple of those guys on the back of those Jeeps."

"Man, I'll say," Jim Bob said, "It was righteous."

"Remember, when our guys were getting fired on after the chopper went down, and I popped a couple of those guys when that one shot went right through both of them!"

"Yeah," Hank added. "And it threw that guy's arm all the way across the street, and it landed right there in that market, where those women were hiding—and they really freaked out!"

"Aw, that was gross," said Bubba. "That was gross."

25

"Well, it was all right with me," John David said. "I always wanted to be a mercenary. I subscribed to Soldier of Fortune magazine from the time I was twelve years old.

"You, too," said Bubba, grinning.

"Anybody got any Red Man?" asked Billy, one of the spotters. The pouch of chewing tobacco landed on his chest.

*   *   *

After the briefing with Brisbane, Garfield and Popeye, who had been tasked to purchase refreshments for the evening, stopped the vehicle at a small concrete building that looked as if it had seen better days. They knocked, and momentarily an attractive young Ethiopian woman with unusually high cheekbones and almond-shaped eyelids opened the door for them and beckoned them to come in. "You have come to see Mr. Ruslan?" she said inquiringly in her soft voice.

Inside the store, walls holding hardware supplies folded inward, revealing a hidden room, the air dense with cigar smoke. They tentatively sat down with Ruslan. When he spoke, his English was heavily inflected with a Russian accent. Pointing a bony, nicotine-stained finger toward his chest, he came straight to the point: "What do you have for me?"

"Well, in the short term, we need some matte black paint," Garfield said.

"Ahhh, that is no problem," the gaunt, pale Ruslan replied as he put a cell phone to his ear. He spoke into the phone in Russian for a sentence or two, and then closed the phone decisively. "What else do you need?"

"I think our price has gone up," Garfield said.

"Oh, it has?" the Russian asked in a foreboding way.

-26-

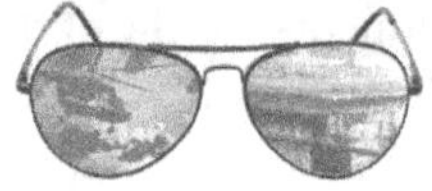

With the body-wiring and sound checks complete, and with the workings of some of the newer equipment having been explained to him, Sam was surprised at how anxious he was for Gordon to continue the explanation. It felt incomplete not to finish the full story of the Lost Ark of the Covenant, and how it had found its way up the Nile into this area.

As far as Sam was aware, the Nile was the only major river that flowed from south to north. It started south of him in East Africa and flowed northward, right through the country he was now visiting.

As he stomped back up the steps, he found that Gordon still had his finger where they had paused. Gordon needed no encouragement to resume his account. After two more hours, Gordon asked if it would be okay to take a brief break. Sam couldn't believe how quickly the time had passed.

"Well, of course, Gordy, what do you need? Can I get you anything?" he asked.

26

"Yes, the dust here is really bothering my sinuses, and I have to go use my inhaler," Gordon replied.

"Where are they letting you stay?" Sam asked as Gordon stood up stiffly, putting his papers carefully to one side.

"Oh, they brought in another trailer for me—it's the one near the gate. Or, at least half of it is for me, and I think the other half of it is for equipment," Gordon said, as he grasped the door handle. "It seems like it never stops coming. Would you want to get together again this evening?"

"Sure, how about right after dinner? I think they are serving at six o'clock tonight," Sam offered.

"Yeah, they are having some kind of buffet tonight. I hope it's something American," Gordon said, lingering but still sniffling.

"Okay, see you tonight," Sam said.

Gordon excused himself, sneezing several times as he left.

"Bless you!" Sam shouted, chuckling. He sat down and ran his finger through his curly black hair. As he leaned over, he put his head between his knees and wondered when the ride would end. In some ways, he felt like a rock star; he even had a bodyguard standing right outside. Researchers were being flown half way around the world just to talk to him. Astonishingly, some people were estimating maybe a billion people would be watching his TV show live—a billion people; one thousand million people. He said to himself in a half-whisper, "I'm not even thirty-two years old!"

As he picked up a production folder, he looked at his notes from an earlier meeting he had had with Drake. He had mentioned that, in addition to CNN and Fox News, it appeared that the Discovery Channel, the Learning Channel, and the National Geographic Channel might all interrupt their regular programming to make way for a live feed from the Archaeology Channel.

As he put on his shoes, he thought about the "A-Channel," as he called the Archaeology Channel. They had been content just two years ago to follow him in the desert, while he dug up some bones. Then a few notable finds had put them all on the map. Now, they were about to uncover the greatest discovery that could ever be made—greater than Noah's Ark, the Dead Sea Scrolls, the Rosetta Stone, King Tut's Tomb, or the Lost City of Pompeii.

He headed back to the production tent to see if he could find his sunglasses which he must have put down over there. Kishor dutifully tailed him over to the production tent and waited for him to emerge. "I would like to urinate, if you don't mind, Kishor," Sam said condescendingly to his bodyguard.

"Go ahead; I will go with you," Kishor said flatly.

"I was afraid that you were gonna to say that. Can you at least stand behind me? I am a little modest," Sam said, his tone somewhat chiding.

"Certainly," Kishor said in a matter-of-fact way.

"This is going to take some getting used to," Sam lamented. "A lot of getting used to."

-27-

BRISBANE'S OFFICE

Brisbane scanned the rest of the CDs that the communication technicians, Speck and Slim, had been continuing to feed him. As the final screen closed on his MacBook Pro, Brisbane was glad that he had ordered pinhole video cameras and microphones to be embedded in the walls of the school. He continued to be amazed at the technology he was able to utilize. The microphone and camera were no more than the width and length of the bristle on a hair brush. The models he had selected were simply pushed through a pinhole in the ceiling. They connected to a small transmitter in the attic unit that sent the signals out to the truck. The pictures that appeared on his screen were small and bit grainy, but he could tell exactly who was talking and he could even pick up the tone and inflection in their voices. With cameras and audio, he could see the roll of an eye that others could not be aware of. He felt it was important to look deeply into the hearts of the men that he was allowing to join him on this historic mission.

He placed the CDs into the file folders and removed a sheet containing a photo of each of the operatives he had selected for the mission. Not all of these men would prove to be loyal, he suspected. Indeed, this had been his view right from the start. "I will just need to sort the wheat from the chaff, or, more precisely, allow them to sort themselves," Brisbane said to himself as he picked up the small digital walkie talkie.

"Speck," he called via the system to the communication van outside.

"Yeah, Boss, right here," Speck replied dutifully.

"Did you wire the other van?" Brisbane asked brusquely.

"No sir, I'm sorry sir, but I don't recall that being discussed, Boss. But it is not a problem at all to do," Speck said, feeling somewhat intimidated by Brisbane's cold tone.

"You know our two Ethiopian nationals, Popeye and his friend, are out doing a lot of running around in that van, and I would like for it to be fully wired as well," Brisbane responded.

"Great! We will get on it tonight after everyone hits the sack. I will make sure that no one knows but the three of us, sir," Speck said.

"Thank you," Brisbane answered.

"No problem, Boss, I am out," Speck said.

-28-

Sam and Gordon sat down again after dinner, and spent time working through more information for about another hour. Eventually, Sam rubbed his eyes and asked if he could meet with Gordon again in the morning. As they broke for the evening, Sam could not believe how exciting it was to hear about a three-thousand-year-old wooden box covered with gold. He had learned, or been reminded of, several things.

He flipped through a yellow legal pad scrawled with notes he had taken. Jewish tradition appeared to agree with Scripture that stated that the Ark originally contained the Ten Commandments, a brass bowl of manna, and Aaron's staff that budded. Interestingly, it also added that it held the remnants of the first set of the Ten Commandments that Moses had thrown down and broken when he saw the people worshipping the golden calf. However, there was also a verse somewhere that indicated that all that was in the Ark when it was finally placed in the Temple was just the Ten Commandments alone.

Sam was always sure that every legend and tradition had some grain of truth to it, but there were so many, and a good number seemed contradictory. He knew from past experience that if the Bible was clear, he had better not contradict it. He had challenged it in the past and, to his own peril, had been shown to be wrong. That is why he boldly named his show "The Truth behind the Bible," even in this secular age.

At the meeting where the name of the show had been approved, the producers had not minded because it sounded like he might be challenging the Bible, he recalled. Some of the executives in charge felt that the Bible was all wrong, and lauded the attempt to try and show the real truth behind it. But the faithful Christians and the Messianic Jews, of which he counted himself one, liked it because they saw the truth of the Bible being corroborated.

As Sam exited Drake's trailer, bidding goodnight to Gordon who strode off in the direction of his sleeping quarters, there stood Kishor, his tall form slightly obscured by some shadows. He was always on watch. It irritated Sam to feel Kishor follow him, always two steps behind and always looking around. Sam stopped, and Kishor halted as well. Sam turned and faced him.

"What is it, exactly, that you are looking for?" Sam finally blurted out, not being able to hold the question in any longer.

"Threats," Kishor responded, his voice sounding ominous.

"What kind of threats? There is nobody here!" Sam said dismissively as he began to walk, waving his arms. "I mean, okay, we are in the middle of a crazy country where, granted, there has been civil unrest and strife and persecution and all those kinds of things. But, we are in a pretty peaceful part, and the government here—even if *we* think it is corrupt—is on board with us on this project. Besides, Kishor, nobody even knows that we are here, or at least why. I just don't understand why I have got to have private security."

Kishor stopped.

"Did I say something that offended you, Kishor?" Sam turned and asked, obviously concerned.

"I am not security," Kishor said.

"Okay, I'm sorry. Really. I meant no offense," Sam said sincerely. "But, you would be what, then? What should I have said?"

"I am a bodyguard; there is a difference," Kishor said, looking away slightly.

"Okay, but you do provide security, right?" Sam confirmed.

Kishor did not respond.

"At least I got him to talk," Sam thought to himself.

"Look, Kishor, I understand the difference, and that was ignorance on my part. I apologize—I did not mean to offend you. If you are going to be sticking to me like white on rice this whole time, I definitely don't want you to be mad at me," Sam said sincerely. "I guess, being a bodyguard and all, you would jump in front of a bullet. That is really different from a rent-a-cop," Sam reasoned aloud.

"I have done that," Kishor said in a measured response.

"No way, man; you got shot? On purpose?" Sam asked, stopping to take it all in.

"I am a bodyguard. It is a code. I would even do that for you, but not because of how I feel about you. I would do that because it is my job, and it is the duty of a bodyguard," Kishor confirmed.

"You won't tell me about the time you got shot, will you?"

"No," Kishor said flatly.

"Well great. Now we understand each other," Sam said, exasperated.

Kishor was back in the guard mode. He stood there and tilted his head back and forth.

Sam engaged the key in the lock, manipulating it until the door finally opened into his trailer. "So are you going to stand around out here all night out here or are you going to come on inside?" Sam asked.

Kishor looked around, and said, "I will come in."

Sam was surprised to find a cot had already been made up for Kishor. "Uh, a lot of stuff is being taken care of here without my knowledge," Sam said hesitantly. "I mean, I see you have a key, too. But I don't really have a problem with you having a key to the trailer, but who gave it to you?"

"Remember we are both working for the same people. I have standards that they must meet," Kishor continued. "I must always have full access; otherwise I cannot guarantee your safety."

"Okay, then; well this is going to be a joyful conversation," Sam exhaled as he flopped down on the couch. "Do you care if I turn on the TV here?"

"Suit yourself," Kishor said, his voice a quiet monotone.

Sam found it a lot harder to relax with another man in the room—especially a man who, at regular intervals, would look out the window and go walk around outside. He was gone again. Sam could not figure out why in the world he was doing it. "Maybe that is part of the point; maybe he is not supposed to have a reason; maybe it keeps somebody off balance," he thought. "Man, how many spy books have I read? I am going to drive myself crazy thinking about this," he said to himself as he surfed the few channels available on the old-fashioned analog TV.

The American classic program, *Knight Rider*, appeared on the screen before him and seemed familiar and somehow comforting to him. The black talking car named Kit, complete with its flashing red strobe in front, roared down the road. He felt he could have been in the United States, or at least it was that way until the show's main character, played by David Hasselhoff, spoke in a language that he did not recognize.

Sam's eyes glazed over as he fell asleep in front of the screen.

-29-

At network headquarters for the Archaeology Channel in Manhattan, Marjorie turned the key in the lock and slipped into the executive suite. The Chrysler Building and other New York skyscrapers stood proudly in view of the window. She woke the private fax machine from its "sleep" mode and inserted three pages, making sure no one noticed what she was sending before she programmed the number. When the confirmation sheet printed out, she cleared the memory of the machine and shredded both the document she had just sent, as well as the journal page.

* * *

IN BRISBANE'S OFFICE

Brisbane gathered the pages from his fax machine, only to see a rather indistinct photo of a man. According to the information secreted to him, this imposing, shaven-headed man was supposedly a bodyguard, a man going by the name of Kishor.

"Well, those idiots must suspect something," Brisbane said under his breath.

The second page had an even more unclear photo of someone sporting what looked like a scraggly goatee beard—this one, supposedly, a researcher. To Brisbane, he looked like some kind of pinhead academic type. He found himself thinking that he could be a member of security, too, and this research stuff could be a cover. However, old Marjorie had never steered him wrong. "Aww," he said, as he read the third page. Marjorie was pathetically pledging her undying love and looking forward to cruising the world with him on his luxury yacht.

In fact, Brisbane did not own any such sailboat. But, the beautiful photo of a sixty-footer, complete with the name "Marjorie" proudly etched in elegant lettering expertly Photoshopped on the stern had evidently looked more than convincing to her. Certainly, this picture had had the desired effect on Marjorie when she had received the email from Brisbane in which he had pledged his love and commitment to her. Little did she really know. . . .

"Some adult American women are easier to fool than even young children are," Brisbane mused. "Give me a divorced, forty-something American woman, frustrated in her life and her dead-end job, and the prospect of a fantasy life on that sailboat will make her do anything," he thought out loud, lowering himself to the floor to do his twice-daily one hundred knuckle push-ups.

-30-

Sam awoke with a start. Through blurry eyes, he could see Kishor looming over him, his form tall against the stark backdrop of the trailer.

"Man, what are you doing? You give me the creeps when you do that," Sam complained, "What time is it?"

"6:30 a.m. local," Kishor answered.

"Well, I knew it wasn't p.m., there, genius," Sam snapped.

Kishor looked at him with narrowing eyes.

"Those are cold, gray eyes," Sam involuntarily thought. "He has killed people. Lots of people. Bigger than me, and certainly meaner than me." He kept the thought to himself.

"Hey Kishor," Sam piped up, "I have gotten into the habit of going over to Drake's trailer every morning, because he has some good Starbucks coffee in there. You want some?"

"No, thank you," Kishor replied politely.

"You are not a coffee drinker, huh?" Sam concluded.

"I've already had some, thank you anyway," Kishor stated.

"What? Do you ever sleep? And aren't you jet-lagged? You were sitting wide awake when I went to sleep last night, and now you are already up, and you have already had some of my coffee this morning!" Sam exclaimed.

"Yes," Kishor confirmed with no visible reaction.

"Okay, whatever. Are you sure you're not like part android or something? You know, were you sent back from the future to save Sarah Conner?" Sam said in an obvious reference to the movie series "Terminator." The allusion seemed totally lost on Kishor.

Kishor stepped outside and shut the door behind him as was his custom without saying anything.

"Kishor, man, you missed your line; you were supposed to say, 'I'll be back,'" Sam joked under his breath.

Dragging himself from the comfort of his cot, Sam peered at himself in the mirror, rubbing some sleep from his left eye. "This dust certainly doesn't help matters," he muttered to himself. After dressing in a fresh, open-necked shirt and light-colored chinos, he opened the door and clamored down the metal stairs outside the trailer, making his way across the yard to where Drake's trailer was parked.

Kishor, of course, appeared behind him from nowhere, as was his habit.

The coffee was still hot at Drake's, and the aroma filled the small trailer. Although smaller than Sam's, it had a more upscale look and feel to it, but he could not tell why, exactly. Sam really enjoyed just having coffee with the guys every morning. He felt that he actually fit in with them. As they sat in the small seating area, Kishor's shadow fell against the narrow window pane, evidence to Sam that he was still standing guard outside.

"What is with your bald friend there?" Mark Simms asked Sam without looking up from his papers.

"Well you know," Sam said, "he is close by because he is supposed to keep me safe. Can't you see all of these thugs lining up to hurt me, all of these warlords coming up with guns?" He stood up and began to pace. "You talk about how *I* spend the network's money, well, *he* is total waste of money. Our channel should be sponsoring digs. We could be sponsoring young men to go through schools and then give them better jobs when they graduate so they are not starving," Sam ranted. "Otherwise, they wind up teaching in a West Virginia coal mining town, or some school up in the rust belt. Instead, we have got Kishor, the assassin, out here ready to shoot somebody."

"Do you think he has ever really shot anybody?" Mark asked, looking up, quite obviously intrigued.

"Man, the way he looks at me—sometimes, I think he would just as soon shoot me," Sam said.

"I feel his pain," Mark said dryly. "Sometimes we all want to shoot you."

"Thanks a lot. He said he is 'duty bound,' or 'honor bound,'" Sam said, still pacing, and making quotation marks with his fingers, "to keep me safe even from myself, I think."

After a pause, Sam sat down and asked: "So, Drake, was this really all Herbert's idea?"

"He runs the channel," Drake said, exhaling.

"He puts the 'M' in micro manager, doesn't he?" Sam jabbed, thinking about the man sitting smugly at his grandiose desk in his oak-paneled suite in the Manhattan office.

"Well, he does when it comes to his star talent," Drake said in deadpan tones, looking right at Sam.

Sam ignored the jab, and said, "I still don't see the need for the security. I do actually appreciate the researcher, though. I really enjoyed talking with Gordy."

"Gordy?" Mark Simms asked in an incredulous tone. "Gordy? What is a Gordy?"

"Uh," Sam stammered, looking away, "Gordon Dew-something, Dewey, uh, Decimal? No, anyway he is really bright. You might even say almost cool, in a way. Well, he is not really cool," Sam thought out loud. "He is actually the opposite of cool, whatever that is."

"Warm?" Mark asked flatly. Drake smiled.

"He certainly knows his stuff. He is really fascinating to talk to. You ought to visit with him; even you might learn something, Simms," Sam added.

"I think I'll pass. I brought my video games to play at night."

"Oh, an intellectual," Sam remarked sarcastically. Drake laughed.

"I am meeting with Gordy again today to finish up. I thought I knew a lot about this topic. I mean, I have spoken on the Ark, but I tell you this, they definitely picked the right guy. This guy eats and breathes the Lost Ark of the Covenant, the Lost Tribe, the whole deal," Sam said admiringly.

"What Lost Tribe? What happened—did they get voted off the island?" Mark asked without looking up.

"The Lost Tribe, you know, the Black Jews," Sam mentioned as he reached over and took the last pastry from the table.

"The what?" Mark said.

"The Black Jews. They are called the 'Falashas,'" Sam said with a mouthful of crème-filled éclair.

"The galoshes? Is that what you said?" Mark asked. "It is bad manners to talk with your mouth full, even for a TV star."

"Not galoshes, dipstick! 'Falashas.' It means 'strangers.' They were the people of the Tribe of Dan that are believed to have come up the Nile to avoid persecution after one of Solomon's sons began to come after them."

"Oh yeah, the truth behind the Bible thing; yeah I got you," Mark said, obviously shrugging it off.

"Why?" Sam asked, instantly exasperated. "Why do you do that?"

"Do what?" Mark said, nonchalantly.

"Act like you know everything, and then blow the Bible off, when you don't know any of it! You don't know the competing theories," Sam said, standing up. "You don't know why the Lost Ark is no longer on Mount Gobi; or under the Temple Mount; or in the Valley of the Kings or over where the Dead Sea Scrolls were!" Sam went on in an increasingly abrasive tone. "You don't know any of that, but yet you blow it all off like it is all myths or something!"

"Yeah, yeah, I know it is not just mythology that somebody parts a sea, or puts every animal that has ever been created on a giant boat. No, no, that doesn't sound like mythology at all," Mark said, his voice dripping with sarcasm.

Drake interrupted, "Give it up, Sam. Mark is a hopeless case. Save your breath."

"What burns me up," Sam continued, "is not that you choose not to believe, but why you act like you know something about it, when you don't know *anything* about it, and you are just too darn lazy to even look into it."

"I guess I am too darn lazy to give you a good answer," Mark said. Sam looked infuriated.

"Only help the willing," Drake admonished, with an air of grandfatherly wisdom.

"You are a jerk sometimes, Simms!" Sam barked.

"Oh, very intellectual there, Cohen," Mark responded in his most patronizing tone.

"I am out of here," Sam said turning to leave. "Thanks for the coffee—I can't survive without a good cup of joe."

"No problem," Drake said.

Sam bounded down the stairs, but as he hit the last metal stair, one end of it became disconnected and yielded, sending his lanky, six-foot-two frame sprawling. He found himself face down on the ground, the gritty sensation of red sand on his lips.

Kishor's shadow fell over him.

"Why didn't you do something?" Sam demanded, as he stood up, brushing red dust from his shirt and khakis.

"My job is to keep someone else from hurting you, not to keep you from hurting yourself, Cohen," Kishor said. Sam thought he caught a glimpse of a smile for the first time. Sam now learned that all he had to do to make Kishor smile was fall, preferably in a particularly awkward, painful way. "This is who is supposed to save my life," he thought. "I am not sure that I am in such great hands, here."

-31-

THE HALLWAY,
FORMER AKSUM UNIVERSITY

Brisbane stood silently in the hallway, listening just outside the room where the three snipers and three spotters were talking. Six bunks had been lined up for them when they arrived. Now, after some days of use, Brisbane could see bunks in disarray all over the room. "Gentlemen, may I borrow one of you spotters, please?" Brisbane said cordially. "Could you bring your equipment?"

"You just want me to have a look with no guns, huh?" asked the most senior spotter, Jim Bob, as he stood up.

"No guns necessary, thank you," Brisbane said as he exited the room.

Jim Bob hoisted up a large black duffel bag and a camouflage backpack, adding, "Suits me, Mr. Aussie. I am bored to tears sitting around here."

Brisbane and Billy took the old white panel truck and drove out down dusty roads in the direction of the temple. Local men walked along the road's edge in long, off-white robes, some with colorful head wraps. The women were tall and slender with long necks, and most of them were much more colorfully arrayed. Many of them carried bulging baskets, and even full pots of water, carefully balanced on their heads. "It always kills me that they can do that," Jim Bob said as he pointed at two local women with giant vase-shaped pottery vessels carefully balanced on their heads as they walked.

Brisbane handed a folder to him and Jim Bob unfolded a three-dimensional satellite photo of the temple in Aksum. "You might like these," Brisbane said, handing him what looked like tiny binoculars.

"What?" Jim Bob said, looking at the small optical device.

"Look at the temple area map through them," Brisbane added.

"Aw, cool!" the seasoned spotter exclaimed as he saw the small trees on the map leap to height as they took on visual three-dimensional properties. The buildings could be seen all the way around by just rotating the map. The hills overlooking the temple were of particular interest to Jim Bob.

"Where would you get the best look at the temple?" Brisbane asked as they bumped down the rough road. "It is about to smooth out somewhat when we get to the paved road up here," he added as the vehicle hit a particularly large pothole.

They began to circle the area. In the distance, the production trailers of the network looked innocent enough. The spotter craned his neck to see through the driver's window. "Well it looks like you have got a shooting position way up there, but there's that eastern position over there at the rock outcropping which will be perfect cover. You could use a third to triangulate fire; go back around there one more time—take the block, please sir," asked.

Brisbane was happy to comply with his request.

"Yeah, yeah," Jim Bob said, shielding his eyes from the bright glare of the sun as it caught his eyes, "you need to get up in that scrub on the side of that hill that would give you your three spots, with the main one the rocky hill to the east," he concluded.

Brisbane was impressed. These were the same three spots that had been previously selected by the Ethiopian men, Popeye and Garfield.

"I would like for you to spend the rest of the day in one of those spots and do a little live reconnaissance for us," Brisbane requested.

"If you see this fellow," (he handed him a copy of the faxed picture of a bald man) "do you think you could identify him through your scope from that distance?"

"Heck yeah, man. I could tell you whether he has had spinach recently by the specks between his teeth," Jim Bob boasted as he grinned.

"Is everyone in the rural American South filled with so much bravado there, Jim Bob?" Brisbane asked curiously, then, without waiting for an answer, he added, "Which spot would you prefer?"

Guided by the spotter, Brisbane parked in an out-of-the-way spot and retrieved a large camera with a huge lens, one like the professional photographers have on sidelines at football games, and a large tripod.

"What is that thing for?" Jim Bob asked.

"People take photos of the temple for calendars, tourist posters, and so forth," Brisbane said. "With your equipment as a kind of decoy, if you are casual and all, it will seem just quite normal. No need to hide. I will see you this afternoon."

* * *

Jim Bob nonchalantly walked up the hill, sat down between the bushes near the top, and looked around. He eyed the temple through the camera's telephoto lens. When he was sure that no one was looking at him, he took out his spotting scope and placed its tripod next to the camera's tripod.

It took him no time at all to see the bald man standing just outside a trailer, along with the other trailers that were arrayed in a semicircle in a lot that was only a quick, two-block walk from the temple site. Adjusting his earpiece, he quickly called up to Brisbane. "I have already spotted him, the bald fella, the trailers, satellite trucks and all. Looks like there is at least one bodyguard and I think that's the bald guy you had a picture of," Jim Bob noted. "What do you want me to do?"

"Just observe the goings on today, and I will pick you up before dark," Brisbane replied.

"Roger to that. I'm out," Jim Bob dutifully said as he resumed his reconnaissance, and snapped a few photos.

* * *

Brisbane pulled back up at the old school house and stuck his head into the communications truck. "Gentlemen, were you able to work on last night's priority?" Brisbane inquired.

"Yes sir, it is all rigged up," Slim assured him, and gave him the thumbs-up sign indicating that the van that Brisbane had just been driving was also wired for surveillance, and properly functioning.

"We picked you up talking to Jim Bob about where to park, and what hill to sit on and so forth."

"Perfect," Brisbane said. "So, it passed the test, and we were far enough away. Excellent job, gentlemen; keep up the good work."

Speck asked, in a cautious tone, "Well, since we have been doing such a good job, is there any chance that we could have some more of that pizza?"

"I will make sure of that," Brisbane replied.

* * *

In the back room, the remaining snipers and spotters were going through the routine of disassembling, cleaning, and reassembling their weapons again, as the snipers discussed Jim Bob's impromptu mission. The matte black paint had arrived and was sitting outside their door. Each of the men lightly painted the silencers with careful attention so as not to clog up the tiny holes that allowed the gases to escape, and that deadened the sound of the firing of the bullet.

"So, did we ever figure out what Vince and Louie have been doing? I have not seen them in a long time," John David queried as he screwed the silencer firmly onto the barrel, admiring its precision.

"No, I don't trust them. I am surprised those Croatian guys didn't just shoot them the other day, when they smarted off outside," Bubba said.

"Yeah, I don't know what they said to them, but those Croat guys don't play," John David concluded.

"I call them Cro-Cops, you know like the guy in the Ultimate Fighting Championship," Bubba joked. "Cro-Cops...get it...Croatian Cops." He pointed his rifle at Hawk, who knocked it away with a dismissive look.

"Were they really Croatian policemen?" Jake asked naively.

"Hey man, I don't know, really," Bubba said, getting louder, "but if those guys are the police, I'd hate to see what the bad guys looked like!" Boisterous laughter echoed in the room.

Jake jammed in the magazine and examined it carefully. "You reckon they are just mercenaries, just like us?" he asked.

"I bet so," Colton, the other spotter, said.

"Colton, I didn't know that you could talk. I never hear you," Bubba said, smiling.

"I guess I don't have a whole lot to say," Colton replied.

"I do all the talking for him," said Jake. "What do you reckon they have Jim Bob doing?" he asked.

"I don't know," Bubba said. "There sure wasn't much warning on that little mission was there?"

"Yeah, what are we now, about three days out?" Hawk asked.

"I am ready to rock and roll," said John David.

"Me too," said Bubba, "One shot—one kill!" Bubba exclaimed to a chorus of enthusiastic agreement.

* * *

Two rooms away, the Croatians, on the other hand, had taken up smoking. At least, a couple of them smoked and the others were trying it.

It was comical for Louie and Vince to watch the men from their upstairs window. They had kept to themselves, correctly sensing that they weren't too appreciated by the others.

"You know, if weren't for our connections, and gambling money out of the four casinos that we got a hand in down in little Tunica County, Mississippi, this operation would never have got going," Louie mentioned.

"They just don't appreciate us," Vince said.

"You're right," Louie agreed. "If it wasn't for the money that we skimmed off of the Tunica deal, those guys there wouldn't be having all of these first-class silencers, guns, and all this communication equipment."

"That communication equipment alone cost a mint," Vince added.

"Yo, maybe we are in the wrong business, huh?" Louie joked, laughing.

"Bottom line, I think we ought to keep our heads down," Vince concluded.

"I'll tell ya, I wouldn't want those Croats, or whatever they are out there, to hear you laughing at them not being able to smoke," Louie said, leaning near the window.

"Yeah, what is it with those guys? Did you notice how they signal to each other even when they don't have to?" Vince said quietly. "I must say, I just don't trust them."

"Well, you know, I'll tell you who we have to watch out for, and that is Brisbane. I think he wants a bigger cut. I think he will take any of us out to get a bigger cut," Louie confided.

"Yeah, it has crossed my mind, too," Vince said.

"You know what happened with Tony Capano in Chicago?" Louie reminded him.

"Sure, his own son killed him to take a bigger cut," Vince retorted.

"There is no honor among thieves is there?" Louie concluded.

"Has there ever been?" Vince replied. "Has there ever been?"

-32-

A Hill Overlooking the Temple

That evening, when Kishor was not in sight for once, Sam slipped out to hurriedly walk up to the nearby hill overlooking the Temple. No Kishor, no production deadlines, no more Ark education.

The sun's glow caused a growing blood-red glow to envelop the arid landscape. The ever-present airborne dust gathered in the low areas like fog. The dry dust coated the back of Sam's throat like a spoonful of cinnamon. Then he realized, to his horror, in his haste to avoid Kishor he had slipped out of the trailer without his insulated water mug. This would be a short walk without water.

A voice from behind him interrupted his thoughts, startling him. He spun around and dark eyes met his from under a dirty white turban. The wiry, robed form was much closer than he expected. It was unnerving.

The man's stillness was also unsettling. He just stared.

"What?" Sam asked.

Without a reply, the wiry man in the turban produced from his dirty, salmon-colored robe, a well-worn machete, that was almost entirely rust colored except for the concave shiny edge, which looked as if it had been sharpened each week for half a hundred years.

Sam registered that the machete was now pointed at his throat. He felt the hot steel press in against his trachea. If he were to gag or cough, it could kill him. He tried to remain calm, but he instinctively knew it likely was not going to work. He held his breath.

The assailant growled a threat that Sam could not understand.

The dust in the back of his throat and the pressing metal blade against his windpipe made it impossible to cough, but time and— more to the point, anxiety—was making it impossible for him to hold his breath.

Sam had to act. He had to devise a way of escape.

The robed man growled something incoherently. His eyes were black, unmoving; they had a cold, deathlike quality to them.

As air escaped his mouth a bit, Sam was planning his moves. He would turn to his left swiftly and sweep his right hand to the left, intending to catch the arm of his assailant—forcing the blade safely away to Sam's left. This would allow him to avoid the blade, and to then push or just bowl over the smaller man and escape, hopefully with his head still on his shoulders!

Clenching his eyes shut and saying a quick prayer of "Lord, please help me!" he tensed his left leg and began digging his right toe into the sand to push off with.

Then, with a rush of breath, he blindly spun left with a powerful, adrenaline-fueled swinging right hand, catching and clamping down on the outstretched elbow of the bandit. As he spun, he pushed forward, but nothing stopped him. Inhaling once again, his breath finally filled his lungs. He felt flushed and light-headed.

The arm he was now clutching in his right hand felt warm, wet, and limp. As he looked around, his knees became weak. The arm, still gripping the machete, came to an end as a bloody stump between the elbow and where the shoulder had been.

"Ugh!" Sam exclaimed as he threw it to the sand, blood still running from his hands.

Kishor was walking back toward the camp.

Sam, breathless, went and stood over the bloodied body of the assailant. The sand had turned a deep red color around his upper torso. He now could see that the man's arm had been cleanly severed, just below the shoulder.

"Hey!" Sam called out. "Where did you come from?"

Kishor did not break stride.

Sam could not even see any blade Kishor had concealed. What was with this man?

* * *

That next morning, Sam stepped outside to face Kishor.

"Look, I don't know what all happened last night; I just needed to get a break from all this," Sam explained. Kishor remained silent, looking past him. "Okay, I'm sorry, okay?" Sam confessed. "I get it, I get it."

Sam noticed the brownish dried blood on the bodyguard's boots. "I guess I do really need you," he volunteered, his tone apologetic.

Kishor cleared his throat.

"Um. Ugh. And, well, thank you," Sam stammered.

Kishor gave an almost imperceptible nod.

"Good talk," Sam quipped as he gave up on any further conversation as he began to move away. Then he stopped. Turning back to Kishor, his tone a little softer: "Does anyone else know this happened? Like Drake?"

Kishor shook his head slightly, eyes still searching in his usual way.

"Good!" Sam concluded. And then he stepped back, adding with a grin, "I had it under control, you know."

Kishor remained solemn.

-33-

BRISBANE'S OFFICE

Downstairs, Brisbane looked out the window, as Speck's hand passed through yet another CD to him. He inserted it into his laptop and adjusted his earpiece. He listened to what the snipers had to say. Then he skipped to the second track, the one that had recorded the Croats' discussions. Finally, he listened in to the hushed tones of Vince and Louie, who still were talking upstairs. "So far, so good," he said to himself. "So far, so good."

Brisbane got up and entered the room where the Ethiopian nationals were, asking loudly, "Gentlemen, do you have any dinner plans yet? What does everybody want?"

"Believe it or not, they all want pizza again, from that same place that we got it before," Garfield said. "That time the delivery guy brought the pizzas, I think he was eyeing us out, wondering what was going on. Best if we go get them ourselves this time. Is it OK if we take the van again?" he asked, turning inquiringly to Brisbane.

"Sure, go ahead and take the van. Have you got enough cash?" Brisbane asked.

"Oh, yes sir, thank you. Same amount as we ordered the last time?"

"Yes, that will be fine," Brisbane replied as he returned to his makeshift office.

* * *

The two men got into the truck and headed off to town to bring back the evening meal; and once again they stopped at the little concrete building. They knocked, a sound pattern of four deliberate, staccato knocks. The same woman servant greeted them shyly through a crack in the door before opening it wide and beckoning them quickly inside, her almond-shaped eyelids open in a neutral expression as she held the door open for them. They entered the small room. Again, she unlatched a bookcase that swung open, revealing a smoky office. After they had been admitted, they noticed that Ruslan stood up to greet them this time.

"Gentlemen, sit, sit," Ruslan politely insisted in his thick Russian accent. "I hope all is well. I have reconsidered. We are willing to pay you more than twice what we originally offered."

Garfield seemed puzzled, looked at Popeye, and said, "But that is not as much as we have asked for."

"I understand, but please believe me when I say that the Russian Mafia is not what it once was. Funds are somewhat, shall we say, limited. But, this could make all of the difference. It is very, very important that you understand how sincere my friends in Moscow and Kiev are about this situation."

"Serious or not, my friend," Popeye popped off in a cocky retort, "I told you the price, you know what it is worth, and it is a bargain even at twice what we ask. But you know what it is going to take. There is not much time left if you want to get your men ready." His voice was firm, and his tone uncompromising.

"I understand," Ruslan said. "Let me make one additional phone call. I will see you in the morning when you come on the journey to get breakfast."

"We will see you in the morning," Garfield said as they walked out.

After they had picked up twenty large pizzas, they piled back into the van. "I just don't understand why they won't pay more. Do they not understand how important this is?" Garfield asked

"I don't know," Popeye said, obviously disgusted. "I have explained everything to them several times. I mean, at least Brisbane totally understands the value of this. He loves to make speeches, about its historical value, and all of that. The Russian mob have already stolen everything that they can get their hands on and sold everything they can sell. The drug trade has dried up and they have few arms left to peddle. They really need this," Popeye concluded.

"But the only reason they even have a chance other than the lack of security is the fact that they have us as insiders," Garfield said. "The key to this is that they can't pull it off without us, and if they expect us to double-cross Brisbane, then it is going to have to be worth it. I mean, there are a bunch of guys that we are sleeping in the same rooms with tonight that would kill us as soon as look at us."

"Let's just check with him in the morning, when we go get all of the eggs everybody wants tomorrow," Popeye advised. "Just be sure not to discuss it in the school building. I have a feeling that the whole place is wired."

"Good idea, Popeye," Garfield said, "Brisbane has probably been being extra careful."

"Well, maybe *he* should be careful, huh?" Popeye said, as they both had a good laugh.

* * *

The CD—another one this time—was handed through the window. Brisbane inserted this one in his MacBook Pro laptop. He was just getting to the good part, the conversation that had taken place in the truck going to town, when the Ethiopian nationals walked in and yelled, "Dinner is ready!" in Amharic, their language, but quickly corrected it to English.

"Did you boys have a nice trip?" Brisbane called out.

"Yes, sir. You will still want scrambled eggs in the morning?" Popeye asked.

"Yes, that would be great," Brisbane said as he looked out the window.

"No problem, I already have the guy on it," Popeye said dutifully.

"Thank you for your efficiency, gentlemen. The only thing I appreciate more than efficiency...is loyalty," Brisbane said, his eyes narrowed in a knowing way. He shut the door loudly. Garfield and Popeye looked at each other.

"You think he knows something?" Popeye asked Garfield. Garfield just shrugged nervously.

"I sure hope not," he said as he exhaled loudly.

* * *

Sam sat down with Gordon, who appeared to be wearing exactly the same clothes as he had the day before. This bothered Sam, but he thought, "What do you say to another grown man?"

Gordon relieved the awkwardness by opening to a place in his notes where a yellow post-it note stuck out. Appearing to ready himself for a marathon, he said, "Now, this is where we were yesterday," and he began to tell the story of Solomon, the Queen of Sheba, the Tribe of Dan, and even the Knights Templar.

Sam settled in for what he knew would be a long haul.

-34-

Brisbane had downloaded an image from the Internet, this one taken somewhere in the Caribbean. The short message he attached to it read simply: "My Darling: Here is another spot I imagine us going; I cannot wait to be sailing the world with you!"

Checking his proxy settings again, he transmitted it in an email through four different servers on two different continents, knowing that it would soon show up at Marjorie's home email address. "That will definitely keep her going a little longer," he said to himself. "She will be sure that we are sailing the world together very soon."

Brisbane then generated one more email using the same circuitous sending path. He needed to be sure that the exit plan was completely failsafe, even if it meant a kind of overkill when it came to preventing the tracing of his emails:

"Victor, I trust everything is still in line for airlift. The coor-

dinates previously given to you, and the time, are still all a 'go.' My vehicle will be a white Chevrolet. Be sure that the helicopter is well fueled. Do not attempt reply. —B"

-35-

Sam was feeling pretty confident as he popped in on Drake. Kishor was always two steps behind, never seeming to stop turning this way and that, his eyes always scanning. As they mounted the stairs to Drake's trailer, Sam could feel the trailer give slightly under his weight on the short metal stairway. Kishor waited dutifully outside, as always.

"It is all coming together. Between my conversations with Gordy, and all my field work, I feel qualified, Drake," Sam continued. "Actually, I can now better explain a lot of unknown or even misunderstood ancient history to my audience."

"Your audience tests out as pretty intellectual, Sam." Drake confirmed, while lighting a pipe. "They do seem to appreciate hearing all of the different theories and the reasons for each." He looked thoughtfully at Sam, then continued, "I have not seen this gleam in your eye in quite a while, Sam."

Sam was ready with the explanation: "Well, see I have spent about a day and a half with Gordy. He has walked me through so many cool things that I just never knew, or had never quite put together," Sam explained as he paced back and forth, a tone of excitement in his voice. "Indeed, the Ark of the Covenant is symbolic of other things, but it has a real-life history of its own, and I get to tell it! Now, some of it is still pretty murky, but it is simply fascinating, and I think the audience will really like it. I just want to know how much time I have to go over everything, because I *am* going to need time. I have got pages and pages of notes on my legal pad, here. It is going to take a while to go through them all." Sam slowed his pace and looked at Drake pleadingly, his notes clasped under his arm.

Drake looked at him strangely. "Sam, I know you love this stuff, but if you are reading the history of the Lost Ark of the Covenant in such detail, well, it would cause people to turn over to the 'Let's watch paint dry channel' or the 'Let's watch grass grow channel.'"

Sam looked sullen.

"No, don't pout," Drake countered, "I am not saying that you can't go into the history of this thing—in fact, you must. We cannot just do a live feed with nothing to prepare the audience. If we have you doing a voice-over narration of some of the history, and we show some artwork, and location photos of some of that, you can do it. Also, keep in mind that there is the blog, and that will give scope for a lot more information to be presented. And didn't I hear there was something about a church?" Drake asked.

"Oh yeah, there is a picture in a church," Sam said, very excited to know what Drake had heard about it. "The painting actually shows the Ark being carried out of Jerusalem."

"And I suppose then winding up here, right? Great! We can take some footage of that and have the landscapes with you giving a brief history of this—but it needs to be brief," Drake reminded him. "You are going to have to review your notes and cut out whatever you absolutely don't need to say. You have to get it down to, well, just get it down to the nut," Drake concluded.

"The nut?" Sam asked, grinning.

"The nut, you know, the point," Drake explained. "People aren't tuning in to hear you teach some kind of long history lesson. They are tuning in to see something that most people don't believe even existed, or if it did exist, it sure wouldn't be around today. Sam, you are going to affect a lot of people with this broadcast. Now, even though you have immersed yourself in this ancient history, I would not want to see that get in the way of this. Remember what my granddaddy always said," Drake continued. "*Always keep the main thing, the main thing.*"

Sam repeated this slogan under his breath. He had heard it before.

"Now, what is the *main thing* in this project?" Drake asked, almost rhetorically, as if a tutor were asking his pupil to recite something that he was supposed to have learned. "The Lost Ark of the Covenants still exists and is to be found within mere feet of here, where we stand!" Drake proclaimed, answering his own question. "Keep that first and foremost, Sam. You still have some time, so go work through all of your notes. But remember, we cannot give clues to our location until after the broadcast. It is exceedingly important that no one in the outside world, outside of the network, should know so much as what country we are in, or, for that matter, what continent we are on—let them guess, if they will, but we cannot reveal it; there is too much at stake, and that's how it has been agreed with the attorneys in New York. The live broadcast must come from the secret underground tunnels in 'an undisclosed location,'" Drake reminded him, making imaginary quote marks in the air with his fingers.

"I heard you guys found out there are even more tunnels, huh?" Sam asked.

"Maybe miles. And, you know they told us that we would find skeletons down there," Drake mentioned.

"Do you know how many?" Sam asked.

"We found a total of twenty-seven earlier, and we only went so deep. Almost all have been Keepers of the Ark. Some of them still have items like weapons or digging tools, so you should be able to roughly date these guys," Drake said.

"Cool," Sam said, leaning forward.

"Apparently, there have been some attempts at the theft of this Ark, as well. Two of the skeletons were said to be thieves' remains," Drake related. "It looks like the keepers were pretty rough on them."

"Can you imagine trying to steal the Ark of the Covenant?" Sam asked. "Well, it would be the biggest theft in history. It would be a bigger theft than the Mona Lisa, bigger than the Hope Diamond, bigger than the Brinks Train Robbery. There would be nothing to compare it with."

"You are starting to sound like the network's liability insurance carrier," Drake said. "He was absolutely seething at the idea that we were over here without plenty of security. I think they only hire paranoid people. But, I am glad that Kishor is here to help keep you safe, and at least we will have somebody armed on the premises, if there is a problem," Drake said.

"There *are* guards here," Sam said emphatically.

"I know," Drake replied, "but they are not exactly holding high-tech weaponry."

"Yeah, they mostly carry Jewish designed swords, a few have old guns, and I have heard that some are experts with a sling," Sam said.

"Sounds like a regular David-and-Goliath thing, huh?" There was a question in Drake's intonation.

"I would love to see that!" Sam exclaimed.

"It was fascinating," Drake said.

"You saw them?" Sam asked excitedly.

"Well, they were out there practicing yesterday afternoon while you were spending time with that librarian, Gordon," Drake explained.

"Uh, he is not a librarian, but, yeah, he sure looks like one. He is a really good research guy, and you'd definitely enjoy talking to him—if you can get past his nasally voice," Sam confided, mockingly imitating Gordon's rather reedy vocal tone.

"Yes, well, I will take your word for it," Drake said drily. "The guards using the slings were impressive. They set a plaster head upon a pole over nine feet tall and spun these long slings. Sam, I didn't know they would be that long."

"What do you mean?" Sam asked.

"Well, I expected a sling to be a few inches long. But, these things are almost two feet long, and they sling them at an incredible velocity. Just a couple of turns and they send these rocks whizzing out. When they hit that plaster head, it shattered it into a million pieces," Drake said.

"Why did they put the head over nine feet tall?" Sam asked.

"Oh, don't tell me the world-renowned biblical archeologist has forgotten the story of David and the nine-and-a-half-foot tall giant Goliath?" Drake said with a tone mixed with mock self-importance and a little sarcasm.

"You got me," Sam humbly acknowledged. "Well, I have got a question for you, then," he continued, in an effort to quickly redeem himself in Drake's eyes. "How many stones did David bring to fight Goliath?"

"According to the Bible, it was five," Drake said.

"Good, but why do you think he brought five?" Sam asked.

"Hmm—in case he missed a few times?" Drake said, half-asking.

"Nope, wrong. Thank you for playing," Sam said, satisfied that he had humbled Drake.

"Well, are you going to share your vast intellect with me?" Drake asked.

"Okay, it is said that Goliath had a father and three brothers, and so there were five of them in total," Sam explained.

"You mean," Drake asked, "if he killed Goliath, he thought he would have to kill every giant in that family from Gath in order to achieve victory?"

"You got it!" Sam said.

"Think you are pretty smart, don't you, Sam?" Drake asked with a sly smile. "Go on back and read over all those notes and get them down to a few pages. We can help you do that, but remember your initial speech cannot give a clue where you are. We will clear out of this place as soon as we are done. In fact, we are going to leave some equipment—it won't be worth the hassle of carting it all the way back. I agree with the insurer about the threat level going up significantly once we announce where we are, or even once it can be figured out. I am not too worried about it between now and then." Drake rose to his feet.

"Well, that makes sense," Sam said, "I will have to be careful about that. I can plant a lot of other theories as to where we are, because there are so many theories as to where the Lost Ark of the Covenant wound up. Some of them have a credible basis, and some of them are just mere conjecture."

"It sounds like you have got your work cut out for you, for at least the next day-and-a-half or so," Drake said.

"You don't need me for any additonal sound checks or any of that?" Sam questioned, as he also stood up to leave.

"No, we are good. And we figured out all of the cabling problems. I am glad that we brought a lot of extra because we are going miles through these tunnels shooting some great shots," Drake mentioned. "In fact, we couldn't do it without the fiber optic technology, and that stuff is so expensive! By the way, we will need to get a couple of takes of you before everything starts—you walking on the outside of the church and near the entrance to the upper parts of the tunnels, and so forth. We will then splice it in with all of the other tunnel shots. They have the light in front, so it will look like you are walking with them the whole time, and you can narrate any of that that is necessary," Drake concluded.

"Great," Sam said as he turned and walked out the door and down the steps. There was Kishor. He had some type of bandana looking thing on his head, perhaps to help against sunburn, Sam thought. Maybe he's not an android.

As Sam headed back, he thought about how last-minute decisions in television always come off looking so professional to the viewers at home. He wondered if any of the viewers realized how haphazardly some of this was strung together, how quickly somebody grabbed on a mic and did something, especially in a live feed like this. "Mind you, I bet it will look great," he thought. "I have got the best production staff in the world and they really want to make us all look good, even if they don't have their mind wrapped around just how big this thing is."

-36-

Inside a nondescript concrete building, not far from the Pizza shop on the outskirts of Aksum, Ruslan Petrov heard the fax machine ring. Tearing the faxed printout off of the old thermal roller, he saw the familiar format of a message directly from his superiors in the Russian Mafia. Perusing the message, it indicated that 2.5 million dollars in current US banknotes was ready for transfer to him via helicopter at an exact location to be agreed, but within a 200-mile radius of Aksum. It instructed him to be sure that he had obtained the loyalties of two local men who had somehow recently obtained the very American-sounding nicknames "Garfield" and "Popeye," but were known to the local townsfolk as Gareib and Popau. As he completed reading the letter he smiled.

"I believe this will do it," Ruslan said to himself, rather pleased with the praise for his hard work that his Russian superior had lavished upon him in the letter. "At least I hope this works," he corrected himself ruefully. "This is probably our last big chance."

"Maria!" He summoned his young woman servant. "When those men in the van call later on, be sure to have some hot coffee ready to offer them!"

-37-

Sᴀᴍ's Tʀᴀɪʟᴇʀ

S am finally got his laptop to work, and began some of his own
research and fact confirmation on the Lost Ark of the Covenant.
He couldn't believe how much Gordon had been able to rattle off
while barely looking at his notes. He had covered something like
three thousand years of history, seemingly almost off of the top of
his head. If he were honest with himself, Sam found himself somewhat jealous—maybe not jealous of Gordon's choice of apparel or
his personal hygiene habits (and certainly not his position or his
apparent multiple doctoral degrees) but he found himself jealous of
his innate ability to scan through thousands of pages of information and be able to briefly summarize their content in a meaningful
way. Now while their discussion would not be described as a brief
one, compared to the length of time, trouble, and material that was
covered, comparatively speaking, it was. But now with Drake telling
Sam that he had to get it considerably shorter, and that some of it
would not even be broadcast until after the whole project in Ethiopia had been completed, he really had to engage further with this
information and see if he could distill the points so that the infor-

mation could be given really succinctly in the pre-broadcast show.

He had once heard a great lawyer try a case while he was sitting in jury duty and the lawyer had told him in a conversation in the men's room later that no lawyer should be able to try a case until he could state his case in as few words as could be put in a fortune cookie. In other words, until you can summarize the matter succinctly, you don't even understand it; you don't know the facts.

He could still remember that case, one where a woman was giving birth with a particularly at-risk type of delivery, and although the doctor was paged thirteen times, he never came. Moreover, the nurses did not seek any other doctors in his place. So, he still remembered the lawyer relating the fortune cookie version—*'a sick mommy; doctor ignored thirteen pages; nurses did nothing and a baby dying.'* That would fit on anybody's fortune cookie. All it lacked was the magic, lucky lottery number they put on the back. He needed to learn to do the same with this information. He would not consider himself successful in this whole venture unless he did. That was something that he could personally take credit for as well. After all, he had arranged for the whole negotiation that allowed for the Ark to be presented like this, and it was his former work that assured them of his sincerity and built confidence within him. A lot of this had actually been handled by other people and negotiated by lawyers that they would never meet (and, for that matter, neither would they want to meet them). However, if he were to take all of this historical information and reduce it to something brief, that would be something that he could be proud of forever. That would be a piece of journalism indeed—and maybe he would be taken seriously by the rest of his journalistic society as well as with the archaeology society. Unfortunately, neither of these parties had taken him all that seriously, and the more popular he had become with the fans, the less they seemed to embrace him. "That is a worthy goal," he found himself saying under his breath. "I will do this!"

"All right," Sam said to himself, "I have got to take this entire pile of research Gordy has handed me and two-and-a-half legal pads full of writing and sketches and get this down to a brief explanation." Sam flopped down into the chair, unsure whether to use the explanation that led all the way to Ethiopia, or to format it in two parts where he talked about where the Ark could be, and then discovered it, finally finishing up in the shows that would follow as to how it got to where they had found it in Ethiopia. Drake had not given him any direction in this—only that he should be much more brief than he probably would be prone to. He was also quite strongly aware that he found the subject incredibly fascinating and could talk about it for hours, though he was certain that not everyone else could.

Sam was ready to practice summarizing all of Gordon's information. He questioned whether to make it very simple and elementary because of the lack of biblical knowledge that regrettably seemed to characterize the free world right then, or whether to gloss over quite a number of the facts so as to not get mired down in Old Testament history. Finally, he decided to do just a little of both. He picked up his Sony digital recorder, set it in front of him, and, imagining the camera and lights in front of him, began to speak in the broadcaster voice he sometimes used.

"Three thousand years ago," he began, "Moses was called to the top of a mountain known as Mount Sinai. The mountain was covered in smoke and rocked by thunder, lightning, and earthquakes. No, the mountain was shrouded with smoke," he corrected himself. He continued in his broadcast voice. "On top of that mountain there was a meeting between a mortal man and the immortal God, or so the Scriptures indicate. Moses descended the mountain, saw a great sin taking place, and threw down what he had in his hands, the Ten Commandments carved by the finger of God in stone tablets. They were shattered, but he later he obtained a second edition and, most importantly, he obtained some very precise rules about how to build a resting place for the Ten Commandments. It was to be a container 2½ cubits long and 1½ cubits wide and tall. A cubit," he said, looking intently before him at the imaginary camera as he practiced his speech, "a cubit is the distance from here to here," (he indicated the end of his middle finger pointing the joint of his elbow). "Now that varies from person to person, obviously, and this measurement was later standardized. We actually see the same measurement being used many years earlier with Noah's Ark, but at any rate you are looking at roughly eighteen inches, so a total of two to three feet high, two to three feet wide, and three to four feet or so long, but certainly no more than that. It was to be covered in gold and it was to have Cherubim or Angels facing each other with their wings outstretched on the top. Rings were made on the side of this box so that poles could be placed through them because the Ark was not to be touched except by the holiest of the priests known as the tribe of Levi or the Levites, Moses' tribe. Then the Ten Commandments were placed inside it.

"If we fast-forward through history, according to the Old Testament, you will find that the Ark will be used in the desert not only symbolically but also as a seat for the actual presence of God between the two angels. The glory of God would rest there while the ark was in a temporary temple known as the Tabernacle which was basically a tent with very thick curtain walls. It was symbolic of an area of the Temple that would later become known as the Holy of Holies. At this point, the person who was allowed to enter the Holy of Holies was the High Priest; everyone else was afraid to touch it or go in there—and they had reason to be afraid. The God whose presence was associated with this box, if you will, or the area right above the box to be more precise, traveled in front of the Hebrews as they walked through the desert. God did this, manifesting Himself as a pillar of cloud by day and a pillar of fire by night. He was certainly no abstract thought that was argued about in philosophy classes, for the Hebrew children grew up watching God interact visibly with them on a daily basis. He even fed them manna each morning.

"The Ark is that important. It is mentioned maybe two hundred times in the Old Testament. It was a symbol of the very presence of God. It was the link between a Holy God and the unholy children of a chosen people, the children of Israel," he corrected himself in the recording and wondered whether he should edit it or just let it go. After all this was only a rough draft in which he was just trying to get the information right. He cleared his throat and continued:

"The Ark was there when the walls of Jericho fell and it caused all kinds of victories to be won by the children of Israel. As long as the Ark was with them, they felt they could not be defeated. Indeed, King David marched to war with this powerful Ark out front. Anyone touching it or defiling it was immediately killed by what is thought to be an electrical charge"—he stumbled a little here—"or thought by many biblical scholars to be an electrical charge."

("Yeah, better make that 'biblical scholars'" he said to himself as he continued the trial recording of his introduction for the show.)

He resumed: "And King David brought the Ark to Jerusalem. This was the most important and sacred thing of the Hebrew religion and would also become important and sacred to the Muslim religion and to all branches of Christianity. Now some of the history on this can get sketchy but we know that David brought the Ark to Jerusalem somewhere around 1,000 BC. We know that David's son, King Solomon, designed a magnificent temple known as the First Temple which he built around 960 BC and that included the Holy of Holies where the Ark was ultimately housed.

"Later the Babylonian invasion took place and the Temple was looted and destroyed in 587 BC. The Babylonians kept exhaustive records. They would put our modern bureaucrats to shame! They listed each item they took from the Temple. Candlesticks, bowls, tables. . .but, it—the Ark—was never even mentioned in their records."

Sam stopped and drank another of his bottles of water. He had sworn not to drink any tap water in Ethiopia and so far he had kept him promise. He continued recording: "Right around the time of the Babylonian invasion, all records of the Ark anywhere ceased. The most important object in all of the history of man disappeared from the pages of Scripture without so much as a word or a whimper. The Babylonians went on to return most of the contents of the Temple and there was still never a trace in the very careful inventory taken that the Ark was ever found in the Temple. It was safe to assume, as scholars did for centuries, that the Ark had been moved prior to the invasion, so the question is, 'Who moved it and where did it go?' Some say Egypt, like the story portrayed in the Indiana Jones film. Others think Jordan. Some scholars think it is near the Dead Sea, where the famous scrolls were found.

"As you might be aware, a leading theory had always been that the Levites had dug underneath the temple through miles and miles of tunnels and somehow secreted away the Ark into a cavity or a cavern or out through some exterior entrance. Indeed, I have walked many of those tunnels and I have still not seen them all. Hezekiah's Tunnel, the wells, cisterns, and even the Pool of Siloam, I can just tell you that there are many, many passages, and as a result, many scholars had concluded that the Ark, if it still existed, was hidden underneath the Temple Mount. Indeed, that was one of the most popular theories. But remember other theories as well—theories that included the Levites destroying the Ark of the Covenant rather than let it fall into the wrong hands. Another theory proposed that the Babylonians kept it and still had it for hundreds of years or that it was defiled by them or other invading sources and melted down, and there was the Ethiopian connection. Numerous versions of the Ethiopian story exist and there are many points where it is believed that the Ark may have rested in its travels. The bottom line is that three thousand years go by, and the most important item known to humankind from a historical, cultural, sociological or religious perspective was gone—but tonight you will find that it never really went away. Now, the part when I am in the tunnels, and can reveal more:

"The Lost Ark of the Covenant was never really 'Lost'. It has been secreted away amidst the tale of intrigue and secrecy and, to some degree, it sounds like a soap opera. You see, the story goes that the Queen of Sheba, who was believed to come from the land of Ethiopia, came to visit the ancient King Solomon; you can read about that visit in the Bible. But the Ethiopians—specifically the Ethiopian Christian Church—believed that there was more to the visit than meets the eye. In this traditional account—it is not mentioned in the Bible—King Solomon and the Queen of Sheba became intimate and she conceived a son, a boy known as Prince Menelik. Prince Menelik returned to Sheba or Ethiopia with his mother but was able to come back as an adult and visit his father, King Solomon. The stories diverge wildly here, but in some manner he took the Ark back to Ethiopia, whether it was for safekeeping or whether he was tricked into taking the real one when he thought he had a replica is not clear; however, what is agreed upon by most of the scholars in this part of the world where I stand right now is that the Ark was taken secretly out of Jerusalem before the Babylonian invasion ever happened—which is why they never logged in anything about it in their inventory. It wasn't there; it had already been taken away. So if we know it's not there by 587BC, we look backward. In the mid 600s BC, the Temple of Elephantine in Egypt, which is about half way to Ethiopia, was built. Why build a Jewish Temple if nothing is available to put in it?

"It was probably moved by priests during the 600s BC well before the invasion. We know that King Manasseh erected an Asherah, an idol, right next to Ark of the Covenant. The vilest of pagan deities right there in the singularly most holy place, the Holy of Holies! Priests could not abide this and probably removed it. Egypt was relatively stable in the Elephantine era, so it is not impossible for this to have taken place, assuming the Jews could keep the Ark safely in that location.

"The Temple there was very similar to the one in Jerusalem, which seems consistent with having the Ark there. But, by 400 BC that temple was razed and the Jews there likely took the Ark with them and followed the Nile upstream to the area that lead to the remote islands of Lake Tana.

"As you can see in this stunning picture from an ancient church you will see the Ark being taken away and an inscription that basically means that you must let this Ark go—it must pass, you must yield to it—and that is probably the only indication that we have of this trip from the archaeological evidence and the documentary evidence of that area.

"But in this ancient writing of the Ethiopians," (Sam pointed to a picture, holding it up to explain it,) "the keeper of the Kebra Negast (The Glory of the Kings) the rest of the story, as Paul Harvey used to say, is told. Prince Menelik moved the Ark but it may not have been a direct journey. There is some evidence that it was taken to a very remote area. Most people don't think of East Africa as having lakes but there is a very large lake called Lake Tana and it's dotted with islands. Several of the islands are very remote and monasteries perch on top of some of them. One particular island, called Tana Qirqos, is edged by sheer cliffs plunging to the waters below, and there is a good measure of evidence that the Ark may have sat there for several hundred years protected by the vast areas of water around it. It's truly immense. . ." Immediately Sam realized that he was wanting to over explain—yet he really had to stay brief. He thought about the last producers' meeting that he had attended, where there had always seemed to be some type of friction between going into greater detail and trying to be scholarly versus trying to spoon-feed the masses who didn't care that much about history but liked to learn a little something every now and then if it was otherwise interesting.

He stopped, stretched, and leaned back adjusting his back and his neck. He took another long drag on a water bottle, then he continued his recording practice: "I have been to that island and I have stood on top of the cliff where the monks live and have allowed me to stand and stare at this area of stone blocks that indicate where the Ark of the Covenant sat for hundreds of years—some people say five hundred years and some say eight hundred years. But when I was there, it struck me how holy this object is. They were still venerating just the area where it once sat hundred years ago. There are these holes bored into the rock that show you how a kind of tabernacle was built on to house this as it sat upon this cliff at this holy site. So, when I was there, I knew I was on the recent trail of the Ark. So this story goes from being a thousand years old in history to my personal desire to locate this treasure, verify it, reveal it to the world. That is what is going to happen in the next hour of our program."

Sam toyed with the idea of telling people to go call someone else to view the next segment seeing as this was the biggest news and surely everyone should know about this. He didn't have too much more time to get this straight, he said to himself. Seeing as this would be live TV, he wouldn't want it to seem too staged or too canned, and he toyed with the idea of whether he wanted teleprompting cards down in the underground cave to cue him or if he just wanted to shoot from the hip, as it were, and tell the story in a more extemporaneous way. Even now he wasn't sure, but he appreciated the producers at least giving him the freedom to deal with this the way that he felt best, even though he was concerned with the way they stressed the need for brevity over and over again. He took a deep breath and began the explanation that it was there on top of that island that he learned where the Ark now rested and where it was still to be found at this very minute.

"Like you, I would have doubted this except for just one relic that was still there," he announced. "You see, there was this old metal chest piece for the linen ephod of the High Priest. Only the High Priest would wear that, and it was passed down from one High Priest to the next. There was only one. It somehow wound up on this island in the middle of a huge lake in the middle of a land far away from Israel. It was accessible, though, as it lies off a part of the Nile River known as the Blue Nile. I knew that the High Priest would never part with this, nor would he leave the Ark, so I knew if he was ever on that island, there had to be a reason *why* he was there. It was claimed that he was buried there between some rocks and initially I was to push for some specific genetic testing of his remains when I first visited that island. That was one of only what seemed like a million dead ends on this road to bring you the Ark of the Covenant on live TV. So, hot on the trail of the Ark, I was quick to discover that the Ark no longer rested on that island. The majority of the stories claim that when Christianity took hold in that area, one of the kings moved the Ark to his capital which was a town to the southeast, and so here I am broadcasting right now." Sam thought this would add something to the imagination of his viewers or add some excitement to this, so he went on to state: "I am right now underneath the streets of a different town many miles away, the very place that I have traced the Ark to, and in the next hour I am going to bring you live the unveiling of the greatest archaeological treasure that could ever be discovered. It is an artifact of absolute priceless value, irreplaceable, and of inconceivable importance to the three major religions of the world." As he recorded these words, there was a knock at the door that startled Sam. "Who is it?" he called.

Kishor stuck his head in. "One of your producers wants to know how you are coming on in your practice and he said to remind you to be very brief."

Sam looked at Kishor quizzically; "I didn't think you were going to get involved in my business. You wouldn't do any running around for me. As a matter of fact. . ." Sam was in mid-sentence, but Kishor simply shut the door and went back to stand at his post. Sam realized that Kishor did not mind passing on criticism or being involved in the business that was, as it were, against Sam but when Sam wanted Kishor to do something, he would simply look at him as if to say that he was no errand boy. This was definitely a one-sided relationship. Thankfully, this part of the trip would be over soon and he would never have to see Kishor again—and it would not be any too soon.

Sam was trying hard to think about all of the shots that had been taken of the small valley of the little town known as Aksum. He wanted to narrate those now but he had about gotten tired of the whole idea. He felt he had made a pretty good first run at this but he wanted to double check his dates and at least write all those down so he wasn't wrong on those. The last thing that he wanted to do when such an immense global audience was looking at him on live TV was to be laughed at by his fellow archeologists because he couldn't keep these details straight. But after all, he wondered, how many of them had ever done live TV? Certainly, they would not have done live TV underground in the middle of a tunnel somewhere in Ethiopia after negotiating for a year to reveal the Ark on live TV to the whole world.

Lying down, he recalled how all his archaeology buddies had laughed at him. They called him an "Indiana Jones wannabe." They all thought if the Ark really ever existed at all, it was long gone. And if did still exist now, by some chance, the last place the academic community felt it would be found was in some quaint church in a remote location in Ethiopia. But Sam had read *The Sign and the Seal* by Graham Heathcock, and other books that had convinced him, along with his firsthand research, that the Ark should be right there.

The existence of the Ark seemed to ring clearly in his ears that the Bible was accurate. Of course, if the Bible was accurate about the existence and the shape and the size and the appearance of the Ark, it would be important to pay attention to what the Bible also seemed to indicate about how risky it might be not to handle it the right way. Or to open it. Some of the Ark's power and mystique was perhaps because it seemed to signify God's presence, and the idea of opening the Ark made him think of the last scene in the "Indiana Jones Raiders of the Lost Ark" movie. Because so many folks called him Indie on account of his travels, he refused to wear a hat for fear that this would reinforce what people were saying about him looking like an Indiana Jones wannabe. It would be about like driving a DeLorean and not expecting jokes about "Back to the Future" and Michael J. Fox. He laughed to himself—"I never really wanted to carry a whip, though," he said to himself. He thought back to the way this little Ethiopian church had been discovered while it was nested in among other buildings in the community. It was a unique, small temple with a red drape curtain over the front door. There was an iron fence all the way around it with spikes that turned outward to make it practically impossible for anyone to climb. And then, too, there was the matter of the keeper of the Ark, something Sam had not yet mentioned. Once the whole unveiling was done, he wanted to focus on this point.

He sat up and started again, "A man chosen as young as seven years old to spend his entire life in virtual seclusion—a direct descendant from the priestly tribe of Levi, they say—that is, the same tribe that was the only tribe alive to approach the Ark and look upon it in the Old Testament. Imagine living from seven years of age to maybe seventy or eighty and never going outside the location of the temple. And outside the fence there are a few men with a few guns and, in general, the whole place is now pockmarked with bandits and revolutionaries and a few war lords and a government sometimes struggling to keep it all together."

He tilted his head again to the imaginary camera and in the tones of his best broadcasting voice, continued: "While many in the academic community and others may not believe that the Ark could be located in this simple shrine almost in the middle of nowhere in the eastern part of Africa, I have been convinced for years that this is the place. Ever since I stood on that island in Lake Tana, I was convinced that I was on the right trail. But there is other evidence, too, and, in all fairness to them, I am not the first scholar to have identified this. There have been books written and documentaries recorded about why Ethiopia is the likely resting spot of the Ark. One of the most convincing things for most people has always been the ceremonies and rituals that are only conducted here. There is a peculiar one, where a version of the Ark is covered up and was carried on a march through the streets. Virtually every single Ethiopian Christian Church has a copy of the Ark, a replica if you will, called a 'tabot.' They don't consider the church sacred if the church does not possess it. But they are all the replicas of something, and there is no replica unless someone had access to the original." Sam paused. "That alone made it interesting to me, but as I said, when I saw the High Priest's ancient breastplate among the other objects that were quite obviously consistent with those taken from Solomon's temple, I knew. Wherever these people said to go and look, that is where the

Ark would be found. Tonight has been a historic moment indeed," Sam concluded. He knew he needed a timeline and to shorten his initial presentation. The problem was, he could talk all night, but people would not just watch and listen all night.

Sam looked down at his well-worn stack of legal pads from his conversations with Gordon. He realized that more revisions would be needed to include—or sift—the historical data that he would like to use and yet still make it read like the story that he had fallen in love with and that he had now been pursuing for years. It had always been a theory that the Ark had stopped at the Elephantine Island for maybe a couple of hundred years where a Jewish temple had been built, and it had always made sense to him and to others that it could have been there because that is the whole point in building a temple in that day and age—to house the Ark—but personally he had never found the theory of Elephantine Island to be sufficiently convincing. It wasn't long before he had felt certain that it had been moved to the island in Lake Tana, the source of the Blue Nile. Looking back, Sam also realized that the source of the tradition of the Falashas (sometimes referred to as the "Lost Tribe of Israel" or the "Black Jews of Ethiopia") dated back to the earliest form of Judaism; and that in connection with the artifacts he had discovered on the Island of Tana and the traditions and the writings (and even the bones of the man believed to be the High Priest who was rumored to have come to that area of Prince Menelik or of his descendants), all of this added up and gave a convincing set of reasons for the Ark's new location. Sam was pleased that he had discovered not only Ark's true resting place but it also that he had pieced together the work of enough people (using his own intuition) to believe that this information was now quite reliable.

At the same time, Sam realized that finding that the Ark's true resting place in Ethiopia may not have been as much of an accomplishment as he might like to think. After all, the Ethiopian Christian Church had never stopped proclaiming that they had the Ark in their possession. They marched in the streets twice a year, dressed in white robes, and carrying candles and torches and generating a replica of the Ark—the item they called a tabot—covered in brightly colored cloths.

There was some confusion in Sam's mind as he realized that he could not go on the program without being sure whether the tabot referred to the Ark itself or the replicas of the Ten Commandments which rested inside these Ark replicas. According to tradition, often the tablets were made of wood rather than stone.

He began on this subject. "The Falashas or the Black Jews of Ethiopia, whom some people call a lost tribe, have many traditions. They venerate the Ark and march though the streets every six months or so with a replica of the Ark called a tabot. No photographs have ever been taken of it, or videos. A series of armed men stand around the outer perimeter fencing. The Temple guards that were sworn to protect this ancient box came at an early age and served for life and one particular guardian would be sworn in at seven and would never leave. Indeed, only the Keeper of the Ark, who is chosen by the keeper before him and the Keeper before him and so on, can actually go into the holy of holiest and see the Ark.

"But what would happen if a man with ulterior motives ever went in to see the Ark? Well according to some legends—and I have had some trouble verifying them—that may have happened at least once. There is a legend of Keepers of the Ark over vast years who were not pure in heart and, upon seeing the Ark, they were struck down dead. It is a great and terrible thing to go in and see the Ark for those who may have active and unconfessed sin in their lives. According to this legend, the Ark is a living fiery item and indeed it is the cause of concern for many in my crew for tonight's show—so stay tuned!"

Sam then sat down heavily into a chair. Here he was, building up the drama that people may be struck dead by waves of fire or light or electricity from a wooden box, and the same concerns could have applied to him. He was convinced this was the true Ark—at least, he was ninety-nine percent convinced—but what if it was not? What if only one person knew that it was not, and that person passed away so there was no one to ever verify that it wasn't the true Ark? If other people had died when they tried to inspect it, that was certainly a vote for its authenticity, but did that happen? Battling with it himself, Sam found himself going from one extreme of wondering if it could still possibly be a fake, all the way to the other extreme which could mean his death if it truly was the Ark. In talking with several well-known Christian and Jewish scholars over the years, he had posited this question. "If the Ark were ever found, could it be approached by someone other than a Levite?" The Jewish answers seemed to be affected by the way the scholars lacked belief that it had survived the destruction of the temple since the destruction was so complete, but eventually they concluded that they felt that only a Levite should approach it, for any other person would be killed. The fact that his last name was Cohen—Hebrew for the word for *priest*—was not entirely sufficient to put him at ease in this matter. Answers from Christian scholars, especially those who emphasized the importance of the letter to the Hebrews in the New Testament, seemed to be different. They favored the theory that the New Testament had fulfilled the Old Testament and therefore the actual purpose of the Ark of the Covenant had been completed. The purpose of the Ark of the Covenant in the Old Testament, they said, was to show God's presence with man in order to guide him, correct him, and so forth; whereas in the Christian tradition, the coming of Jesus Christ the man 2,000 years ago fulfilled that and therefore the Ark would have no supernatural power because the Spirit of God no longer rested on it in the same way. The law had been fulfilled in the work of Christ as a perfect man. Jesus Christ was the first true man who fulfilled all of the Ten Commandments perfectly all through his life and then scarified his life on behalf of other people. That was the whole redemptive purpose of the cross and the resurrection, they had explained. While Jesus was a true man, he was also truly God.

Sam recalled a sermon that he had heard when he had attended the well-known Bellevue Baptist Church in Memphis some years previously when he was visiting with Angela and he had heard the late Dr. Adrian Rogers. He said something to the effect that "Jesus, being infinite, had sacrificed Himself for us who are finite." "No," Sam thought, "I haven't got that quote right. I don't want to use it unless I learn it right." Sam looked around for his well-worn Bible to see if he had written the quote down correctly. It actually went like this: "We—being finite—will suffer for an infinite period of time for our sin, but Jesus—being infinite—suffered for a finite period of time for our sin and paid for it." Sam smiled, thinking that was the way Dr. Rogers would say it, and nobody could ever say it like him.

His thoughts turned back to that sprawling campus where he

had held the hand of the only girl that he had ever really loved while he listened to the fiery preaching of the statesman of Christianity. He wondered how much his own faith may come out in this message that they would be airing so soon and would be live for all the world to see. His faith had become an issue for some of the producers and several of the folks back in New York, so he tried to be a little less specific at times. He wondered how faithful that was to be vague about his faith, but he felt that he was doing more good for it by helping to reveal the authenticity of the Bible through archaeology, and thereby undermining the position of those who said that the Bible was unreliable. After all, the Dead Sea Scrolls included remnants of every single book of the Old Testament except for the book of Ruth which is barely a page long anyway. Other discoveries also supported the authenticity of the Bible. He understood this better than most because of his Jewish background. But the archaeology that he had commissioned and now popularized almost single-handedly—he felt was doing an important work. If his influence caused people to realize that of all of the world's religions—Hinduism, Buddhism, Taoism, Confucianism, Voodoo or others—that only the three great western religions have a source of truth, that would have been a worthy accomplishment. In fact, he had come to believe that Evangelical Christianity, with its roots in Judaism, was the only true religion because its followers worship the only true God who has revealed Himself in the Old and New Testaments.

The heaviness of this thought hit Sam anew. He was going to see with his own eyes something God had used in revealing Himself; and what if some of those old Jewish scholars were right? What if it still had the same deadly outcome when an unworthy person encountered it? What if there was a glow about it that had to be covered up with all of those cloths? What if, what if he or his crew were to be struck dead? While he had given this possibility little thought, he could not honestly say that it had completely left his mind. "Well, I guess me frying will make for good television," he wryly replied to himself. It wasn't funny, and it did not quell the butterflies that filled his stomach at that thought. He wasn't afraid to die. But he sure felt. . .unworthy.

-38-

Brisbane sat down with the glossy photographs. For two days, two of the sniper teams who had been doing reconnaissance exercises from the hills that surrounded this little valley of Aksum had taken hourly photographs with the Sony camera and its powerful zoom lens. It was clear that the small cluster of soldiers outside the temple somehow overlapped their shifts so as to not all be changing shifts at one time, or never to leave a particular post unguarded. They seemed somewhat casual about their duties, even to the point where they blended in, and Brisbane was surprised that the original researchers he had commissioned had not accurately counted the number of soldiers around the temple at any given time. It was clear that there were more soldiers and more armed security personnel here than his initial research and reports had indicated. He didn't feel that would be a problem, but he did consider his credibility might be damaged by this information.

He called in Raphael and pushed the pictures across to him. "You see all these fellows?" Brisbane indicated, pointing to the photos.

38

"There is more of them there, Boss, than what we discussed," he said.

"Exactly," Brisbane said, "so what can you do about it?"

"Well, it does look like they may be putting on additional security for the event. You know some anti-personnel mines like the old claymores would be very effective all along the sides of the complex."

"That is the reason that I brought you in here," Brisbane said, "but I doubt that these fellows are just going to walk up and watch you mount Claymore mines on trees and rocks. Go out in the van and talk to the AV guys. They have got boxes and camera equipment, satellite hook-ups, and all kinds of stuff out there. Maybe you can just make it look just like the TV equipment. It's possible that you could put some of those mines facing the complex inside some official-looking equipment that the Ethiopians are not going to bother about; after all they could still be outside the fence and just blow through the fence, right? What is the effective range of these things?" Brisbane asked.

Raphael studied the photos, his dreadlocks hanging heavily around his face: "Looking at this photograph, if we cross these three corners by having six mines angled toward one another, you know, one on each corner facing the other, we will have a killing zone that will take all of those three corners out. Of course, we just don't want it to reach over to the place where we are coming in and out, so I would probably angle them downward a bit," he observed.

"Like a speaker array at a concert, almost?" Brisbane interjected, more than pleased with the idea.

"Yes, but the important thing is that we somehow sell the guards on not moving the containers that they are in. I mean, if I had more time, maybe I could get them to be placed in, like, artificial rocks or something."

Brisbane said, "Good idea—but there's no time for that. Rather, go out there anyway and see what you can put together. If you can't get enough mines, at least try one pair on a corner or two, like you said. Our snipers will take out many of these folks as necessary. There is just quite a few of them, and I don't want it to become an issue for our men. I definitely don't need any cold feet," Brisbane said flatly.

"Okay, let me go out to the van. I will take care of it, Boss," he said.

"I know you will," Brisbane said as Raphael left.

Alone in his makeshift office once more, Brisbane quickly got back on the Internet and searched the term "love poetry." There were quite a few hits. He selected the fourth screen, and hit the last one down that list, copied and pasted it into an email, and typed "Dear Marjorie," across the top. The text underneath, recorded in rather ugly capital letters, read:

ALL I EVER WANTED WAS TO BE PART OF YOUR HEART,
AND FOR US TO BE TOGETHER, TO NEVER BE APART.
NO ONE ELSE IN THE WORLD CAN EVEN COMPARE,
YOU'RE PERFECT AND SO IS THIS LOVE THAT WE SHARE.
WE HAVE SO MUCH MORE THAN I EVER THOUGHT WE WOULD,
I LOVE YOU MORE THAN I EVER THOUGHT I COULD.
I PROMISE TO GIVE YOU ALL I HAVE TO GIVE,
I'LL DO ANYTHING FOR YOU AS LONG AS I LIVE.
IN YOUR EYES I SEE OUR PRESENT, OUR FUTURE AND PAST,
BY THE WAY YOU LOOK AT ME I KNOW WE WILL LAST.
I HOPE THAT ONE DAY YOU'LL COME TO REALIZE,
HOW PERFECT YOU ARE WHEN SEEN THROUGH MY EYES.

He ended with his assumed name at the bottom, and sent it through the same untraceable, secure network to Marjorie's private email address.

"One more to keep her going a little longer," he said to himself, a small smile quivering around the corners of his thin lips.

-39-

Ruslan was sitting in the back of his office when he finally got the call. "This is Moscow," the speakerphone crackled in Russian. "We have authorized the payment, but we want more assurances than just that your two little fellows have delivered. How do we know for sure that they will actually have the information to intercept the Ark?"

Ruslan responded, his voice slightly hesitant, "To a degree, we have to trust them."

"I trust no one. Not even you, Comrade." The unseen voice cleared his throat: "What if this Brisbane fellow, what if he just betrays the locals, or does not tell them where he is taking it?"

"He needs the locals to get it out of the country, I believe," Ruslan countered. Ruslan did not want to be the one Russian mobster that had taken money from an ever-dwindling supply, and spent it on a hunch with nothing to show for it. Without doubt, he would be killed in a dreadful manner. Recently, they had killed slowly with radioactivity.

However, if the plan worked, it would be exactly what was needed. Already the contacts that he had made throughout the Middle East had pushed the price that he could anticipate well up into the hundreds of millions of dollars. If this worked, he would be set for life many times over, and the Russian mob would finally have the worldwide respect that they had craved ever since the fall of the motherland. And, if the Jewish contacts wanted to prevent the Muslims and Christians from getting it, they could continue to push the price to a billion dollars or more by the time the operation was complete.

"So, as you understand it, the Ark is to be moved within underground tunnels to a new secret underground location, but Brisbane will grab it, slip it out, and then the tunnels will be blasted for security after it has passed through, right?" the phone crackled.

"Yes, Comrade, that is exactly so," Ruslan answered. "According to our intelligence, they will do so by a cargo helicopter with plenty of supplemental fuel tanks. They are planning on heading all the way to Switzerland, I am told, though there will be an aircraft change in either Libya or Morocco. So we need the resources allotted to take care of it, and to take the Ark back by force by armed helicopter gunship escort. They will only have small arms with them."

"And once we escort their helicopter with our gunship over through Eastern Europe back into Russian air space, our men could not be followed by anyone else. . . ." the Russian voice on the other side began to laugh and then to cough, an obvious smoker's hack. "Pardon," he said while clearing his throat. "This is where having bribed or threatened all of the key members of what's left of the country's defense department will really pay off, Ruslan. If the pesky Israelis, or the Americans, or even some African air force remnant pursues us into our airspace, they will find out that a few of the MiG fighter jets we control are still flying."

"So, we do have the helicopter gunship acquired then?" Ruslan asked anxiously.

"Yes, an Mi-24 'Crocodile' with the newest version of the GSh-23 twin-barreled automatic cannon on it. Much better than the models we lost in Afghanistan, and that we sold to Somalia and Ethiopia. We will also have air-to-air-capable missiles on the pods, though I do not expect our staff will need to use them" his Comrade boasted. "And, plenty of fuel."

39

"What about detection locally? That's one big bird!" Ruslan commented.

"We have removable markings on it, so we can intercept marked with either Ethiopian or Somali Air Forces' insignias, if necessary," the Muscovite noted.

"Okay, excellent. They both still fly a few Crocodiles here," Ruslan replied.

"Hell, Mother Russia sold these things to anyone who looked like a country and had a checkbook. They are tough to get parts for, which helps our black market. But, no need for that petty crime when this comes through, huh?"

"No, Comrade, no need then!" Ruslan said excitedly.

"This box is the key, Ruslan! Give them what they ask. A courier will bring you the cash, and the secure cell phones to give the locals. You are going be a very rich man, and a hero to your whole village near Kiev! So," he paused, "so don't screw this up, Comrade." The line went dead.

-40-

In the pre-dawn darkness, Drake assembled the crew in the glare of a utility light stand. He and his assistants worked through each crewmember's equipment of on the four-man "shoot crew." They checked batteries, backups, connections, and almost a quarter-mile of ultra-lightweight broadcasting cables that had been assembled just for long-reaching, underground shots like this.

The two cameramen, Mike and Marcus, were both big fellows with brown hair and they resembled each other except that Marcus sported a graying goatee. They would do the shooting with powerful light-equipped cameras. Jeremy, a tall athletic man with bushy blond hair sticking out around his earphones, was the audio technician who would run the sound boom and deal with the echo chambers they expected. It was going to be challenging to get sound crisp enough to hear without muffling it in the precautions to avoid undue echoing. His young assistant, Brad, a wiry little guy with spiky black hair, would spool out line, carry a pack with backup equipment, and generally help out.

"Gentlemen, you have been selected especially for this shoot," Drake began his speech in an important tone. "We have flown you—quite literally—halfway around the world under absolute secrecy." He began to pace back and forth, somewhat like a general reviewing his troops: "We've exposed you to untold germs and diseases, put you on the edge of a continent that can be lawless at times, where there are warlords and zealots who probably would kill you without a thought, and now you are about to descend underground into an area no white man has ever even tried to go—and lived to tell about it—to find an object some say does not exist, and others say will kill you."

"Is this a pep rally?" Marcus whispered.

Mike laughed quietly.

"This is the most priceless artifact in all of human history," Drake continued, "worth more than the next ten most valuable items still thought to exist. We have taken great care to ensure your security and the secrecy of this endeavor. However, as you are aware, we can provide no guarantees. So, if you do not possess the intestinal fortitude to carry out your mission, please tell us now. There are stories about the Lost Ark of the Covenant that scare people, even now. I am not here to tell you that there is nothing to be scared of, as there well may be. However, after more than a year of preparation, money, time and massive expenditure, if we can pull this off, you will be participating in the most-watched, historic, television event that mankind has ever known!"

"He's in rare form today," Mike whispered to Marcus.

Drake continued, "I have taken the liberty of providing your beneficiaries with additional life insurance coverage at the Archaeology Channel's expense, because, if something goes wrong down there, your remains will not be recovered. Your loved ones will be well taken care of. Do you understand the risk you are both taking?" Drake asked.

"Yes sir," they all answered, almost in unison. Two men came to them with clipboards and pens.

"Good," Drake concluded, "then please do sign these releases and these waivers. And verify your next of kin on these forms."

The crew looked at one another.

"Man, what did we get ourselves into?" Marcus exclaimed softly.

"Probably an early grave," Mike sighed.

He had no idea how prophetically he had just spoken.

-41-

"Come in here, Angela!" Sherry, the heavyset African-American charge nurse said. "Paula is going to cover your shift while your super boyfriend goes digging for the Ark on TV!" She smiled and high-fived another nurse, Sandy, who was sitting with her. The television was tuned to the Archaeology Channel, and a commentator was giving a countdown to the discovery, while showing clips of Sam Cohen and his other finds. They switched between the "A-Channel," as it had become known, and CNN.

Angela stuck her head in breathlessly, pushing back her honey-blonde hair and inquiring, "Is he on yet?"

"Not yet on live TV, honey-child, but I sure do like watching him. Umm, he is one fine looking white boy," Sherry smirked. "You two ever gonna get hitched?"

"Okay, I will be right back!" Angela said, ducking out before she could be stopped, and leaving the question floating in midair unanswered.

"What is with that girl?" Sherry asked aloud. "If my man would just get off the dern couch, I would be dancin' down Beale Street! Her man is on TV and a big star, and she is too busy to even watch all of it!"

"She cares about these kids, though," Sandy said.

A somewhat frail looking older nurse, Ms. Pat, agreed, "She is a class act. More like the nurses back in my day."

"Ms. Pat, no offense and all, but the nurses back in your day took notes on stone tablets with a chisel!" Sherry blurted out and everyone, including Ms. Pat, had a good laugh.

Sam's longtime girlfriend went about her duties. A few reporters had gotten wind of her relationship with Sam, but they had been kept at bay outside the sprawling St. Jude complex. The security division had been alerted.

The folks that had known her pretty well were aware of her relationship with Sam, and it was clear that almost every television station was going to be carrying this event live. As Angela entered the room and perched on the arm of a couch, a CNN correspondent on the break room television had said that this would be ". . .cable news' finest hour—not a plane crash or a terrorist attack, but a time when the whole world could view a positive, thought-provoking historic moment at the same time, one that may truly unite us all."

Others still insisted on comparing the enormity of the audience with 9/11 during the plane attacks on New York City, the moon landing, or the Kennedy assassination. But that was not why Angela ran out of the room.

As they flipped channels, Fox News cut to their morning crew that was covering this event on special assignment. The well-dressed, blonde news anchor noted how "cute" Sam was, and even commented that she didn't mind having him look for anything that he would like to look for with her. Whistles and cat-calls from her co-hosts followed, along with a ripple of laughter, and Angela's face reddened as she blushed.

She wanted to disappear. She felt a bit dizzy as she headed toward the vacant ladies room. On so many levels, she had not been ready for this. Resentment surged. Staring at the bathroom mirror, she said out loud, speaking solemnly as if the blonde anchor was on the other side of the mirror, "Okay. First of all, he is a scientist, you bimbo; second of all, he is not interested in girls like you who are intellectual, I don't know. . .door knobs!" She laughed at herself, unable to come up with a suitably sassy insult. "Door knobs?" She washed her face, and paused again. "Anyway, he is cute, isn't he?" she said in a somewhat catty way. "And we will be together, forever, one day. Or at least I pray we will."

She headed back to the break room. As she passed by the folks in the hall, she was getting congratulatory greetings from those who knew. She had to watch. But, what would she really be watching Sam do? What if Sam was wrong on some of this? What if the host country back-pedaled and didn't let the Ark be seen after all? The secret negotiations had lasted about a year, with a lot of crawfishing. Sam had said that it was set up with all of the folks at the temple, and all the leaders of the country, but she knew things could still go wrong. There had also been talk about whether some thought they would even be safe from the Ark itself. She had convinced herself that the Ark was an important artifact and nothing more. After all, there had been curses of the mummy that made great movies and great stories, but many people had opened up hundreds of sarcophagus sites in Egypt and had not been struck dead. Of course, the God of the Ark was real, in her belief. But still, a modern-day curse? However, it made great television. They cut to yet another clip of the melting faces in "Indiana Jones and the Raiders of the Lost Ark."

With Angela in mind, her friends sensitively switched back to the A-Channel, where Sam's pre-recorded program was now on air, giving information on the search for the mysterious Lost Ark of the Covenant and its history.

Angela checked herself from biting her nails. It was hard to describe the tension in the air—it was more than palpable.

Sherry noticed and patted her leg. "Don't worry there, honey, your Sam is going be just fine. I know he'll come here to see me real soon, and you can visit with him then," she added for comic relief. "I'm his favorite anyway."

Angela half-laughed, and then settled in for the next part of the broadcast.

-42-

THE CHURCH AT AKSUM

Behind the temple—the Church of Our Lady Mary of Zion—as planned, the local guide met up with Sam and the designated camera crew. He directed them to stand against a wall. One of the cameramen, Marcus, nervously asked under his breath, "Sam, what is this?"

"Apparently, they think you need a cleansing ritual," Sam whispered back and winked at him. A haunting chant was said over them by a group of church leaders dressed in spectacularly colored tunics.

Sam looked around awkwardly.

"Are they all coming in?" Brad whispered to Sam.

"Ha. No way. They would never try to enter," Sam chided.

"Fan-freaking-tastic," Brad humphed.

Once that seemed to be completed, the guide signaled that they should go into the temple. "I am Berhanu," he introduced himself in his best English. "With this matter complete, we now go into the temple. We then go underground from there."

Brad, the audio assistant, nervously ran his fingers through his gleaming hair and whispered, "I thought we weren't supposed to go into the temple itself, but only into a tunnel or whatever."

"It's okay; my research indicated that the entrance to the tunnel labyrinth is somewhere just under the temple. We've got to go in," Sam indicated. Brad did not seem reassured.

Kishor stood nearby, always keeping a close eye upon his charge.

Again Berhanu spoke: "Everyone welcome here who keeps his heart right with Almighty; we go inside, then we go downstairs. Come, and I will show."

"You think I will be okay down here?" Sam whispered to Kishor sarcastically. Kishor made no answer, as usual, and simply stood by as Sam, the two cameramen, the audio technician, and assistant entered the temple through an ancient, ornate door.

Immediately, they encountered what felt like a wall of incense fragrance. Marcus sneezed loudly and involuntarily. "Sorry," he said weakly.

Inside, the chamber in the temple was not as large as they had imagined it would be. But, what it lacked in size, it made up for in artistic beauty. Each of the four walls had various scenes from the Pentateuch, also known as the first five books of the Old Testament. "Look guys," Sam pointed at each scene, "Creation, look—Garden, and the fall of Eden, on that wall."

"Over here, there's the violent flood with the fountains of the earth bursting forth, and Noah's ark with many perishing outside the ark," Sam explained reverently.

"There, that is Abraham ready to sacrifice Isaac—see, he has his hand with a raised knife," Sam stopped as his gaze fell on what the others were already staring at.

"What in the world?" Mike, the other cameramen asked, as Jeremy whistled slightly.

An immense painting showed the Ark of the Covenant carried by priests depicted standing on a high hill. From the Ark, golden beams of light powerfully emanated from it in all directions, grotesquely ending the lives of the enemies of God's people.

"They're burning alive, look," Brad said, "like burning from the inside out! They have this 'art' in a church? Isn't that at least a PG-13 for violence?" He quietly whispered this to Sam.

"Gross," Marcus, the cameraman said under his breath.

"Shhh!" Sam hushed them.

The guide pointed to a large column, one of two in the rear of the temple sanctuary. Sam and the crew stared at it blankly. Archaic writing of some type circled the pillar, carved deeply in the aged stone.

Coming closer, Sam translated the words on the old column:

"I CALL HEAVEN AND EARTH AS WITNESSES TODAY AGAINST YOU, THAT I HAVE SET BEFORE YOU LIFE AND DEATH, BLESSING AND CURSING; THEREFORE CHOOSE LIFE, THAT BOTH YOU AND YOUR DESCENDANTS MAY LIVE; THAT YOU MAY LOVE THE LORD YOUR GOD, THAT YOU MAY OBEY HIS VOICE, AND THAT YOU MAY CLING TO HIM, FOR HE IS YOUR LIFE AND THE LENGTH OF YOUR DAYS; AND THAT YOU MAY DWELL IN THE LAND WHICH THE LORD SWORE TO YOUR FATHERS, TO ABRAHAM, ISAAC, AND JACOB, TO GIVE THEM."

"That's Deuteronomy the thirtieth chapter," Sam said, pleased that he had identified the passage straightaway.

"Choose life, huh? Sounds like some statement on abortion," Jeremy, the audio technician, quietly mentioned to Sam.

"I am still kind of wondering about the death and cursing part," Brad, added in a subdued voice, lingering for long moment. "He curses people? Umm. . . ."

"It's like the Ark. It is a blessing or curse to you, life or death to you, depending on your heart," Sam said as he approached the engraved column.

"Was that supposed to help me feel better? Because, you know, it didn't," Brad quipped, half smiling, looking around nervously.

Berhanu stepped forward and ran his hands up and down a seam in the column to the left of the group. When his hand felt the inset, he pulled. The column creaked open like a door. "Look! It's the entrance," Sam said. He pointed downward into the dark aperture. The crew each looked at Sam and then at one another.

"Sure about this?" someone asked, but Sam had already begun his descent down the ancient spiral staircase.

"You coming?" Sam's voice echoed up from the darkness below.

Once down in the musty cave-like tunnels, Berhanu led the way, with Marcus helping direct the beam of the light from over his shoulder. Sam checked the time. There was only a minute or two to go to the commencement of the schedule to begin the broadcast. "Let's start the transmission feed now. I want some anticipation to build," Sam said, smiling.

Facing the first camera, Sam began broadcasting underground. As he walked, he gave a brief summary of the Ark's recent history, points he had been rehearsing to himself ever since his final meeting with Gordon. He had already touched on this in the prerecorded program that had just aired. Once he had completed the additional background information on the Ark, he stopped, smiled broadly, looked into the camera and said, "Hello. This Sam Cohen, deep underground in...well," he smiled, "I cannot tell you where we are just yet. But I can say that I'm delighted that you have joined us to view this most fantastic discovery, ever! This entire operation is only possible with absolute secrecy as to our present location. Sometime later, well after this broadcast, the location we are in now will be made known. But, do not come here looking for it yourself. For one reason, you could be killed!" Sam smiled again. "Secondly, after we have completed this live video feed of the discovery of the biblical Ark of the Covenant, it will be moved to new secure location that none of us has been allowed to know. In the meantime, I invite you to walk with me as we make our way further into the depths of the earth, and as we prepare to reveal to you what has lain hidden from most people's sight for over two thousand years."

Turning away from the camera, Sam instructed Berhanu to proceed. As they moved forward, they began to navigate a series of tunnels, most of which were on a gradual decline. The cables made a steady swishing sound as they played out. After several seconds, they had to negotiate a rocky staircase, and at the bottom, two other stairways intersected it, as well as two other passages—each one looking almost exactly alike. "Intruders over the years have no doubt perished, lost down here," Sam said as he continued his narration. "These passages all look alike—running for perhaps miles in all. A person down here without knowledge of this labyrinth would be doomed, and would face a long, lingering death in this cold darkness." He brushed a cobweb from his ear; they draped the wall at intervals along the way, and their silky stickiness gave the setting an even more eerie feeling to it.

After another several moments, they came into a round room with seven tunnels branching out from it, rather like a child's drawing of the sunshine and its rays. One of the lights mounted on the cameras glinted on some words on a wall.

Sam looked at it in the light. "This is in Aramaic!" he exclaimed. "That is an ancient version of Aramaic. We have to be close."

"What does it mean?" Jeremy whispered, prompting the narrator.

"Uh, it's just. . .it's just an ancient curse," Sam said, trying to look calm, but feeling as if he were about to explode inside. "Looks like they are on all these walls," Sam said nonchalantly as he had the light point and the camera pan to show the tunnel walls, "All curses, warning against, well, pretty much what we are doing," Sam tried a smile for the camera.

"So, which tunnel is the right one, Doc?" Jeremy wondered under his breath.

Knowing he was not supposed to speak during a live broadcast, but unable to remain silent, the audio assistant, Brad, asked in a pleading but quiet voice, "Aren't there, like, traps and things that shoot poisonous darts at us?"

"You watch too many movies, Brad," Sam chided. Turning to the camera, he explained, "In the movies, you will see traps, poison dart shooting caves, pressure-sensitive idol holders, and ancient pivoting walls. From an engineering perspective, those cannot still operate, if they even ever existed. These tunnels pre-date the time of Christ by over half a century!"

"Truthfully, just having these various tunnels go on in so many directions is quite the trap enough," Sam explained to the camera. "Any ancient intruders carrying reed torches would not have enough light to even make it back out in all likelihood."

They continued on deeper in to the tunnels. Sam narrated as he moved, explaining, "There is no evidence of bat 'guano' which is bat excrement, and that tells me that there are no other ways in, or out, of these tunnels. All possible entrances are well-sealed, or have only tiny venting or bats would find a way down here."

Sam stopped for a moment and faced the camera: "Let me say that if you kids out there have dreamed of an adventure, you should really consider a career in the science field. Kids, this has been a dream of mine since my Abba—that means 'Papa'—read me the stories about the Ark of the Covenant, and here I am. And you are here with me as you view this. Maybe one day, I will be watching you on television as you make a great discovery!" His voice, without being patronizing, had a strong note of sincerity in it as he cautioned, "But, you must stay in school, stay off drugs, and make wise choices if you are to live your dreams."

The impromptu notice over, they descended a succession of three narrow staircases that wound down into the blackness, and which made it very challenging to spool cables out and to shoot good video. At the bottom of the third one, the tunnel seemed to widen somewhat. The walls looked smoother, and there was no writing. "This is a deeper layer of bedrock. It's so much cooler down this deep—and interestingly, the air is quite clean smelling. This is because of a system of rudimentary ventilation tunnels that have been constructed to supply air for the keepers. We must surely be getting closer," Sam said to the camera.

As they came to yet another intersection, the local guide stopped, obviously fearful.

"Are you not coming?" Sam asked him.

Berhanu, anxiety etched over his light features, his face gleaming with perspiration in the reflected light from the camera apparatus, fearfully pointed to words upon a wall. Sam had the crew shine their powerful lights on it, and as the camera etched it in clear relief, the sounds of Berhanu's feet carrying him back in the direction from which they had come receded into the distance.

"Ugh, Sam? Where'd he go?" Brad asked fearfully.

"It's written in Hebrew, this text is!" Sam said, ignoring the question as he brushed off the wall with a special archaeological hand broom. Getting closer, he carefully blew the dust off of the ancient Hebrew lettering, translating it to English out loud as he read:

"Then God's Temple in Heaven was opened, and within His Temple was seen the Ark of His Covenant. And there came flashes of lightning, rumblings, peals of thunder, an earthquake and a great hailstorm."

Turning to the camera, Sam exclaimed, "That's the Book of the Revelation, the eleventh chapter, umm, I think, the nineteenth verse! But that was written years later in Greek, not in Hebrew. When would they have had this revealed to them? Who would have told them?" Sam wondered out loud. The crew's lights filled the cavern. "Well, that might be my answer," he continued, as he pointed to an immense and imposing image of an angel, towering maybe twelve feet tall, carved into the wall opposite the inscription of the verse.

"That's not the angels I picture," Jeremy whispered to no one in particular.

"Guys! Guys!" Brad, the audio assistant, exclaimed, his voice quavering, "Look!" The cameraman followed his direction and as he did so, the skeletons came into focus.

They lay in shelves, like beds carved into the rock, along three tunnels intersecting the area. "These must be the remains of the keepers of the Ark," Sam said. "There are more of them, from hundreds of years."

Sam looked at the camera and continued: "The keepers took an oath. They are sworn in as a young man, and they never leave the temple for the rest of their life, never."

"These men *sure* never left," he commented ruefully as the camera panned over the skeletons. Some of the bones glinted white, but most were parchment colored, almost like stone. "The new keeper's first duty was probably to bring the old keeper's remains here. He knew, all his life, that his fate would be the same as these men of God. Only a Keeper has been past the point where we now stand," Sam narrated as they moved their feet cautiously on the rock floor.

Finally, they entered another room with a tall ceiling carved into the rock, and there was a dark-colored veil about six inches thick. As the lights hit it, the deep purple color became visible. It was heavy to move, and dust flew in the harsh glare of the camera lights as they touched it. Then another veil was moved, and the Keeper of the Ark seemed to appear from nowhere.

"Ahhh!" the members of the startled crew exclaimed, and cameras jostled. Brad hid.

Standing before them was an elderly black man, with a rather kind face. He wore an ancient tunic—perhaps it had once been white, but now it appeared a light grayish-tan color—with long tassels all over it, looking almost like liquid as they moved with him.

As Sam approached, he could see that the Keeper's eyes were dull with cataracts. His grizzled beard was long, seeming to reach past his navel. His features were oddly Jewish in character, but that might just make sense, Sam thought. The Keeper appeared to be feeling his way as he moved, almost floating in the darkness. His hands seemed to read the texture of the rock wall as he walked.

Sam realized he had been silent for too long, and needed to narrate, but almost hated to. In a hushed voice, he began, "We are in the underground part of the temple. The Keeper is with me now. This area has never been seen by the eyes of Westerners, let alone by people on a television broadcast."

Unexpectedly, the Keeper moved his weight against the far wall, evidently made of smooth marble. There was a heavy rumble. Brad, fear filling his eyes, seemed ready to run. His heart in his mouth, he asked, "Is it a 'quake or what?" The cameramen tried to get into a position for the best shot of this happening.

The entire wall slowly pivoted, with a billow of dust filling the area. It opened with an ominous grinding sound, like an old locomotive coming back to life. The pungent odor of incense almost overwhelmed their senses. Marcus had to hold his nose to prevent himself from sneezing once more. Mike whispered to Marcus, "I thought Doc said old walls like this don't pivot right?"

"Yeah—wonder what else this guy is wrong about?" Marcus replied snidely.

Undertaking a live TV feed underground certainly had its own very specific challenges. With more jostling to get into position, the camera crew found that light from the chamber hurt their eyes and kept interfering with the cameras' exposure settings. "What's. . .What's happening?" Brad asked.

-43-

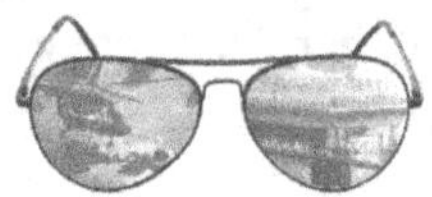

There it sat. History. . .Truth. . .There stood the symbol of the appearance of God—the Ark of the Covenant.

Next to it, several golden candelabras, somewhat like menorahs, lined the room and the light danced on the golden surface of Solomon's ancient treasure. A golden set of bowls sat on a small stand in the far corner from which the smoke of burning incense steadily rose.

The Keeper suddenly began to whisper to himself. Sam could not make out all the words, but this much was clear to him as he listened: he was talking about the glory and power of God in a mixture of Hebrew and Amharic. Sam did not want to interrupt, even though he felt again he should have been narrating this.

The camera lights gleamed back into Sam's face, reflected from the pure gold overlay. His eyes lit up as he slowly approached the box sitting upon an ancient stone altar. He turned to the camera and began to narrate in a hushed reverential tone, "For more than a thousand years, only the eyes of the Keepers have seen this sight. Ancient Hebrew Scripture records this ornate golden box—that's what the word 'Ark' means, 'box'—leveling mountains, causing whole armies to flee, and killing any of those who dare to touch it, even by accident. We are not going to touch it, but the Keeper will. This Keeper has been the sole guardian of the ark for seventy-seven years. He is almost blind, as he has severe cataracts. All the Keepers have sight difficulties, perhaps from being underground so much, and some people assume from the rays the Ark is believed to emanate. The Ark has been the cause of death of many. Some will not believe that this is the real Ark of the Bible. But, I am assured that he can demonstrate—and will now prove—that it is indeed the real lost Ark of the Covenant."

The Keeper approached the Ark with obvious reverence and respect, but with no noticeable fear.

Sam positioned himself with the Priest behind his right shoulder and spoke directly to the camera, "Every night for seventy-seven years, this Keeper, the High Priest as they sometimes call him, has been here, keeping the incense lit before the Lord. Many believed that the Keeper only worshipped before the Ark once a year, as in ancient times, but I have discovered that is not the case. The Keepers view themselves almost as the husbands and the Ark as their wife. They worship each night. He is now going to prove to all of us that this is the true Lost Ark of the Covenant, that King David himself—the one that killed Goliath—had before him in every major battle. . . ."

As he spoke, suddenly a popping sound rang out and echoed from somewhere above them.

"What was that?" Sam asked.

"Sounds electrical, maybe? It could be our high pressure bulbs popping?" Brad wondered out loud.

"Those are not bulbs bursting; that's gunfire," Kishor announced as he looked back over his shoulder.

"Hey, keep the camera on me and the Ark!" Sam chided.

The staccato sounds repeated themselves, this time sounding much closer. There was no doubt this time that these were gunshots, much closer now, ringing out, echoing dramatically in the confined space. "Keep rolling, man, just keep rolling," Sam instructed the cameramen, his tone serious. There was movement somewhere down the tunnel. Quick steps could be heard.

"Get down!" Kishor commanded as he seized Sam by the arm and began to run down the adjacent tunnel away from the approaching sound. "Down! Down!" he repeated. Brad, the young audio assistant, dropped his pack and ran closely behind Kishor.

"What about the rest of the crew?" Sam shouted to Kishor, as he looked back over his shoulder. Brad, obviously terrified, was the only one behind him, and was gaining fast. At his side, Kishor shoved Sam forward abruptly, only saying tersely, "Shut up and run."

Kishor herded Sam even further down into the dark tunnel. The small tactical flashlight he had pulled from his cargo vest illuminated the way ahead of them, but he quickly switched it off. Rounding a corner, with Sam and Brad panting heavily, the three men stood for several moments without speech.

-44-

"What's happening?" Angela screamed, her knees pulled up in front of her face on the couch. "What's happening?"

The screen displaying the feed from the A-Channel had suddenly gone black and there was no sound. On Fox News, a reporter was going back over the feed and summarizing, "So, this is what we know so far, in this developing story. Dr. Samuel Cohen, the ever-popular archeologist, was broadcasting live, just moments ago, when a man who remains unidentified apparently ambushed his crew, appears to have hijacked the Ark of the Covenant, and apparently executed the crew. This seems not unlike a terror attack!"

Angela shrieked, and ran from the room, down four flights of the stairway to the ground floor. She emerged outside and felt the air, thick with cigarette smoke wafting from a waiting room where a small cluster of parents were chain-smoking as they anxiously awaited news of their children's struggle with cancer. Exiting from a side door marked "Staff Only," she felt better being outside—but only for a few moments when a well-groomed but supercilious look-ing local news reporter had just parked his car. Seeing her, he began shouting questions at her.

"Ma'am, aren't you Angela, Sam Cohen's girlfriend? Were you actually engaged? What will you do now that he is dead?" His tone was rude as he pushed his microphone toward her face.

Angela turned and, before she knew it (with strength that she had never known she possessed) she had slapped him hard in the face. The reporter—he was a small man—crumpled under the im-pact, blood running from his nose.

"Wait, that's assault!" he cried weakly.

"So is what you said, you, you. . .you vulture!" she shouted, tears running from the corners of her eyes.

Turning into the parking lot, two mobile satellite trucks from competing TV stations pulled up nearby and turning their cameras on the scene their crews began to film the reporter on the ground. Moments later, two thickset security agents appeared from inside the building. One of them quickly escorted Angela back inside the "Staff Only" door.

"She assaulted me," the reporter said, getting to his feet, speak-ing in the direction of the other security agent.

"Yeah, I saw it on surveillance. You had it coming, you punk. Now get lost! Don't make me have the rest of the nursing staff rough you up!" the second security guard admonished him, chuckling.

-45-

The snipers counted down through ear pieces, more grunting numbers than counting. On the third such sound, muffled cracks seemed to come from all directions. The guard nearest the entrance fell over stiffly. A second guard grabbed his chest and screamed, just as the man next him appeared to disappear in a blast of pink mist as his head detonated like a bomb.

Brisbane looked at Raphael, and ordered tersely, "Go ahead. Hit the first claymores!" The man responded, his dreadlocks hanging heavily and swinging as he hit a board with each number in sequence. Successive explosions came one after another as each corner of the complex erupted with screaming scrapes of sharp, heavy lead. The claymore mines shredded any flesh nearby. And remaining temple guards whose positions had been identified began to explode in the place he was crouching or lying, a horrible slow-motion cycle of death. The acrid burning smell and of powdered metal wafted along with the smoke as it billowed through the area.

"Execute! Izvršiti!" Brisbane commanded in English and Croation.

The four Croat gunmen, running as one, rushed the entrance firing. They signaled to each other in the "smooth is fast, fast is smooth" manner of leap-frogging each other.

Oslo and Gundy followed behind them.

Response from the local militia was fairly much as Brisbane had expected, and the ensuing firefight was not nearly so dramatic as it could have been. The local police presence in the form of three motorcycle-bearing policemen was soon sequenced by the sound of military Jeeps that had been dispatched from barracks on the other side of the city. The snipers made easy work of the three policemen, picking them off before they even reached the temple complex. The revving of one of the engines continued for a couple of minutes where the motorcycle had come to rest, lying halfway in a culvert on the roadside.

Taken almost completely by surprise, the military personnel in the three Jeeps barely had time to assess what was taking place. With no visible foes to fight or apprehend, and with the outline of the temple looming elegantly above them as their vehicles screeched into the complex, it seemed almost as if a freak accident had taken place and ended the lives of the policemen.

The ensuing scene of carnage built quickly on the landscape as the first Jeep exploded under the watchful marksmanship of John David's armor-piercing round, each one followed by incendiary bullets, whose momentary flame is 3,000 degrees Fahrenheit. The second and third Jeeps stopped and began to try to and reverse. The second Jeep rammed into the third, backing over its turned front tire and overturning. Three men rolled out awkwardly and took cover.

As the third Jeep backed away, its windshield exploded and it rolled backward to a stop.

All three soldiers crawled away from the wreckage of the second Jeep.

"Watch this," Bubba mumbled as he shot one man in the leg, causing him to scream out in pain. He waited, and, as he expected, the other two soldiers helped him to his feet and tried to get him to safety, as if helping a player off a football field. Bubba then released a single round that shattered one rescuer's left shoulder and continued on into the already-wounded man. The third soldier took off running into the haze.

With the temporary respite in firing, it was opportune for the large forms of Oslo and Gundy to emerge from the temple under the cover of the snipers, a large object borne on long poles and covered by a purple embroidered cloth to be seen between them.

From behind a bush at the perimeter of the property, one of the temple guards that had not been accounted for took careful aim. His rifle, an old British .303, had seen better days, but he had kept it in good condition. Never expecting to have to use it under conditions such as this, his finger tightened on the trigger. He had spotted one of the flashes of fire in the distance and down the scope, in the bright light of the engulfed Jeeps, drew a bead on what looked like a sniper's head. He filled the sights of old scope with the tan-colored bump—it was a head—only to see a glint of glass. It was a scope. One moment later, the temple guard lay sprawled under the bush.

Once more, the large forms of Oslo and Gundy could be seen traversing the temple yard. For a moment, they were huddled in conversation with Louie and Vince. They, too, carried a large, rect-angular-shaped object under an ornate cloth. For a few seconds, Brisbane joined them. His arms gesturing in the direction of the smaller of the panel trucks, it was evident that he was ordering that the box that Louie and Vince held should be placed in it. Retreating several steps, he lifted the small Sony handheld video recorder and pointed it in their direction as they loaded the item on the van and drove off. "Get straight to the airport now," he ordered. "We will clear this joint and be on our way soon."

With that, placing the camera on a stone wall where he stood, he pointed it in the direction of the disappearing panel van, as it drove off at high speed, dust rising and spreading in its wake. With his cell phone pressed to his ear once again, he issued his next set of orders: "Explosives, please, so that all trucks are disabled; you may then turn your attention to the trailers where the TV crew are positioned· but I want all vehicles out of action within 200 yards of this complex."

Within seconds, the sound of several more explosions rocked the vicinity and the atmosphere became darkened with clouds of smoke. Breathing heavily, Oslo and Gundy once again lifted the Ark carefully on its poles, and manhandled it into the white second-hand Chevrolet that Brisbane had secured. At the wheel, seated three-across on the front bench of the car, Brisbane was thankful that the large forms of Oslo and Gundy would not have to travel many miles this way. He would much prefer piloting the helicopter that would be arriving from the source in southern Somalia from unnamed personnel affiliated with the rebels there. With a clattering sound, the Chevy's engine came to life. Adjusting his sunglasses, Brisbane observed to his traveling companions, "Nice work so far, men; let's get to the next part of the operation now!" As he reversed out of the parking space, his watchful eye noticed the car clock reading 10:03. Turning on to the main road, he directed the car not toward the airport—and not toward the town—but in a southwesterly direction.

-46-

In the chamber beneath the temple, deep underground, the remaining camera crew had stayed put, the men evidently too unsure to move, and still recording as instructed. The Keeper, sensing danger, had taken leave of the group, stepping away quietly and disappearing into yet another adjacent tunnel.

The Croatian gunmen were ruthless. They fired short, controlled bursts of automatic gunfire into anyone they saw, always continuing their forward movement into the labyrinth of tunnels, using their customary hand signals to communicate with one another. The four gunmen surrounded the camera crew—the two camera operators and the remaining technician who was operating the boom microphone.

"Freeze! Nobody move!" one of the gunmen said in heavily accented English.

From behind them, Brisbane sauntered up to the cameramen. "You still rolling?"

Mike, his camera shaking with his emotion, stuttered, "Y-yes sir."

"Good!" Brisbane smiled emotionlessly. "Get me here, with the Ark behind me. This has been a long time coming. Good? Ready?" Both camera operators nodded compliantly.

"Good morning—or evening—to America, and to the whole world," Brisbane began with calm, cold smile. "As you can see, this is the lost Ark of the Covenant, the single most sought-after item in the history of the world. Nothing else even comes close to its value. It is, quite literally, 'priceless.' We followed Dr. Cohen and his crew here, and we are showing it to you. Is it real? They think so. The great Dr. Samuel Cohen thinks so. And *we* think so. Why am I here? I came here to take it. I now have the Ark. Why? It is simple. Ransom! Money! You know, 'the root of all kinds of evil'!" Brisbane alluded to a statement in the Bible with a smirk. "It is no longer 'priceless.' The high bidder gets it. The reserve is one billion—that's with a 'B'—dollars, and no, we do not accept checks or PayPal. If you win the auction, and the money is wired through my account chain, you will receive instructions on how to retrieve it. Bidding opens now online at the following website: www.Treasure-ofSolomon.com. Ain't capitalism grand? Happy bidding!"

He stood to one side of the camera. "Get all that?" Brisbane turned and asked the crew. They all nodded. Brisbane then leveled a pistol at Mike's camera as it was broadcasting, and shot right thought the lens, causing both the camera and the head of the obedient operator to explode. The broadcast video signal faded to black, but the sound continued. The other cameraman, Marcus, fainted, his equipment shattering on impact with the stone floor. With screens now black, viewers around the world heard the gunshots that ended the unconscious cameraman's life.

Jeremy, the audio boom operator, began to make run for it. The audio was still broadcasting when Brisbane coldly said, "Gentlemen," and three or four submachine guns rang out in staccato bursts, followed by a faint scream and thud. The metallic ringing of shell casings hitting the stone floor echoed, and gave way to silence.

-47-

Kishor shoved Sam though one dark, narrow passage after an-other at full speed. "Do you even know where we are going?" Sam asked indignantly, as Kishor's strong arm propelled him fur-ther yet again.

"Yes, I do. Up here," Kishor calmly replied.

"It must have been at least a mile!" Sam panted.

"It's been six hundred yards; about two hundred more yards to go," Kishor said, pushing Sam onward. "They're going to blow the tunnels. I saw the detonation wires that they were trailing behind them."

"Why?" Sam slowed to ask. "They are taking out the Ark first, aren't they?"

"I don't know, probably they will, but just go—keep moving!" Kishor chided, propelling his questioner by the arm.

"Where are we going?" Sam asked, careful not to slow down this time.

"The new temple chamber," Kishor said impatiently.

"The what?" Sam slowed again. Kishor pushed him along the wall roughly, and Sam grabbed his shoulder. They ran further. The light from Kishor's flashlight probed and danced ahead of them.

Kishor continued, his breath in sharp bursts as they stumbled along the passageway, Brad's heavy breathing and footfall loud behind them: "I think we will be able to get out through the air vent system. I found out about it from one of the townsfolk the day before yesterday. It's not that well known, and I will tell you everything I know later when we get out, assuming we do, but three years ago the temple bosses ordered that a more comprehensive ventilation system be installed to allow enough oxygen into the system for the lamps to work and for overall better conditions for the Keepers of the Ark in the new section. It's a relatively large vent that is wide enough for an ordinary man to climb up, and it comes out about 330 yards to the east of the main complex behind the scrub of trees out past the perimeter fence. The main challenge will be to dislodge the hidden grid and netting that is mounted at the top end to keep vermin out."

"Oh, so you know more about this ventilation system than I ever realized," Sam replied, his breath heavy with the exertions he had been making.

Kishor came to a halt at the T-intersection and looked at the freshly hewn walls. "Look, the letters have just recently been carved into these walls," Sam observed.

Kishor began to run his hands along the edges of the wall.

"I will have to decipher these. Do you have any paper?" Sam asked.

"Yeah," Kishor said as pushed hard on one section of the massive wall. With a grinding rumble, it pivoted, opening into a large square room, complete with an altar. An oil lantern cast a low gleam in a corner of the chamber.

Sam stood dumbstruck. Kishor grabbed him and slung him into the room; Brad bolted in after them. Quickly, Kishor closed the opening in the wall, pushing Sam and Brad across the chamber to other side.

At that very moment, a massive rumble seemed to come from all directions at once. The reverberations entered their skulls and vibrated their spines. It was as if they were in an earthquake simulation machine. The floors and walls undulated as if they were made of Jell-O.

Just when they thought that it could not get any louder, it did. Kishor tackled them and covered their prone bodies with his. Small rocks and dust dislodged, falling from the roof, and rained down on Kishor's back, covering all of them with debris, knocking over the lantern and plunging the chamber into complete darkness.

-48-

Brisbane's eyes had a quality that his men had never seen before. The gunmen thought back to their last sight of the inner chamber, the Ark reflecting the light that cameramen had held earlier, as well as the more muted tones of the oil lamps standing around the edge of the room, and the inert bodies of the television crew lying at his feet.

The silence settled heavily around them. The Ark had been easy enough to move once they had gotten it into position and had inserted the poles for carrying it. Laying out the detonation cables had gone according to plan, and, as expected, as they emerged from the back of the temple, the snipers had established secure possession of the building.

Berhanu's lifeless form lay outside the rear entrance, the flagstones colored with a large semicircle of red, the mute testimony to an invisible wound where a well-aimed bullet from one of the snipers had pierced his heart.

-49-

AIRPORT

For Vince and Louie, their bumpy ride did not take long to conduct. "Brisbane is as cold as a fish, but you have to agree that he is an outstanding planner and action man when it comes to things like this," observed Louie. "I dunno where he gets all these ideas, and he is phenomenally well networked the way he can pull all these things together."

"Sure," responded Vince. "Didn't you love the way it all came together and we were able to eliminate all resistance. And we only lost one of our guys; not bad all things considered!"

Louie pressed his cell phone to his ear. "Yes, Boss, that's so. . . . Yes, we are getting near the perimeter now and we have eyeball on the southern horizon. It looks as if the plane is just visible as we speak." He turned to Vince, gesturing for him to take his binoculars and survey the distant hills. "Do you see the plane coming in there?" he asked.

"Yeah, it looks like a Beechcraft, so that's probably the one that Brisbane arranged to be sent from Nairobi or wherever in Kenya," came Vince's response.

"Uh oh, what's that?" asked Louie. His eyes turned to the rear view mirror. Quickly gaining on them was a speeding police vehicle, its blue light flashing, dust from its rapidly revolving wheels being kicked up from the edge of the paved road each time the driver took a bend too quickly. "I think here's trouble after all; be prepared to fire if needs be when we stop. There's no way we can outrun him."

Pulling to the edge of the road, Vince wound down the window as low as it would go. Looking as nonchalant as he could, he regarded the Ethiopian police officer with a mixture of politeness and contempt. "What can we do for you, officer?" he asked. As he did so, the Beechcraft—it had been making rapid progress through the skies to the south—swooped overhead, touching down on the runway not more than two hundred yards away.

The form of the Ethiopian police officer filled the window from where Vince observed him. "We wish to inspect your vehicle for any contraband equipment; we require your compliance," he stated, pulling police identification from his shirt pocket. "There have been some incidents in Aksum."

They were the last words he spoke. A well-placed shot from Louie, his weapon concealed in a plastic bag he held on his lap, ended the unfortunate policeman's life.

As the officer's crumpled form sank to the ground, Vince put the vehicle back in gear, and wiped the blood splatter from his face. The vehicle sped onward to the airport's entrance.

-50-

Deep Underground

Kishor grunted and shifted his position in the dark. One of the falling rocks had gashed his head just behind his left ear, and some blood was trickling down toward his shirt. He could feel it wet and warm against his skin.

Sam had fared a little better, as had Brad. Kishor's form had protected them both from most of whatever had dislodged from the roof of the new chamber. His voice hoarse from the dust, Sam coughed as he tried to speak. After spluttering a couple of times, he managed to say, "We're very fortunate; I know from my other digs that these chambers can be quite resistant to tremors and such like. Kishor, that explosion could've killed us."

Brad's voice, less raspy than Sam's, pleaded from the darkness: "Can we get out of this cave somehow? I cannot stand being in confined places like this. I can't even get an MRI!"

The darkness dissolved somewhat as Kishor, fumbling, announced, "Well, that's good, my flashlight is still working. We're going to have to move quickly—this place may not be as secure as we think it is, and there could still be an aftershock or some subsidence brought about by the explosion. I don't know what explosive they used, but it's probably made any exit virtually impossible the way we came. We're going to have to see if the ventilation system is still operational. I think it might be, as the explosion would have been much worse if everything down here was sealed up completely. Sam, what do you know about ventilation systems in the digs you have done?"

"Not a whole lot," Sam responded hoarsely. "But I agree, the force of the blast would have been much worse if you hadn't managed to close the entrance back to how it was, and I think we could have been put completely out of action if there had been a pressure wave that couldn't have gotten out of the system; even if there are maybe scores of tunnels, if they go nowhere in the end, the blast wave has to go somewhere—I guess the air in the tunnels acts like something of a shock absorber."

"Hold it, guys," came Brad's voice again. This dust is really irritating my throat, but I think I can feel fresh air over here; it's, it's like some kind of wafting feeling. Come here and feel what I mean."

Kishor strode over to the wall and shone his flashlight upward.

"This is it!" he exclaimed. Look, there is the grid. "Sam, you're slightly taller than I am. See what happens if you pull that part sticking out over there." Sam reached up and tugged the object. It had a metallic feel to it.

"Hmph, it feels like it should move, but it doesn't want to budge," he said through clenched teeth. "Let me move over here a bit, and see." As he did so, another stone dislodged from near the top of the wall, narrowly missing his head.

"Be careful," Brad advised warily.

"I'll try it from this angle," Sam announced. As he stepped to the left, his foot snagged on a fallen rock and he stumbled heavily to the ground. "Ouch!" he exclaimed, a whimper of pain unwittingly coming from his lips as he fell.

"Oh, I'll do it," Kishor announced impatiently. Gripping the flashlight between his teeth, to assume the position that Sam had intended to, his height increased by the upturned rock on which he was able to stand. With a violent heave, suddenly his body contorted. Momentarily a large metallic structure came crashing down, this time narrowly missing Brad who had to jump out of the way.

50

"So that's what it is!" exclaimed Sam from where he sat cradling his foot. "Yes, I see, it's the end piece of a ventilation tunnel fixture. I've only ever seen one like this in the digs I have done. Could you shine the light up a bit higher, Kishor," he pointed. "Can you see how there is what looks like it might be a service tunnel here, going upward and disappearing around a corner? What you have done is to disconnect the end piece. I think what we will find is that, further up, there is a rudimentary fan system, maybe even driven by a windmill device, that pushes air down. There will likely be a barricade above to stop small animals, and creatures like bats and rats, from getting in. But this could be a way out for us."

Kishor stood on tiptoe as his flashlight probed the darkness. "Dr. Sam Cohen, I believe you are right." he said. "Brad, you are the shortest of us. I'll give you a leg up, and you can see whether we can make our way out from here."

"Me?" Brad asked sheepishly.

"Get up this hole now," Kishor said through clinched teeth.

Brad vaulted up and caught hold of the edge. Kishor pushed Brad's legs up till his feet disappeared.

-51-

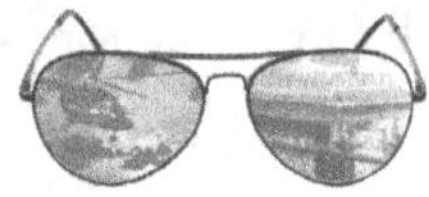

After some careful maneuvering, Brad's head cautiously emerged from where he had pushed out the metallic gauze meshing that prevented wildlife from entering the ventilation aperture. Sure enough, there was a small solar device above that drove a simple fan system to draw air into the underground tunnel system. Reaching up, Brad's fingers encountered the roots of a nearby thorn tree. Getting a good grip, he heaved himself upward and soon his whole body emerged from the darkness. "I never thought I would love the open space of Ethiopia so much!" he exclaimed as he looked down on the curls of Sam's emerging head.

"Whatever we do, we must be quiet," Sam hushed. As the rest of his head came into view, he became aware not only of the brightness of the mid-morning light, but also of the ambience of burning and death. Looking through the small thicket that surrounded the outcropping, he could see the temple in the distance shrouded in smoke. Its siren wailing and lights flashing, another police vehicle was approaching at speed, its occupants brandishing submachine guns from three of the windows.

51

Kishor's head was last to emerge. The gash to his head was raw looking in the dappled light of the cluster of trees, but Sam could see that although it was a wide wound, it was not deep. Passing him a handkerchief, he said, "Use this on your head, Kishor; you are going to need to keep that gash from getting infected."

"We must stay completely concealed," Kishor whispered. "I'm not sure that this place is yet safe. My guess is that the bastards who did this heist have made a getaway, and have taken the Ark with them, but we need to be on the lookout for booby traps and unexploded devices."

"What's happened to the Ark, do you think?" asked Sam. "It will be gone forever if they get out of the country."

"We'll only be able to find out once we know where these devils have gone," came Kishor's response. "Whatever happened, it looks like it was a really well-planned operation; that's professionals that they used.

Sam grimaced at the thought of his colleagues under fire, wondering what might have become of his new friend, Gordon. Smoke rising above the area where the trailers were parked near the compound did nothing to encourage him.

They made their way stealthily through the wilderness area and crouched nearer the road to get a better look.

A moment later, the comparative stillness was shattered by a piercing cry, part wailing, part an agonized, gut-wrenching series of gasps. It appeared to be coming from not far away from their concealed position. "It's coming from over there; sounds like a woman or a girl," confirmed Kishor, pointing to a side road adjacent to the thicket. "Making his way in short, sharp movements, as he ducked from one tree to the next, instinctively taking cover momentarily in the lee of a wall, he reached the road. A car—it looked like a taxi of sorts—was parked at an angle on the edge of the roadway.

On the side of the road, a light-skinned Ethiopian, a man of perhaps fifty years of age with grizzled hair and a light mustache, was crouching over the lifeless form of another man, perhaps in his mid-thirties. Next to him stood a boy, maybe seven to ten years of age. The boy's shoulders were heaving with uncontrollable grief, his small face wet with tears.

"It's not a woman screaming, it's a boy," he called to Sam over his shoulder.

"What's wrong?" Kishor inquired, with a tone of compassion that Sam had never before heard in his voice. "Did you see what happened?" he asked.

The man spoke, his English uncertain, yet his words deliberately chosen. "Yes, I drive taxi. I was bringing my friend and his boy to the temple area for a school report his boy was doing. I was going to drop them off, but suddenly there was lots of commotion, so I drive my taxi onward, very fast. Bullets come this way," he gestured to his car, "then bullet come in glass and get my friend, but he already died when I took him out of car. His head just. . .you can see." He pointed to the injury that had evidently ended the life of the boy's father. "His son. . . ." he pointed to the boy.

"So, this boy is his son?" Kishor inquired. "I'm so sorry." He placed a strong arm on the boy's head and shoulders. "I'm so sorry for you," he said. "So sorry. We must find the man who killed your father, and he must die, too." It was evident to Sam that, for Kishor, life had to be evened out. He found himself beginning to warm in his appreciation for the bodyguard that the A-Channel had decided to hire for him.

"No child should ever have to see his father killed like this," said the terrified taxi driver "His mother, she died three years ago when there was a land mine explosion and she was killed. I knew her. Now this boy is a complete, how you say, orphan?"

Sam, who had remained quiet up to this point, was listening to the exchange. "What happened at the temple, do you know?" he inquired.

"Explosions many," uttered the taxi driver. "I was drive here to take my friend," he repeated. "Then I see something, like big fireworks, and smoke it come out of temple and men are firing bullets from long way away to kill temple guards. One bullet hit my car here." (He pointed again to a hole in the windshield on the passenger's side of the vehicle and then to the corpse at his feet.) "My passenger die, I take him out of car—he boy's father."

"Scum," uttered Kishor scornfully, his eyes once more surveying the horizon. "This poor kid—an orphan, thanks to your friends, Sam, who have taken the Ark."

"Hey, did you see what happened after the temple was attacked?"

Kishor asked the man. "How many men? Which way did they go? What vehicles did they use?" His questions were probing and urgent. Sam could sense the intensity of the discipline in his background in his quick and proactive response, signs of a rigorous training, perhaps from a special division of the military.

"Yes, I see what happen," came his answer, "but not everything; I only see what there was when I was driving on other side of the temple building. It was very bad, very bad. One of the people from town got hit by a bullet—blood everywhere. His chest all bloody, especially."

-52-

Couching behind the Taxi

"We've got to find out what has happened to the Ark. It's the most valuable artifact that could ever be found, and it could be worth millions of dollars in the wrong people's hands; that seems to be what is happening here. That blond man, whoever he is, is up to no good. We've got to find a way to stop him." Sam's voice had a note of determination in it that Kishor had not heard before.

"Hey, my brief from your employers is to look after you, not to go chasing after old archaeological stuff," responded Kishor, the lenses of his sunglasses reflecting a distorted image of the distant temple complex in the background as Sam regarded him.

"Sure, understood," rejoined Sam, "but the thing is, an item like this in the wrong hands could precipitate another major international conflict. Who knows what happened after we scrambled before they blew up the tunnel system; my colleagues lying dead somewhere here under our feet, a megalomaniac who has probably demanded a fat ransom for the Ark, people dead and dying all around us, who knows what as far as police and military are concerned here in this country. . . . I think we must try to *do something* to get it back."

The Sam Cohen who spoke now had a new and steely determination in his voice. Yes, the nice-guy Sam was still there, but the passion of his calling—the years of his investigations, the conviction of his commitment to be an archaeologist, the sense of the importance of the discovery and the indignation of having it snatched from under his very nose—were emotions that fueled his anger and his newfound determination.

"I am Dar," suddenly announced the taxi driver. "I attend worship at this temple often as well as my other church where we preach the Bible. The Ark, we know it was there underneath, and we not want it to be stolen. If we move quick now, maybe we can find where bad men take it. I think we must drive, maybe to airport, to see if we can find where it go. We all go in my car here, windshield OK," he pointed once more to the hole made by the bullet; it was a clean puncture with no fracture around it. "Because windshield OK, we drive OK and see if we find what happened."

"I'm Kishor," announced Kishor. "And this is Mr. Samuel Cohen. Mr. Sam knows everything about your Ark."

"Nice to meet you, too," said Sam, his hand outstretched in greeting. "Yes, we must do what we can. Please, tell me the name of the boy."

"Boy is called Adane," answered Dar. The boy had calmed down somewhat now. Kishor's strong yet kind touch had been a calming influence on him as he stood nearby. Dar removed a blanket from the trunk and spread it over the upper part of Adane's father's body. "Rest in peace, my friend," he said, as he made the sign of the cross.

The car's motor sprang to life as Dar turned the key in the ignition. "I think these many men are bad men. I think they go in many different directions. Perhaps they try to meet again somewhere else in Ethiopia, maybe Kenya, maybe Sudan or Somalia. Somehow maybe we find them. You can stop them. Let us start and try to drive near airport."

As the car gathered speed, the scale of the destruction from the armed men became more apparent to Sam and Kishor. A pall of smoke hung heavily over where the trailers had been, their burntout wreckage lying eerily in the compound. All that remained of the main satellite truck was a shell, and a distorted dish, charred by fire that had almost burned out now. "It's doubtful whether there will be any survivors there," Kishor said as he shook his head in unbelief. And all this done because of greed."

"Greed! Yes, my people know about greed and why greed very bad," rejoined Dar. It was a surprising comment for Sam to hear. Here he was, a young, successful TV journalist, well salaried, well liked, much respected, on a dusty road in Ethiopia in search of and maybe in pursuit of criminals who had just conducted maybe the greatest heist in the history of the world, being counseled by a middle-aged Ethiopian driving him and his bodyguard in a beaten up old taxi. "Yes, I know some American missionaries," Dar continued. They come from the United States, how you say, Tennessee, Memphis?"

"Memphis! Hey, I am from Memphis, Tennessee!" exclaimed Sam.

"Yes, Memphis. They bring old recorded messages from a preacher, a good man, he called Dr. Rogers, Dr. Adrian Rogers. He have big church in America, and he preach very good messages, also another man from there, Johnny Hunt. One time I listen to his messages in my taxi, his English help me to learn good English like I speak now, and Dr. Rogers, he say greed very bad thing." He laughed as he recollected one of the memorable statements that he had heard. "Greed like this, it is a sin:

'And Sin takes you places you did not want to go;
Sin keeps you longer than you want to stay; and
Sin costs you more than you want to pay.'"

Kishor grimaced: "Hmm, it's gonna cost them all right," he growled through clenched teeth.

"So, what else do you know about Memphis?" inquired Sam.

"Oh, lots of American missionaries come to us from there, good people," Dar answered. Our Ethiopian people like them very much. They tell us about gospel of Jesus, how He is Savior and He lived and kept God's law and then die for us to set us free from sin. Then, one day He will come to judge all people."

Sam was astonished at the driver's clear recital of the facts of the gospel: Jesus, the fulfillment of the Old Testament, the long-awaited Savior. He thought of the sacrificial system, the temple, and how it all pointed to Him and found its fulfillment in His life, death, burial, and resurrection.

"Yes, Jesus is now in heaven, and will come back for everyone who is looking forward to His appearing," agreed Sam.

It was quite clear that Kishor was not enjoying this religious discussion. "Hey, we've got to track down these people," he reminded them, "not be having a long-winded discussion about these things from long ago."

As they neared the airport perimeter, Kishor stiffened and said, "Dar, don't drive in the gates—it looks like there is something going on there. Just pull up there on that incline overlooking the airport."

After winding up a bumpy, dusty road to the low hilltop in Dar's taxi, Kishor said, "Wait, stop here; let me get a look." He produced a spotting scope from his small black backpack. He had managed to get his pack out from the temple tunnels by pulling it behind him as he eased himself through the ventilation tunnel after Brad and Sam had made their exit.

"What else do you have in there?" Sam asked.

Kishor ignored him and focused the dials on the scope. "The white truck is backing up behind a hanger," Kishor narrated. "Okay, it's definitely them. Five, no, six men in black, bulletproof vests. They are offloading a large, heavy-looking, wooden crate onto that plane."

"Yeah, but who are *they*?" Brad asked, pointing at some movement at the airport entrance. Several military vehicles could be seen rolling onto the airport property from the opposite side, three of them plunging though the perimeter fencing, and evidently about to surround the Beechcraft aircraft. As they did so, soldiers from a troop carrier fired a round of automatic gunfire into the tires of the aircraft, effectively preventing the flight's departure. As Kishor looked, he could clearly see teams of soldiers pouring out and surrounding the aircraft.

"That's too fast," Kishor said. "Something is not adding up in what we're seeing."

"What do you mean?" Sam asked.

"This must be a decoy. A division of their military was tipped off ahead of time. They mobilized the vehicles, and look, there are photographers, probably from the local press or another nearby town—they will have missed whatever took place back at the temple in Aksum. . .it's just all too fast," Kishor kept saying. "I'm pretty sure that this is all a diversion. Come on, let's go! My hunch is that the Ark has been taken in a different direction altogether. And if we are wrong, and it is in the plane that these security guys have just taken out, we'll find out, but the fact that media are here already just does not fit."

"You have a point," came Sam's reply. "Dar, we think that we need to go back toward Aksum; maybe see if we can figure out what has happened."

The taxi engine roared to life once more. Dar accelerated carefully as they descended the outcrop and entered the main road once again. The sight of the airport disappeared behind them as they drew nearer to the town, smoke from the temple complex and the trailer compound still dispersing into the blueness of the morning sky.

* * *

Around the temple, deafening sounds rang out in quick succession as each rigged vest C4 explosive detonated inward. Several of Brisbane's men were blown in half.

-53-

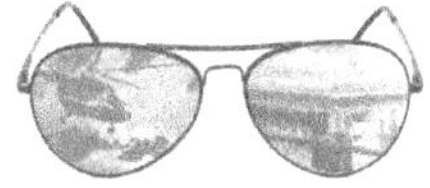

A Road Approaching the Temple

Suddenly, Dar applied the car's brakes. "Over there, look!" he pointed. To his right, next to the road, a woman was gesturing urgently toward the taxi, her hands waving dramatically from side to side. "This is Biftu," he announced. "She is my late wife's sister; in English, you say her name is 'Dawn.'" Reversing quickly from where he had gone past her, and rolling down his window, he called something to her in Amharic. A short conversation ensued, with animated gestures on the part of both speakers. The boy, Adane, looked on from the back seat next to Brad, his eyes growing wider and wider in astonishment.

"So, what's going on?" Kishor spoke again.

Dar turned the motor off. "My wife sister, Biftu, she says she was working in the field near temple about forty-five minutes ago, and when she saw bad people shooting, she leave quickly by running this way. She not get bombed or shot like other people. She say that she see one bad man who get hurt. She hid nearby. He was a local man." Biftu nodded in agreement; she evidently understood enough English to be able to track the conversation.

"Then she hear this bad man say he know he going to die and now there is nothing he can do. He was talking out loud but not making a lot of sense. She tried to help him. He said was going to get money, a lot of money, for helping them, but now it too late. He thought I was his mother. He was bleeding really bad. He said that the big truck that was leaving only had men on it—they the men with black vests—but the car, a white Chevy sedan, that car with three men, it have a big box put inside it with a colored cloth, this was valuable thing stolen from temple. I do not know what he was talking about. He called out for his mother."

Kishor interjected: "So Dar, is this lady saying that the Ark got taken somewhere that was not going to be the airport? That would confirm that what we just saw out at the airport was a decoy event."

Biftu started saying something in her language to Dar, pointing animatedly in the direction in which they had been driving. The word "Tana" was repeated several times.

"This man, this man who died," explained Dar, "This man kept saying before he die that the very bad men, they go to Tana, they take big box to Tana, but want to trick others that box goes to airport. Box not go to airport, that is other box to look like the real box that got take to airport. Real box go to Tana."

"Tana!" exclaimed Sam. "Why would they go to Lake Tana?" Then, with an expression of understanding breaking over his face, he continued, "Tana—yes, they would know to go to Tana because they could have viewed my report—the report I did before we were broadcasting live! They had to, to know when to strike. I had a report prerecorded on Lake Tana and all the relics out there and my search. Remember, I had a villager try on the ephod; also, we showed the original laver, as well as a range of the other relics that are hidden there from my archived footage back in the US. He knows that the whole lot, the Ark and all the other relics from the temple, will be worth even more if they can get them together—a package deal!"

"So that's it," said Kishor, understanding also breaking over his face. So the airport thing was just a complete ruse. Likely thing is that they had a decoy plane to take a decoy Ark—very smart thinking. That would've been the Beechcraft we saw them storming. That will lead everyone a whole song and dance. Dar, you can drive us to Tana?" His statement was intoned as a question.

"Yes, sir, I can drive to Tana, but it is quite long way," he said. "Road bumpy, but we go as fast as I can drive."

"Good!" Kishor retorted. "But we need more information to know what we are looking for. The car that the men took—please ask the lady to describe it more exactly."

Dar turned to Biftu. In their exchange, it was clear that she was describing the men as well as the vehicle. "One man so big, he is, you say, like a, like a giant man, veeeery big!" exclaimed Dar as he translated, gesturing dramatically to give a sense of the size of the men. "Other man also very big, with very thick neck, not a lot of hair. And the man, the driver, he seem to have very white hair, not long hair. They drive this sedan, a Chevy, and very big box in the back where they take out the back seat."

"That's it!" exclaimed Kishor. "They would have modified the back part of the car. All they would need to do would be to remove the back seat. The Ark is big and heavy, right, Sam? What, maybe three hundred pounds? We must trail them and somehow get to Tana if there is any way we can intercept them. Dar, please confirm the color of the vehicle we are having to locate."

Biftu immediately interjected, her English evidently quite good enough for this question. "White, white, car white" she exclaimed emphatically.

"OK, so it's a white Chevy we are following. Dar, step on it! We can maybe intercept them. This gang is tricky and organized. That theft went far too smoothly. I wouldn't put it past them to have an aircraft or two lined up for another getaway for the Ark."

In the back seat, Brad was sitting quietly, wishing he could be anywhere else on earth at that moment. Sam was by the other window, the young Adane between them. As Sam's mind tried to process the events of the morning, he felt almost overcome. What would Angela think if she could know what was going on? "Why would you chase these murdering thugs?" she would ask. What would be the response of his elderly mother back in the United States?

What had come of his colleagues and crew—and would any of them have survived? Drake? And good old Gordy—what of him?

He could not remove the thought of them from his mind. He felt numb.

-54-

A Rural Road Leaving Aksum

The route that lay before them from Aksum to Tana was typical for the terrain. Sam recalled from his research before he had come to Ethiopia that, if he should travel in the region round about, he should expect to see some mountainous topography as well as desert or semi-desert countryside.

"Dar, how far is it to Tana?" inquired Sam from where he was seated in the back of the vehicle.

"By road, nearly 200 miles; if we could fly, it would be less, maybe 125 miles, but by car we go through many bends on roads, and the mountains and hills, they can be steep in parts," he answered.

"Hmph, we need an aircraft. Some luck we would need to get one now," grumbled Kishor, his sunglasses reflecting the moving scenery from outside his window. Air coming through the bullet hole in the windshield in front of him made an eerie whistling sound. He tried plugging it with his finger, which quietened it. Taking out a magazine from his vest, he popped out a pistol round. Odd looks were exchanged by the occupants of the car. Kishor then stuffed the brass cartridge into the into the round hole. "You can still see OK?" he asked Dar. The driver nodded his response. Dar looked at Sam, who just shrugged.

"I think we should pray for aircraft so we fly there quick," Dar suddenly announced while staring the bullet lodged in the windshield. Sam felt a gentle flush, a warmth of encouragement surge through him. It seemed that the taxi driver was truly a believer.

"Yes, why not?" he found himself agreeing aloud. "The true and living God is able to help us in our time of need. That's what the Bible says, anyway."

"Dr. Adrian Rogers, he say we should always pray. Bible say 'Men ought always to pray and not faint,'" he quoted, remembering the recordings he had used to help him learn to speak English better. He thought of how much he had learned from listening, and also from time to time meeting with the missionaries who would sometimes make use of his driving services.

Kishor let out an irritated sound through his nose, something between a snort and a cough.

"Yes, maybe we could pray that there will be some way of stopping these guys, some way we could prevent them from making off with the Ark," Sam found himself emboldened to say.

"Might as well pray to your God for a storm to stop these thugs from flying, as far as I am concerned," muttered Kishor. "Actually, what we *really* need ourselves is a chopper or a plane," he continued. "Sam, you can add that to Santa's wish list," he added scornfully.

Sam was thankful that he was in the back of the car and did not have to respond.

He bowed his head silently.

-55-

On a Road Southwest toward Lake Tana

With the sun beating down from almost directly overhead, the occupants of the car were feeling the heat. Air conditioning in vehicles in Ethiopia seemed to be more of a luxury than a necessity. The boy, Adane, still sat mutely between Brad and Sam. In the front, riding in the passenger seat, Kishor sat, his spine erect, his eyes traversing from the sides of the road to the view ahead, and occasionally squinting into the external rearview mirror.

As they passed just west of a well signposted area informing them they were in the vicinity of Simien National Park, movement erupted in the bushes ahead, on the side of the road. "Elephant!" he exclaimed as he slowed the car. "A herd of elephants!" He slid the old car to a stop as dust engulfed them.

As impatient as he could be, Kishor knew that stopping and waiting was all they could reasonably do. The risks of colliding with one of these great beasts were too great, and he knew that they would soon be on their way once they had trooped over the road. And then he noticed something else: "Dar, these elephants are agitated; this is not how I know elephants from when I visited Kenya three years ago, when they would be peaceful. These ones are waving their ears, and their trunks are swaying quite wildly. I think there is something agitating them."

"Something not right," Dar confirmed. "We have to wait here for some moments." He turned off the motor.

In the relative stillness, the reason for the elephants' distress immediately became apparent: the staccato sounds of helicopter blades chopping the hot air nearby became clear. Even as they sat in Dar's car, the rushing down-current of the helicopter sent a whoosh of dust and small twigs into the atmosphere, shrouding the car as it passed over them. Above the sounds of the rotors came a roar. Then a second ear-crushing report echoed.

"They're shooting at us," cried Brad, his head wincing away from the window on his side of the car.

"Yes, they are shooting,' agreed Kishor, "but not at us; they are trying to get those jumbos in front of us over there!" Through the trees, he could just make out the form of a man hanging from the side of the helicopter, a long, scoped weapon in hand, the largest of the elephant evidently in his sights.

And sure enough, through the billowing dust, they could see a large bull elephant, evidently in distress, beginning to thrash with his trunk, his massive ivory tusks pointing heavenward.

In a clearing a little further ahead, the helicopter touched down. In the excitement of their poaching, and the dust of the blades, the filthy car was not even noticed. As the occupants of the car watched in horror, it was evident that if the car had been seen through the dust, the helicopter snipers were either too brazen or too brave to care about being apprehended. The chopper sat down in in roiling mushroom cloud of reddish-tan dust.

The forms of two men exiting the chopper were seen hurrying through the small trees as the dust settled. Lifting his scope to his eyes once more, Kishor commented: "Hmm; nasty pieces of work they are; they're dressed like beggars, but they're probably amongst the top income earners in the nation. Often these kinds of guys are in a cartel, and they make a killing—out of killing innocent beasts."

"Yes, these, bad men," Dar informed his passengers. "They poach elephants for their tusks. Ivory of their tusks is luxury in many countries. Very valuable in parts of the world, cost a lot of money to buy, so they get rich *veeeery* quick."

"You mean they kill the whole old elephant just to cut off his tusks to make some carving? That is so wrong!" Brad's voice from the back was indignant.

"Maybe your prayer is being answered!" exclaimed Kishor. "I think we could use a helicopter."

Just as he spoke, two loud shots rang out from inside the car. The boy screamed and Brad held his head. "My ears!" he exclaimed. Kishor's weapon had emerged from somewhere concealed on his person and two well-placed shots had been made from his side window. Sam's beliefs were confirmed—Kishor was a deadly accurate marksman.

One of the men who had stepped off the chopper staggered. He was quite evidently a poacher—he held a cordless hacksaw in his hand in readiness to remove the tusks from the dying animal. The other, the one with the elephant gun, crumpled next to his prey. The whites of his eyes showed him, clearly fear-struck, even from the distance he could be observed from the car. Kishor was out of the taxi in a split second, sprinting low to the prone form of the first man. He was followed at quick pace by Sam. Suddenly it was as if the hunter had become the prey. Kishor seized the gun. He quickly threw the gun to Sam who had almost caught up with him. They left them there, bleeding in the dust next to the elephant, his companion just yards away.

At the chopper's controls, the rotors still spinning above, the pilot was quite evidently at a loss to know what to do. Kishor moved quickly and within moments had him at gunpoint. He needed no encouragement to put his hands up. By now Dar, too, had emerged from the car and was running up to the scene. Only Brad and Adane remained in the vehicle.

"Come here, Dar, translate," ordered Kishor.

Dar pushed his way through some small bushes, avoiding the blood pooling by one of the injured men, and made his way to the helicopter.

"Tell him to fly us to Tana Qirqos, on the lake," Kishor instructed. The pilot looked at the two poachers who were crying out for help, grasping their bleeding wounds. Looking away from them, he nodded his compliance to Dar.

"Come on, get in," Kishor yelled, summoning Brad and the boy from the car. Sam, Kishor, the boy, Brad, and Dar all clambered into the aircraft.

A large helicopter, there was plenty of space inside, though most of the seats had been removed to make way for cargo.

Seated next to the pilot, Kishor was making it quite plain that his weapon would be an encouragement to him to do whatever he decreed. As the craft took waveringly to the air, the tops of the trees dropped below them and from the open door the poachers, who just moments earlier had been in control, could be seen below. The elephants began to surround them. The abandoned taxi stood on the side of the road, only just visible through the dust the helicopter was fanning into the atmosphere.

From this vantage point, they could also see the fallen elephant lying inert on the ground. Two of the other elephants had come up to him, gently prodding him with their trunks, but with no noticeable response.

The poachers, both incapacitated by their wounds, were looking up wide-eyed at their disappearing chopper. "Hover one moment, still," instructed Kishor. Even as he watched, four of the other elephants began to close the circle around the downed poachers. One of the men was frantically waving a branch from a bush that he had managed to break off, but his feeble attempts to ward off the giant animal were unheeded. With one of its tusks, the first elephant began to maul and gore him. The front feet of one of the other elephants were raised in readiness to crash down on the head of the second poacher.

From Brad's vantage point as he peered out of the helicopter, he could see that the situation was not going to end happily for the poachers.

"An elephant, he never forget," Dar said. "They are better to one another than humans are, that's for sure."

"I'd agree with that," Sam added.

<h1 style="text-align:center">-56-</h1>

The elephant scene rapidly receding behind them, the chopper sped forward as it rose in a southwesterly direction. With a gesture, the pilot—he was about thirty years old, had a wiry build, sallow skin, short sideburns, a closely cropped mustache, and sported tinted spectacles under his aviator's cap—indicated he wished to speak to Dar. Dar moved forward and, with his ear near the pilot's mouth, listened attentively, his face taking on a more and more anxious expression.

Motioning above the sound of the rotor overhead, Dar translated, "Pilot say we are overloaded, by three extra peoples, and we may not have enough fuel to get to the island of Tana Qirkos."

Kishor surveyed the bank of instruments in front of him. "Can he at least get us to the edge of the lake?" he asked.

"He says he thinks so, but it will be very close."

Brad's neck was stretched forward so he could hear at least some of the conversation. "Why can't we just get more fuel? I thought there was a little airport slightly to the north. Assuming we can use a credit card, I can cover the cost—really, I can pay. I have my credit card," Brad pleaded.

"I already asked about that, but he say he cannot refuel in public place. The poachers have their own stash of fuel, but that is over one hour to the south, completely in the wrong direction for us to go. And he say that the authorities want to arrest him for flying poachers. Poachers have killed park rangers—murdered them—so they know him and his chopper. He say authorities will arrest us all on suspicion of poaching if we land anywhere," Dar explained over the rotor noise.

Brad's face whitened. "Oh no, oh my gosh," he exclaimed limply, his voice mostly drowned by the noise of the helicopter.

Kishor's firm voice asserted itself above the noise: "Tell him I want my feet in the water before he sets down or I will try to fly this thing—and he can try to learn to fly without a helicopter."

Dar translated to the pilot, making violent gestures and pointing to the door. Behind his tinted lenses, the pilot's eyes widened, his Adam's apple rising and falling as he swallowed several times violently in quick succession. He reached over to some of the supplies and equipment he could do without and began to throw several items out of his side window.

"He say we need to reduce the load, throw everything out we don't need!" Dar yelled. The boy, who had had been completely silent through the developments of the last fifteen minutes, suddenly started to whimper and to cling to Kishor.

"What is he doing?" Kishor asked, as the boy tightened a death grip upon him.

Dar asked the boy, and then gave a knowing nod. "He say he worried you do not need orphan with you."

"What?" Kishor looked stunned. "He thinks I am going to throw him out?"

"He is scared, sir. He has no one now," Dar explained. "He is at your mercy." The boy's crying stopped all talk for moment.

"Tell him I have him, and I will not let him go" Kishor said as he patted the boy's head and deftly wiped a tear trickling next to his nose.

Sitting to the side, Sam saw it, and found himself thinking that it was time to reassess his views of his bodyguard yet again. "Underneath the tough exterior, there looks to be a real heart, a hurting heart," he found himself reflecting, and wishing there were some way in which he could help Kishor to overcome the hardness that he felt and that boiled so easily to the surface when it came to the mention of spiritual matters.

The boy smiled faintly for the first time. Kishor hugged him. "What is the meaning of his name 'Adane'?" Kishor asked Dar.

"The real name 'Adane,' it's pronounced like your English name 'Aiden,' Mr. Kishor," Dar said helpfully.

"'Adane,' huh?" Kishor said, and the boy's face creased into a smile on hearing his own name called.

Dar continued: "In Ethiopia, his name means 'He saved, he rescued, he healed,'" Dar added, with a knowing look.

"Really? Maybe it should mean 'needed to be saved, rescued and healed' and not the other way around?" Kishor said, looking pleased.

"Well, sir, the story of his life with you is just beginning, is it not?" Dar asked, a knowing smile with missing teeth playing out under his grizzly mustache.

Feeling the excitement of the moment, the sense of destiny in it all, Sam could not contain himself and blurted out, "Hey, but God came through for us on the chopper, huh?"

"*I* got this chopper. *I* got it!" Kishor yelled much louder than he had to. "Some God of yours! These guys are out here killing innocent animals. Boys like him, who did nothing wrong, are left with no parents! Yeah, what an awesome 'God' you serve. How can you expect me to believe in a Being who allows bad things like this to happen to good, innocent animals and people?"

Sam was almost completely taken aback by the rage that consumed Kishor in an instant. There had to be a reason. "A very deep hurt somewhere in his life," Sam thought.

In the rear of the helicopter, Brad, taking his cue from their pilot, was throwing out whatever he could find that looked as if it could be gotten rid of through the open door—there were some sleeping bags, two small gas cooking stoves, camping equipment, and supplies of canned food that the poachers had evidently been using. He worked his way along something bulky he could feel under a tarpaulin. Lifting the edge, he saw what was concealed: a pile of long, heavy elephant tusks. Steadying himself, and taking a deep breath as he grasped the handle next to the doorway, he heaved the pile to the edge, then pushed them out with a mighty effort. The helicopter surged upward and forward with the lightening of the load.

Looking over his shoulder, Dar said: "Every one of those tusks costs enough feed one of these poor villages for a year." He pointed to a small settlement below them. His brow was furrowed with concern, his eyes angry. "They are illegal to hunt, but not illegal to sell. What a waste."

"We need the weight off!" Kishor hollered over the chopper's roar. "There's just no choice in this matter."

*   *   *

At ground level, some distance beneath the scudding helicopter, life was proceeding as usual in a missions tent. It was located near one of the many small villages that were clustered along the edge of the hills. The staff were well acclimated to the dry Ethiopian days, the dust, the poverty, and the challenges of ministering to such poverty-stricken people.

The sign outside indicated in four languages it was a prayer center. As well as inviting local villagers to come for prayer, there was a range of service ministries that were used to help reinforce their message of God's love and care, including a small medical facility, a classroom teaching area, a room used for young mothers, and a room used for general counseling.

Weaver Stevens, the coordinating missionary, veteran of twenty years in East Africa, was feeling keenly the needs of the mission organization. Not only were drought, poverty and disease ongoing ministry challenges, but there was also the ever-present risk of attacks by bandits, and the potentially volatile political situation, not to mention the new risk of terrorism and hostage-taking. News he had heard earlier on his satellite radio of disruptions in Aksum at the temple had concerned him, but he figured there was nothing that could be done from his remote location in the bush.

Calling to his white-coated assistant Rachel, a young Ethiopian woman, he beckoned her to ring the bell and call the lunchtime prayer meeting before serving the meal to the children who gathered each noon in the compound. "We give you thanks, O God, for your great mercies to us in the gospel," he began. "For every good gift that descends from the Father, receive our thanks," he continued.

At that very moment, a crashing and splintering sound was heard on the playing field outside, the place where the children would engage in recreation after their lunchtime meal. As he opened his eyes and rushed to the window, to his great surprise, the missionary could see some large, long white objects scattered along the field, dust rising from where they had impacted the dry ground. Craning his neck up, he could also see a helicopter making its way in a southwesterly direction.

"Ivory! It looks like ivory!" exclaimed Rachel.

"Yes, it's fallen from the heavens, from the sky, maybe from that helicopter," responded Weaver. "Perhaps this is the answer to our prayers—but this is different from the old song 'Pennies from heaven'!"

Rachel said, "He has provided!"

-57-

The helicopter and its unusual crew made good progress through the noon skies of Ethiopia. The hilltops slid past them not far below. The intense glare of the sky made Kishor glad for his sunglasses. The pilot continued his anxious and frequent glances at the fuel gauge as they crossed the final range of hills. In the distance, a gathering haze could be seen.

"There, see!" Dar shouted above the noise of the engine. "Lake Tana." Through the haze, on the horizon, the large, deep blue lake looked out of place in the dusty aridness of its setting. It stood out from the sea of brown mountains and plains that surrounded it.

"It's shaped kind of like Australia," Brad observed as they drew nearer.

"There's the island of Qirkos on the southern end of the lake," Sam pointed. "I know that from when I was researching this and the pictures I viewed then; still a good way to go."

At this, the pilot then spoke to Dar and gestured to the instrument panel. A buzzing alarm sounded.

"What did he say?" Kishor shouted over the noise.

"He say we must put down soon!" Dar explained.

"Feet in the water," Kishor said. "Tell him, 'Feet wet!' I want to at least get to the lake!"

The engine sputtered, seemed to fade, then restarted, sputtering again, but they continued to move forward as they descended. The lake seemed much closer now, hopefully within reach, and Kishor could see trees located on the shore, a band of welcome greenery against the brown backdrop.

"Please God." Sam muttered under his breath. "Please!"

"Put down there," ordered Kishor, pointing to a flat, open space a little to their left. "That will have to do." The pilot nudged his controls, adjusted a switch, and eased the throttle back.

The helicopter's engine quieted just as they hit the ground, while the buzzing alarm echoed. On rough contact with the earth, the craft lurched uneasily to one side. The ground was not as level as it had seemed from the air. There was the sound of something metallic fracturing as one of the skids partially gave way and the chopper settled at an awkward angle, still upright, but the rotors continued to spin freely, gradually slowing.

"Hold on!" Dar pleaded.

The rotors at first skimmed and then impaled in the dirt. Dust and twigs billowed around them.

Brad yelled something, and the boy clung to Kishor.

"Everybody out!" Kishor ordered.

"Yeah, everyone out!" Sam added, realizing again he was not in charge of anything today.

As he flipped the remaining switches, the pilot turned to Dar and asked him something urgently in his own language. Dar translated, "Uhh, Mr. Kishor, sir, the pilot say he want to come with us, that he will be arrested here because they know him and his poaching."

"Tell him it's that, or I kill him," Kishor said coldly without looking back at them.

"No problem," the pilot said in stilted English, holding up his hands. "I stay."

Brad observed, "Hey, he speaks English—at least a bit of English."

Kishor, his hand shielding his brow, surveyed the coastline. A dozen papyrus boats were lined up along the shore. "Those will never do," he muttered, some disgust in his voice.

"Look, find me a proper boat—a motor boat—and a guide. The boat must be fully fueled!" Kishor ordered Dar. Dar dutifully ran off in the direction of a nearby dock. "Brad, get me those elephant guns, and every one of those shells; we are probably gonna need the ammo!" Kishor ordered.

"Man, these are heavy!" Brad complained as he lifted two huge hunting rifles, mentally noting that, in light of Kishor's orders, it was probably good that he had not thrown these from the helicopter in his attempt to lighten the craft and conserve fuel. He noticed the boy observing the shiny brass shells, almost six inches long. "Want one there, little buddy? Here you go." He held one out and the boy grasped the silver-tipped shell as if it were a treasure. He smiled broadly, his teeth white against his face.

"How come different shells have different colored tips?" Brad asked Kishor. "There are lots of regular lead ones, but also a few of three-colored kinds: red, black, and silver,"

Without even stopping his work ably disassembling and checking the rifles, Kishor explained, "Reds are tracers; they use magnesium burning on the back so you can see where you are shooting. Those are great against aircraft or at night in general. Anything with black is armor-piercing, known as 'AP rounds.'" Kishor held one up, and explained, "These are .50 caliber sniper rounds. Effective at more than a mile! Oh, and the silver tips are a nasty combo, called an 'API Round,' or an armor-piercing-incendiary round."

"What's an incendiary round, again?" Brad asked.

"Whatever they hit, they catch on fire, especially if they hit things like fuel tanks. Regular bullets rarely ignite fuel tanks, except in movies. But these will," Kishor assured him, as he held up a massive, silver-tipped bullet.

Kishor located a satellite phone that had been lying in the helicopter, but the battery was dead. As Kishor finished assessing his equipment, Dar ran up and proposed breathlessly, "We get a boat for one hundred dollars, U.S.?"

"Is it fast, and fueled?" Kishor asked as he lifted a large rifle with a massive scope on it.

"Yes, the owner say it is. And, he know the lake. He was raised here," Dar said.

"Does anyone in this place have a phone that works?" Kishor asked Dar.

Dar only laughed in reply.

"Fine, let's go." Kishor slipped him a one-hundred-dollar bill for him to pass on to the owner of the boat. With that, they clambered aboard the craft. It lurched somewhat and subsided in the water as the party embarked.

It was a nineteen-foot ,mostly white, cruising boat with faded red vinyl seats. It was obviously used for tours, and well equipped with a powerful 90 horsepower outboard motor. It had a white solid top and canvas curtain shades on both sides to protect tourists and their delicate skin from the harsh glare of the African sun that blazed down on the immense lake.

"This is too slow—and it's too far!" Kishor said, glancing up at the sun which had now passed its zenith overhead.

"Isn't it great that God got us a helicopter—and all this cool weaponry, huh?" Sam said, smiling.

Kishor hollered over the roar of the engines, "A storm would impress me. A storm! Something to delay them. We know that those devils could get here pretty soon, even if they have to drive all the way, though I have to say that it wouldn't surprise me if they got some kind of aircraft to get them here."

Sam looked around. It would be good to know how God was working out His purposes in this, he thought to himself. A storm might well be the way they could be stopped from reaching the island but, humanly speaking, this did not seem a likely event, especially at this time of the year. Yes, there were some cumulus clouds marshaled on the horizon, but that they did not appear significant.

"God, you did it for Elijah; please do it for us," he prayed silently.

-58-

After surging through the choppy water at full speed for what seemed like an eternity, the once-distant but imposing island grew increasingly tall out of the water as they approached it. "Tell him take us to the side with the monastery, where I can see it!" Kishor told Dar, who translated this to the boatman as he was ordered.

The boatman indicated he had approached the island in just that way, and they should be able to see the monastery soon.

Kishor regarded the apprehensive faces around him. Only the boy, who had sustained the worst of tragedies of all of them, seemed the most at peace—it was strange, but perhaps an indication of the boy's quiet faith in his newfound friends and his sense that somehow things would work out. The boy squeezed Kishor's arm, and they exchanged smiles. Kishor directed Adane to curl up under the shade of the rear bench on a mat, and the boy was soon asleep in the boat's rocking motion.

"He's had a tough time," Sam said, smiling at Kishor and indicating the sleeping form at the back of the vessel.

"The toughest. Now, let's just hope we can stop them," Kishor said, sounding determined, and yet with a slight tone of discouragement in his voice.

As they spoke, the beating duf-duf sound of helicopter rotors could suddenly be heard overhead and to the east, quickly becoming almost deafening in volume, the sound seeming to emanate from everywhere at once. A large, matte black, unmarked chopper flew not very high above them as it approached the island.

"What's that? Is that them, do you think?" Brad asked. "Could we have gotten here ahead of them after all?"

"Yeah, stay under this cover here. Dar, tell him to kill the engine and drop anchor. We will just look like an ordinary tour group and we won't attract any attention that way," Kishor directed. He placed the bag of ammunition that he had taken from the poachers on the driver's console.

Kishor propped a massive .50 caliber Barrett sniper rifle across the bow, but still slightly under the canvas, deliberately out of view from any aircraft overhead, and settled low in the boat. He adjusted the giant scope.

"You can't do that! The Ark will be on the chopper!" Sam said as he as he tried to wrest the rifle from Kishor's steady grip.

Kishor brutally chopped him in his torso with his free hand in a karate-style punch, and Sam doubled up in pain, dropping to the bottom of the boat. "Ouch!" Brad reacted to seeing the sharp impact to Sam's midsection.

The bodyguard continued squinting into the scope. Sam tried to get his breath but for a moment couldn't. He coughed and heaved.

"I'm not going to shoot the chopper or the Ark, stupid! The gun is not even loaded. I did not want you to shoot yourself," Kishor spat out condescendingly from the side of his mouth. "Our only chance is disable the chopper after it lands. It's gonna be a tough shot, especially trying to hit the right spot, and not to hit the Ark, and shooting from a boat bobbing in the waves, over a quarter mile away, and especially with no practice shots."

"You mean, you think you could take that bird out with the elephant gun from here once it's landed?" questioned Brad. "Wow, that's some idea!"

"It's our only chance," came Kishor's response.

In the distance, the pilot of the large black chopper seemed to have difficulty finding the best place to land on the surface of the steep, heavily treed island plateau. Lurching somewhat in the air currents, he circled for a minute or two, birds rising up in fright as the draught of his craft's rotors pulverized the air around them.

"It's landing now!" Brad said.

"I see it. There is that white-haired guy and he is the one flying it. He's got two immense guys with him. They look huge," Kishor said, his face contorted as he squinted through massive scope.

"What are they doing?" Sam asked anxiously once the craft had settled and the rotors had almost come to a complete standstill.

"The white-haired guy looks like he's talking to the people who have come out—the locals—the short black ones wearing white turbans. Who are they?" Kishor asked without looking up from his scope.

"That'll be the priests from the monastery," Sam said. "The main priests would approach him. They're really the only ones on the island apart from one or two other people who are meant to help them get supplies from the mainland."

"It looks, I think, like they are celebrating?" Kishor turned and shot a puzzled look at Sam.

"What?" Sam asked, incredulous.

"Yeah, the two big dudes are unloading the Ark from the chopper. It is on the sticks that you carry it with," Kishor said. "Man, it is golden in this bright daylight, isn't it? I can just see it as the covers come up a bit in the wind."

"You can see the Ark?" Sam jumped up, the boat lurching noticeably as he clambered to his feet.

"Sit *down*!" Kishor commanded.

Sam did as he was told, but then noticed the second rifle equipped with a similar scope. Carefully he pulled it up, surprised by how heavy it felt to him, even in his firm grip. He placed it into position near Kishor's, inhaling at every sound or vibration. Kishor noticed this out of the corner of his eye, but he did not intervene.

Sam squinted his eyes, and tried to focus the scope. He turned dials, and heard clicks.

After a minute, Kishor reached over and removed the black protective lens cap from the far end of the scope.

"Oh, thanks," Sam said, chagrined. Once Sam figured out how to focus it, the Ark came into view. "That's it. Oh Lord, that's it!" he said to himself. "It is more beautiful in the daylight than I imagined!"

"What's happening now?" Brad asked.

"It looks like they are installing it back at the old temple site, where it was kept hundreds of years ago," Sam explained. "The ancient stone altar is still there. I have seen it myself."

"So, why would he give it to the priests way out here?" Brad asked.

"I don't believe he is," Kishor corrected. "He is using it to lure out all the other relics because he is greedy, like all thieves. Remember what Dar was saying about that preacher guy from Memphis, and the things greed does."

"Greedy—really?" Brad said, as if the thought had never occurred to him.

"Did you ever read 'Where the Red Fern Grows,' a story about a boy and his dog?" Sam asked Brad.

"I don't know, maybe. Don't recall it, though," Brad replied.

"The boy could catch a raccoon by putting something shiny in a narrow crack in the log," Sam explained. "The 'coon could reach in to get it, and they love shiny things, but when its fist was balled up grasping the item, he could not pull out his paw. Then he could be captured."

"Why didn't the 'coon just turn loose of the shiny object and set himself free?" Brad asked.

"Because of greed. He no longer had it—it had him," Sam said.

"Greed is like that, huh?" Brad said. "Hey, I am not feeling so well. Anyone got sea-sickness pills?"

"Sure," Sam said, grimacing at Kishor. "I always carry motion sickness pills when I am planning to spend the day underground in secret African tunnels!" His voice sounded a bit exasperated, but there was a slightly playful tone nevertheless in his otherwise rather caustic comment.

"Sorry, uhhh. . . ." Brad clambered to the back of the boat holding his hand over his mouth, and flung his head over the rail. In a moment, loud sounds of his violent retching confirmed that he had not spoken too soon.

58

Looking up from the rifle he was holding, Sam asked: "Kishor, can't you just shoot the engine of the chopper now?"

"Maybe," Kishor said. The Ark is out now." Without removing his eye from the scope, he slowly reached out for the black bag of the heavy shells for the rifle, saying, "If I use an armor-piercing shell, and I can try to hit the chopper's transmission, and that would put it completely out of action."

As he spoke, he was interrupted by a loud thudding splash as something heavy fell into the water.

"What was that?" asked Sam, concerned.

"You're kidding me! You're kidding me! God!. . ." Kishor checked himself, as Sam looked at him, concern etched in his features.

"Those were the shells, weren't they? You just knocked them over the edge by mistake, didn't you?" Sam asked, as Brad noisily continued his retching at the rear of the boat. Kishor nodded, his head dropping and shoulders sagging momentarily.

"How deep is the water here, Dar?" Sam asked. Dar inquired of the captain, and replied, "More than fifty feet, Mr. Sam."

"And, none of these guns are loaded?" Sam asked.

Kishor shook his head to indicate that they were not.

"What about your handgun? Is it loaded?" Sam persisted.

"Yeah, but it's just a nine-millimeter with Dum-dum bullets; that would be a joke at this range," Kishor said, having obviously thought of this already.

"What are Dum-dum bullets?" Sam asked blankly.

"Hollowed-out bullets, on both ends, that completely collapse on impact—designed for use indoors, in hostage situations, and in places like tunnels, because they splat and don't ricochet," Kishor explained. "Ask him what other weapons he might have on board."

Dar translated the answer, "Just a flare gun."

"Great. So, what's Plan B?" Sam asked Kishor.

"Good question," Kishor said, removing his sunglasses and masking his face with his hands.

Sam was reflective. Annoyed as he felt, he knew that God was with them, he found himself affirming.

Surely the one, true, living God was able to help, even in a situation such as this. Had they not seen His hand of care already so many times in just this day alone? The helicopter had been provided.

"I think we should pray," he announced. "What can I pray for?" he asked, putting his hand on Kishor's shoulder.

"I thought we were waiting on your God's little storm, so we could have beaten them up there, on that path and thrown a little welcoming party for those mercenaries!" Kishor ranted, angrily pushing Sam's outstretched hand away. "We could have warned the priests, and we would have been able to capture those thugs, or kill them, and save your Ark! Guys like that kill innocent women and children, and they all have to die!" Kishor looked intently into Sam's eyes, his emotion etched in his usually stoic face.

"What happened, Kishor?" Sam rejoined, his voice calm and firm, sensing a moment of insight, and leaning forward toward him. "What happened to your wife and children? Something happened, didn't it?" Instinctively, he understood the bodyguard's vulnerability.

Tears gleamed and burned in Kishor's eyes as he fought them back. He looked far off in the distance. "They were killed. Murdered by thieves and thugs just like these ones we are dealing with!"

"What happened?" Sam asked patiently.

Kishor let out a long breath. "It was years ago, now. My wife and children were visiting an art museum on holiday—it was a special vacation I had sent them on in Europe. They were in Sweden at the time. A whole batch of sophisticated thugs hit the art museum in Stockholm. That's the same day and place where the thieves just walked away with the art. My family were amongst the casualties; the kids died outright; Maya was in intensive care for three days before she died."

"Man, I am so sorry," Sam said compassionately. "What happened? What did you learn about the killers—surely the security guys and police got a lead on them eventually?"

"There were no witnesses, and they foiled the security. They were really well planned, just like the guys here, and all we ever got was a photo from a security camera that they did not disable—it's of the guy they identified as the ringleader, and a name." Unfolding a well-worn wadded photo from his breast pocket, he passed it to Sam. "He's called Brisbane. He's from Australia and used to do art theft. I have been tracking him for years now, and I try to get jobs that might put us together. Let me tell you now that this was one reason why I was keen to accept the assignment to guard this archaeologist, Sam Cohen, as the word I had was that this Brisbane creature had an operation planned somewhere in the eastern section of Africa."

"You mean, you try to guard stuff he might want to steal?" Sam asked, studying the photo. The hard features of the man's face—eyes cold as they stared from under a brow crowned by thinning white-blond hair, and narrow, straight lips—looked strangely familiar, as if he had seen him somewhere sometime recently. It was an eerie sensation he felt as he looked.

"Something like that."

"What will you do if you find him?" Sam asked, but was suddenly sorry for he had done so.

Kishor just stared at him, a craving for revenge etched in his features.

"God's Word tells us to make room for His revenge." Sam stated gently.

Kishor yelled back, "I don't care one whit! Your 'God' let us both down a lot!"

"You are right," Sam said calmly. "You know, often God takes away from us those very things upon which we lean—those things that matter to us."

"Hold on, there's movement again." Kishor said.

Sam re-focused his scope on the distant scene happening far above them. "Look, they are bringing out all the relics now, and bowing!" Sam exclaimed. "This is so wrong. It's all my fault!"

Brad retched loudly once more in the rear of the boat, largely oblivious to all that had gone on.

"They can't stay up there, chanting and bowing forever, Kishor. What happens when they get all the relics out?" Sam asked, not sure he wanted to know the answer.

"He'll kill them all, probably with small explosives or grenades," Kishor said calmly as he observed the scene, his lips slightly pulled back as his right eye squinted through the scope.

"Is that what you would do?" Sam asked hesitantly.

"Don't ever confuse us," Kishor said coldly. Then he added, "We've got to stop that chopper."

-59-

Almost at once, the air around them became noticeably cooler. "What is that?" Sam exclaimed as he felt something sting him. "Look!" His face still pale, Brad yelled from the back of the boat. "It's starting to rain!"

"I feel it!" Dar said, grinning, his uneven teeth and one or two gaps in them noticeably displayed between his lips. Sure enough, a growing bank of storm clouds was rising up behind them. "But storm not usually come from that way."

From the back, the boatman spoke to Dar, and Dar translated, "He say we have to get to land! This could be big squall."

"No!" Kishor retorted. "We're staying here."

"But we cannot be caught in the storm!" Dar pleaded. Lighting gashed its way across the darkening sky from the ominous-looking bank of clouds, followed by another rumbling wave of thunder.

"It's getting bigger; we've got to get to shore!" Brad urged, wiping his mouth and picking his way gingerly toward to the front of the boat. "I have been shot at, barely survived the trip here, survived a helicopter crash, and I don't want to drown out here!"

Seeing that no one even acknowledged his litany of complaints, Brad asked, "So, what's happening up on the island now?"

"Relics are being produced," Kishor answered, and turned to Sam, "You're the expert—how many relics are there?" His tone was urgent this time.

"Sorry, believe it or not, the monastery goes about seven stories down into the solid rock, with secret tunnels and passageways," Sam explained. His thoughts were drawn back to events earlier that morning. "You know what it was like earlier this morning back in Aksum."

"Yes, that sounds unpleasantly familiar," Kishor interrupted.

"Each level underground has relics. I have only seen a few brought up from the first level. I know they have much more," Sam continued.

"So these guys have had nothing to do for like a thousand years but dig tunnels into solid rock with small tools?" Brad asked, his voice incredulous.

"Pretty much so," Sam agreed, "Like the ant, they avoid the sun, stay cool, and safely guard their treasures. It gets to 122 degrees in this valley sometimes," he explained, gesturing to the outline of the distant hills binding the horizon.

"Hey, Professor, how long have I got, based on what you are seeing up there so far?" Kishor asked impatiently.

Peering through the scope was much more difficult, now, as the intensifying wind had made the waves much larger, and they were choppy, causing the boat to ride up and down in an erratic, unpredictable way. "It's hard to tell," Sam said, "but with the pattern we are seeing, I think the storm may reach them before the artifacts are all up from the tunnels."

"That might be our only chance," came Kishor's response. It was obvious he did not like the look of the odds. "Look, I am not sure what to do. I would be able to shoot the helicopter, but we have no shells," he lamented.

"What happened to that whole bag of shells we brought from the chopper into the boat?" Brad asked impetuously. More lightning followed quickly by rolling thunder erupting overhead.

"Don't ask," Sam warned. The wind was picking up speed. It

was getting hard for the men to even hear one another clearly. Spray kept getting on the scopes.

Roused by the change of weather and the rocking motion of the boat, Adane had awoken and crawled hesitantly forward to sit next to Kishor.

"I knocked the bag of shells overboard," Kishor admitted, taking it like a man. "So, we are left with two options—either climb the side of the mountain in a driving storm or sit here and watch them take everything, kill a bunch of priests, and escape scot-free with the Ark that Sam here deserved to find," Kishor stopped, looking down at Adane's face as the boy rubbed his eyes.

Sam looked at him in amazement. "What did you say? I deserved it?"

"Nothing, Professor." Kishor tried to adjust Adane's position and look through the scope, but the wind, the waves, Adane's form leaning next to him, and the blowing rain made it almost impossible for him to see the island. Peals of thunder and flashes of lightning interrupted one another in rapid succession, and all the while the wind felt more cutting as it drove the rain in stinging drops before it.

With a spluttering sound, the engine started, and the captain began to quickly pull in the rope tied to the anchor. "Hey, what's he doing?" Kishor demanded of Dar.

"He says we have to go!" Dar translated.

"No, we stay here; we *must* stay," insisted Kishor from his position. "Tell him he must drop anchor again and switch off the engine." His tone left no doubt that the order had to be obeyed. Even without his words being translated for him, the boatman reached out, cut the motor, and released the anchor overboard again.

"How can you see?" Brad asked, taking a turn at the scope of the rifle that Sam had put down for a moment.

"In between the blowing rain gusts, I can just see the island. The storm has still not yet quite hit them," Sam explained.

"I can't see a thing! We are totally helpless!" Brad declared.

The comment triggered a thought in Sam. "Kishor, the storm! You wanted a storm; God has given us a storm!"

"Yeah, it's sitting on us—not them! Once again, your misguided God is at work!" Kishor grunted. It was hard to hear what he said with the thunder rumbling so intensely.

59

Sam asked, "So what should I pray for now?"

"I am out of options and ideas. I just. . .give up," Kishor admitted. The words had a harsh and bitter note to them.

"If the storm hits them. . . ." Sam began.

Kishor interrupted, "If the storm hits them, the priests will try to protect he ark and the relics by taking them back underground, and the thieves will probably kill them all, and then just escape in the helicopter whenever it is safe to fly, and there's nothing I can do about it from down here!"

It was clear to Sam that Kishor's thinking had already anticipated every likely scenario. "I would hate to play you in chess," Sam said.

"Huh?" Kishor asked, as the wind howled, and as he pulled Adane closer to him. Lightning was now flashing so frequently that the rumble of the thunder was nearly constant.

"Nothing!" Sam said.

"That's it, then! Brad is right. We are totally helpless!" Kishor exclaimed loudly, as if stating the realization out loud changed it. He suddenly startled Adane, who dropped the shell had been clutching. It fell to the floor of the boat with a sharp thud and it rolled over toward Sam.

"What was that?" Brad asked.

Sam held up the massive, black-tipped shell. "God at work," Sam smiled, presenting Kishor the cartridge. Kishor smiled at Adane, whose face creased into a smile in return, as a boy does when he truly helps a grown-up.

"Oh yeah, I remember: I gave him one of those big shiny shells before we got on the boat!" Brad added weakly.

Dar smiled his near-toothless grin. "Adane. . . .He 'rescues'. . .he rescues the Ark that we are trying to get!" He broke into a little song no one could make out.

"Now, what do you need?" Sam asked.

"The storm. It needs to go to the island, and off us, so I can aim!" Kishor hollered over the blowing winds, "This stupid storm!" Kishor growled at Sam, "Not only is it late, it is now hitting us and not them! I've only got one shot! One bullet! I have got to make it hit the exact point on the transmission."

"Well don't just sit there, get in position," Sam said, feeling more confident in his faith at this recent turn of events, and bowing his head in silent prayer.

Kishor told Dar to explain to Adane that the shot would be the loudest thing he could imagine, and the enormous boom would actually move the boat. The dark-skinned little boy retreated and hunched himself up in the back of the boat, with his fingers securely lodged in his ears.

The storm continued to play around them, still seeming to be centered on the boat. "Can't your God do anything right?" Kishor yelled, frustrated.

"He's not done yet," Sam said, assured, now looking through his scope.

"Look!" Kishor said to Sam.

"I see it!" Sam responded with concern. The vista before them seemed suddenly so much clearer, as if the rain had washed all the haze away and everything stood in crystal-clear relief.

On the island, through the scopes, three priests could be seen reverently carrying what looked like relics wrapped in ancient cloths up from the deep chambers carved down into the solid rock plateau.

"Can you hit the 'copter?" Sam asked.

"I don't know, with the waves, wind and rain," Kishor uttered. "I would have to hit the transmission—that would completely disable it. Lots of the copter is not vital. It has redundant systems. If I cannot take it out with one shot, is your God going to let this thief steal the Ark, get away with it, kill all these innocent priests, and escape in his black helicopter to some tropical paradise?"

"I don't know what's going to happen, Kishor," Sam admitted. "But, I believe," Sam said reassuringly.

"That makes one of us," Kishor stated flatly as he tried to hold the scope in position on the bobbing waves. "What do you believe?"

"I believe you need to take your one shot soon," Sam countered. "And, I believe that God can direct its course like He directed the arrows of warriors in the Bible so that it will go right to its target; Kishor, don't waste any more time."

"He can direct the path of the arrow," Sam assured both Kishor and himself.

-60-

As they watched, the storm raging over them changed course and approached the edge of the island. The priests could be seen running for cover as the first drops of rain began to fall, pelting them wildly. From their position in the boat on the water, it looked as if large hailstones were also falling with the rain.

"It's happening!" Kishor said as he squinted into the scope.

"They are taking the relics back in!" Sam yelled. "The blond guy—he's carrying a gun, too!"

"I see it," Kishor said, "I see him! Oh no, oh my God!"

"What?" Sam asked urgently.

"It's *that* Australian bastard!"

"What?" Sam asked, surprised at the visceral reaction of the usually composed Kishor.

"It's him," Kishor growled through clinched teeth.

"No way, you mean the man in the photo you showed me? The one you said was called Brisbane?" Sam asked, incredulously.

Kishor's finger deftly deactivated the safety catch on the massive rifle he was cradling.

"Ahh, you are going to shoot the transmission, right? Kishor?"

"I'm going to blow that murdering son-of-a-bitch's head clean off!" Kishor thundered. Sensing the tension of the moment, Adane began to whimper in the rear of the boat.

"Please, no Kishor," Sam pleaded.

"Kishor, you have the rest of your life to chase him, but that Ark is going be gone in minutes, and it all depends on you. All history really turns on your decision," Sam stated solemnly.

The crosshairs bobbed across the forehead of Brisbane who could be seen proudly standing next to the helicopter, looking over the world that he felt now belonged to him. The cargo door was still open, and inside could be seen several objects that had been carefully wrapped and stowed in readiness for the next leg of the helicopter's flight.

"Sorry, Sam, but he's history!" Kishor whispered. With the precision and deliberate care of a sniper, his finger tightened on the trigger.

"Hold your ears!" Sam yelled, startled by an unseen wave that moved the boat just as Kishor fired. A burst of wind joined the roar from the enormous .50 caliber Barrett and seemed to shove the boat backward and violently jolted everyone on board, as it pitched in recoil.

The massive bullet tore directly into the transmission of the helicopter, and sparks flew out in all directions, A gaping hole was evident. Sam could see Brisbane and the priests all diving to the ground.

"Good shot!" Sam said, as the scope's view revealed sparks dancing and fire flickering from the smoking area just under the place where the rotor blades were attached to the fuselage.

"What the. . .?" Kishor stammered. He stared through his rifle's scope in disbelief.

"Great shot! It was perfect!" Sam exclaimed victoriously. "God really came through with that precision shot from this bobbing boat and through the wind!"

Sam slapped Kishor on the back, assuring him, "I know that was toughest decision of your life, but you made the right call," Sam congratulated him. "Now what?" he asked, anxious for the plan to unfold.

60

"Uh. . . Well. . .we have created a hostage situation," Kishor said. "But at least they cannot leave."

Just as Kishor finished speaking, popping sounds erupted from a distant point above them, and there were several splashes in the water nearby. "What's that sound?" Brad asked.

"Gunfire," Kishor said calmly. "Submachine guns. Stay down!" Plopping water flew up around the boat.

Pinging metallic sounds began to come from the edge of the boat. "Those two big gorillas are shooting at us, aren't they?" Sam said, ducking away from where the sounds were coming.

"Yes, they're finding their range, so we have got to move!" Kishor urged, pulling up the anchor himself. Even as he spoke, the outboard motor roared to life and the bow of the boat rose high in the water as they pulled away. The boatman had needed no instruction to start the engine. "Thank God for a 90-horsepower motor," shouted Sam above the sound of the wind in their ears.

"Heads down!" yelled Kishor. "Everybody's head *down*," he repeated, his voice urgent. "Those devils know that the shot came from us. We've got to get well out of their range, otherwise we'll be dead men."

A sharp metallic whizzing sound caused Kishor to instinctively cover Sam with his body and shove him lower in the boat. Brad had joined Adane underneath the seats in the rear of the boat. The driver began to steer the vessel in an erratic zigzag pattern to avoid the rifle fire as he put more distance between them and the two large men on the island shooting at their boat. As they drew away, the storm began to recede.

"Now, what's that sound?" Brad asked. He cocked his ear toward the side of the boat, cupping it with one hand as he tried to cancel the noise of the wind as the boat skimmed over the lake.

It was a thumping noise and it grew louder and louder, becoming clearly audible even over the lingering rumbles of thunder, as the storm moved on.

With the throttle eased back, the boat began to slow. "No, don't slow down yet," commanded Kishor. "We could still be in the range of their guns." Dar shouted his translation over his shoulder to the boatman. It was too late. Even as the words left Dar's lips, a lone bullet cut its way through the air and knocked over a metal bucket used for an ashtray near the driver's console, a practical demonstration of the wisdom of his advice.

Looking over his shoulder, Sam could see a large, military chopper approaching the island. It was dark army green in color, and it was massive as it lumbered through the air, hovering slowly, almost directly overhead. The helmeted figures of the crew could be seen behind the side windows.

"It's Russian," Kishor said over the deafening thunder of the rotor blades. "An Mi-24 Crocodile."

"Who is it?" Sam asked. "I mean, are they good guys?"

"There are no good guys anymore," Kishor observed flatly. The hulking 'copter made wide circles overhead and its crew appeared to be surveying the island.

"It looks like it has Ethiopian markings, but I don't know for sure," Kishor said, his neck at an awkward angle as he peered upward. "It could be anyone."

The 'copter hovered between the boat and the island. Suddenly the noise seemed to intensify, overcoming their dulled senses.

"Look, there are more of them!" Brad suddenly shouted, pointing over toward the island. The forms of several more helicopters filled the sky in the distance.

"No, those aren't Crocs!" Kishor corrected him. "Those are ours."

"What do you mean?" Brad asked incredulously. "American forces all the way over here?"

"No, I mean they are American-made, helicopter gunships; Apache Longbows," Kishor clarified. "Only one nation other than us is allowed to use Apaches with that equipment," Kishor said.

"Israel?" Sam surmised.

"Look out!" Kishor pointed at the two long grayish-white streaks that formed instantly with swirling vortices.

At high speed they stretched across the sky from the first of the Israeli helicopters until they met at the rear of the Russian Crocodile helicopter almost directly overhead as it continued its circling motion. "Rockets! Get down again!" Kishor yelled as he tried to cover Adane and Sam with his body.

The orange glow of an explosion above them dramatically mimicked the colors of a sunset. Lurching violently, the craft began to fall from the sky, sideslipping away from the boat. Debris began raining down into their boat as the rumbling surrounded them and as the side of the aircraft blew out in a large fiery explosion. A massive surge of water raced toward them as the chopper hit the water, the rotors flaying the surface before the heavy aircraft disappeared beneath the surface.

"Ahhh!" Dar screamed as he clutched his neck; his shoulder was already red with blood, spreading over his shirt. A small piece of shrapnel had pierced his flesh.

Kishor said, "It got his carotid artery!" and instinctively ripped off his belt. "Give me a clean cloth," he ordered.

Adane took off and held up his own shirt, which was certainly cleaner than that of those who had been in the tunnels. Kishor seized it from him, deftly applying it to the wound. Even as he did so, Dar dizzily collapsed to the bottom of the boat. Kishor managed to dress the wound and make a gun belt strap under one arm and across his neck to help keep pressure on it. "Thanks, Adane'" he called over his shoulder. "That was good thinking." The boy's face glowed with pride.

Shrapnel had not only entered Dar's flesh; the boat itself was now steadily filling with water from the holes the raining debris had made. The boatman was pulling the cord to start the motor once more, but with no response. There was the smell of gasoline, evidence that a fuel line had become detached or punctured.

In what seemed to Sam one of the most bizarre moments he had ever witnessed, paper money, mostly in the form of $50 bills, some of them on fire from the explosion in the helicopter, began drifting down from the sky from where one of the Israeli rockets had hit the Russian helicopter. Brad seized one of them, extinguishing the smoldering flame by dipping it in the water forming in pools at his feet. "Dollars from the sky!" he exclaimed. "They'll never believe me back at home when I tell them about this," he exclaimed.

"The fuel line's cut. I can smell it. Okay, grab anything that floats. Brad, pull those benches up—they have plywood tops under the vinyl." Kishor's order was curtly delivered

"Yeah, that is what I was thinking, too," Brad responded as he discovered that Kishor was right. He began to pull at the hinged padded tops, but got distracted by another shower, this time of $100 bills that were wafting down on them. He began to gather what he could, burning himself on one of them.

"No, now's *not* the time to harvest money," shouted Kishor over his shoulder.

Reaching out, Sam located a solitary, ancient life preserver and placed it over Adane's head.

Kishor frowned at Brad, who pulled fruitlessly on the first of the benches. Kishor grabbed the one he was struggling with and ripped it from the boat with one arm.

"Uh, I loosened it for you there, huh?" Brad managed.

Kishor and Sam ripped out others and tied one in front and one behind Dar, so they reached from his chest to his knees. "Now, you will not have to fight to stay afloat," Sam urged Dar.

"He looks like a giant bobber," Brad noted to Sam. His humor somewhat lightened the intensity of the moment.

"Look!" Brad pointed. The Israeli gunships by had now flown much nearer them and were hovering overhead and to one side. The crew of the two leading machines appeared to be looking down at them through their visors as they peered through the windows. Misting water began to pelt them.

Detaching the scope from one of the rifles, and placing it in one of his pockets, Kishor threw the weapons overboard, waving his arms in a dramatic gesture for help.

The Apache gunships, bearing the white and blue Star of David insignia, continued to hover, violent gusts of wind buffeting Kishor and his party as they looked upward, eyes half-closed against the wind stream.

"Are they going to help us?" Brad shouted as he shook the water off the bills he was frantically collecting from the water.

"They aren't rescue 'copters. I don't know. I think probably not. But we should be able to get to shore as we have drifted quite a bit in the last ten minutes," Kishor answered.

-61-

The boat, now foundering badly with all the water it was taking on, was becoming dangerously waterlogged. Sam shouted out to Kishor: "Look; the last two choppers are now moving closer to the island." He pointed, and surely enough they were now almost directly above the monastery.

Kishor put the scope to his eye and peered through it once more.

"It looks like there's starting to be a firefight there now," he observed. I can see those men taking cover behind some of the gravestones and firing up at the helicopters.

"They're shooting at the 'copters?" Sam asked, surprised.

"That would maybe be like peeing on a forest fire!" Brad joked as he gathered a soggy bill from the water.

"No, actually I think they are just firing in the air," Kishor assured him. "They have taken the priests hostage."

"What happens now?" Sam asked as he attempted to bail water.

"Depends on if they have a sniper team with them," Kishor said.

"Who? The Israelis?" Sam asked while continuing to pour water from the boat back into the lake.

"Yeah. They can take out those guys from the air," Kishor said as he finished securing ancient life preservers to Adane and Brad.

"Take them out? Like you were going to do?" Sam asked, but immediately was sorry he had brought it up.

Kishor did not answer but made sure everyone would be able to survive in the water. Dar was now drifting in and out of consciousness. "My friend, you must get this water down," he urged him. It was vital that he drink all the fresh bottled water they had from the sinking boat. "We've got to keep his blood pressure up. He's lost a lot of blood," Kishor said to the others, his voice urgent.

While Kishor continued to attend to Dar, Sam seized the scope from the weapon that Kishor had detached before throwing it overboard. His face creased as he squinted through it. "I think they may have got them!" he exclaimed.

"Who? Who got who?" Kishor asked, while tending to Dar. "Pass me the scope and let me see!" Putting the device to his eye, he continued: "The Israelis have a different philosophy about sniper rifles. They use very small, very high velocity rounds. There's no movement from the graves, so I think that was the three bad guys buying it."

"So, we use those big 50 calibers and they use little ones?" Sam asked.

"Yep. Israeli snipers are usually shooting in urban areas, and much closer than us. Our .50 cals were perfect in the hills of Afghanistan for one-mile shots," Kishor mentioned.

"They were perfect?" Sam asked. "You were there, too, weren't you?"

"Classified," Kishor said flatly.

*　*　*

Another, much larger 'copter appeared.

"Look! That one looks like it is landing," Brad pointed.

"I don't think that's an Apache," Sam noted.

"No, you are right. That's one of the transports we sold them. Looks like a version of our Sea Stallion. High fuel capacity, it has lots of room, lots of power in it," Kishor noted as he watched.

Soldiers, in all black with face masks, roped onto the plateau from the transport helicopter under covering fire from the Apaches. "They are throwing off...the dead guys!" Sam exclaimed.

Adane, who had been attempting to bail water from the boat, suddenly exclaimed, "Aya, Aya, Look!" In his hand, he held a pair of powerful but well-worn Zeiss binoculars. They had apparently fallen from a compartment he had opened near the back of the boat.

"Give them to me," ordered Kishor. He passed the rifle's scope to Sam who put it to his eyes. Through the lenses of the binoculars, Kishor focused his eyes and blinked. To his astonishment, in crystal-clear view, the inert and crumpled forms of two men—they were those large men, Oslo and Gundy—were being lifted unceremoniously by several of the troops and, even as he watched, were thrown over the edge of the cliff. Their descent into the water below was marked by a splash, and then they were out of sight. Then it was Brisbane's turn to be cast unceremoniously into the lake from the towering cliffs.

"There goes Whitey!" exclaimed Sam as a much smaller corpse careened into the deeper water.

Turning his scope again to the top of the island, the sight that met Sam's eyes was even more unforgettable: six men in ceremonial garb were exiting the large helicopter together. "What are they doing? Who could *they* be?" Sam asked, astonished.

"I don't know," Kishor said, his binoculars trained on the same scene unfolding.

"Wait! Wait! I know!" Sam exclaimed.

"What?" Brad asked. "What is going on there? Can I have a look?"

"Watch, those guys are going to get the Ark," Sam said beaming.

"Why are they dressed like that?" Kishor asked.

"Those are ancient priestly garb, ephods, and Levitical tunics," Sam explained.

"Leav-what-it-cull?" Brad asked.

"Levitical!" Sam almost shouted. "Didn't you go to Sunday school? The only people that could touch the Ark were from the tribe of Levi. They are Levites!"

"Sam, what are you talking about?" Kishor asked, as he kept direct pressure on Dar's neck wound.

"They, the Levites, were the only ones who could touch the Ark.

These guys must be direct descendants! See, the ones that are putting the long sticks in it to pick it up," Sam said excitedly.

"Okay, so they are taking it back to Israel?" Kishor surmised.

"Yes! They will probably hold it there until the third temple is built," Sam said confidently.

"What are those things on their legs?" Kishor asked. "They look modern, made out of shiny, silver metal."

"You're kidding me! That's right!" Sam said with obvious recognition.

"Mind sharing your little secret and please tell me what is going on?" Brad asked in an irritated tone.

"Sorry. Man, I can't believe we are getting to see this! Okay, the men carrying the Ark. . . . They cannot sit down with the Ark, so those must be braces to hold their legs straight on the long flight!"

"All the way to Jerusalem?" Kishor asked.

"Yes sir," Sam said.

"They would probably be made out of titanium to cut down on weight," Kishor surmised. "Their security division must have known about this for weeks or even months."

"Really?" Sam asked.

"Your little secret was not very well kept," Kishor said. "Whitey knew all about it, and so did the Moussad."

"The who?" Brad asked.

"The Moussad!" Sam answered. "The Israeli CIA."

"Look, the rotors on the transport are turning!" Kishor observed.

"They are leaving. . . .I got so close!" Sam said sadly.

"You got really close—to meeting your God." Kishor flatly reminded him.

"So, you believe in Him now?" Sam chided gently.

"I don't know what to think. . .my aim was off, Sam. The boat moved," Kishor confided with obvious difficulty. "My bullet should not have hit. . . .I didn't do it. . . ."

"You hit in the perfect place on the 'copter," Brad reminded him.

"I. . .I missed it," Kishor concluded.

Sam stared at him.

"W-what?" Sam stammered.

"I was on the Aussie's forehead, Sam," Kishor confessed. "I

don't understand. . . ."

"There a burst of wind, and a wave. Right when you fired. . . . So God. . .directed the arrow?" Sam asked expectantly.

Kishor put his face in his hands.

-62-

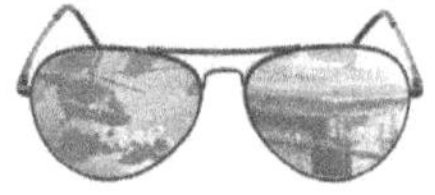

WATERS OF LAKE TANA

The boat had taken on so much water that they held each other while floating on debris. "I think we've drifted almost to shore," said Brad. "We should be able to wade over to the bank. Sam, please help me with Dar so that we keep his nose and mouth well above the water."

Dar's form was almost completely inert, but as Brad helped guide him, held safely as he was between the wooden seats, he could see his eyelids flickering faintly, and his mouth opened and closed with each breath.

Adane needed no encouragement to kick and thrash his way to the shore, the life preserver keeping his face well above the warm waters of the lake.

One of the Israeli helicopters, piloted by a tanned and well-toned man of about twenty-eight years of age, had no difficulty in landing near where the small party had swum and then waded to shore. The medical personnel were able to stabilize Dar and started an IV using emergency equipment and supplies carried on board.

A transport with a backet later hovered and winched each of

them up. Kishor was the last to allow himself to be taken up.

As Sam later recollected when he was outlining the major events from that point onward to Angela, the flight south to the covert US air base outside Nairobi was relatively uneventful following on from the dramatic sequence of the earlier events.

Mop-up operations back in Aksum were not anything that he had to be involved in and it was with a great sense of relief that he heard of the survival of Gordon who had been in a restroom at the time of the attack on the TV trailer compound, and had miraculously escaped serious injury. Others from the A Channel were less fortunate.

Sam's speedy transfer back to the United States of America in sequential stages, partly on a cargo aircraft to a base in Germany, and then by connection on a regular airline from Frankfurt and Amsterdam, was characterized by a complete lack of drama. He had never been so tired.

He had only been able to speak to Angela for a few moments from his brief transit in Nairobi. Her sobs of relief that he was relatively uninjured confirmed his conviction that he would put the proposal of marriage to her the moment his feet were once again on the firm soil of Tennessee.

It was what transpired in the debriefing exercise back in the United States that brought all Sam's investigative journalistic curiosity back to the fore once more.

-63-

MIDDLE EAST BRIEFING ROOM, CIA HEADQUARTERS, LANGLEY, VIRGINIA, USA

"Then God's temple in heaven was opened, and within his temple was seen the Ark of his Covenant. And there came flashes of lightning, rumblings, peals of thunder, an earthquake and a great hailstorm," CIA Director Robert Mullins read aloud. "So, what is this stuff supposed to mean?"

"That's the Book of the Revelation, chapter eleven, umm, verse nineteen," Sam explained. "That's the only mention of the Ark after it disappeared thousands of years ago."

"Okay, well," Mullins thought as he spoke, "So you are saying that they just took this Ark?" He was seated behind a large desk, a map of the world adorning the wall to his left. Two phones, one white, the other a dark blue one, sat prominently on his desk. His jotter was arranged neatly next to his laptop computer, one of the LEDs blinking incessantly next to a cluster of cables that was connected to it.

"Right," Sam confirmed.

"Okay. So, if I understand, you survived gunmen, a tunnel explosion, made an improbable escape through a hidden ventilation system, got a car, got an intelligence briefing from a scared local woman, witnessed elephant poachers being gored to death, stole their 'copter on fumes, then commandeered a boat, and shot the transmission out of a helicopter on top of an island in the middle of the storm with only one bullet available?" Mullins' tone was even as he summarized events as he understood from their meeting.

"Yep, that about covers it," Sam confirmed.

All that, and you couldn't stop them?" Mullins asked, his tone not a little exasperated toward Kishor.

"Uh, sir, they had our well-armed Apache longbow helicopter gunships. . . . Sir, we had just had a flare gun," Kishor stated flatly.

Mullins stood up, sighed, and stared at an open folder marked "Classified: Above Top Secret: Eyes Only"

"The Ark is retracing steps, sir," Sam added helpfully.

"Do what?" Mullins looked up quizzically.

Sam stood up and began to pace as he often did when he was deep in thought—not unlike a professor in a classroom, "You know how in Scripture, events happen that seem to mirror each other, like it is all planned out in advance by one author."

"I am aware of that belief from my church," Mullins confirmed. "Go on."

Sam continued, "Like how there was the first man, Adam, and later, the Bible calls Jesus the second Adam? Jesus was also like Moses."

"How so?" Mullins asked, leaning back and brushing into place the strands of his receding gray hairline. One eye ticked slightly as he spoke.

"In the book of Exodus, you had Moses," Sam picked up a dry erase marker and began to sketch on a whiteboard on the wall opposite the map of the world. "Pharaoh, at the time Moses was born, ordered the all Hebrew baby boys to be killed. In the New Testament, King Herod also killed all the Hebrew male children at the time of Jesus' birth."

Mullins sat leaning forward, the fingers of both hands touching their corresponding ones as his hands formed the shape of a pyramid in front of his face.

Sam continued, "Moses was rescued from the slaughter by entering Egypt. So was Jesus; he was carried off by his father to, of all places, Egypt," Sam drew parallel arrows.

"Moses was put in the covered basket, floating down the Nile, right?" Mullins asked.

"Right, but what you call a basket is what the Hebrews called an ark," Sam said with a smile. "It just means 'box.'"

"Is there more?" Mullins asked, now obviously much more engrossed in the explanation that Sam was giving, and feeling resigned that he needed to hear this out.

"Yes sir, as a matter of fact, there is," replied Sam, while drawing lines to indicate a blue sea.

"There is always more," Kishor added.

Ignoring Kishor, Sam continued, "Then the chosen people of Israel, after crossing the waters of the parted Red Sea, were tested in the wilderness for forty years. Jesus also left His baptismal waters of the Jordan River and was then tempted by the devil in the wilderness for forty days and nights."

"Wait, forty days and nights?" Mullins almost stood up.

"Yes, that was also the length of the rainfall of Noah's Flood," Sam agreed. "In the Bible, 'forty' indicates judgment." He sat back down. "In Scripture, these events mirror each other, because there is only one author. The Ark is retracing its steps to Jerusalem, for the eventual building of the third Temple."

"This is really fascinating," Mullins exclaimed, though Sam could not tell if he was being sincere or sarcastic.

Reaching for his jotter, he began inscribing several key points in his neat, well-formed handwriting. As he did so, his cell phone vibrated. Reaching for it from his pocket, he read a text message. His face paled.

He looked around.

Standing up, his demeanor visibly changed, he took control and said tersely: "Gentlemen, this event never happened. The Israelis have denied that they were even there."

"But. . . ." Sam began to interrupt.

"I know, of course, we tracked their choppers by satellite, and we know you guys are being entirely truthful. But, you must never talk of the Ark making it out," Mullins sternly warned.

"What's wrong with telling the truth, sir?" Kishor asked.

"If it gets out that the Ark was taken to Israel, it would undermine the entire Eastern African region. The Ethiopians have to believe that they will have gotten it back," explained Mullins.

"Why would they buy that?" Kishor asked.

"They have been given a perfect replica by Israel, to prove to them it was recovered," Mullins explained, "And, since no one left alive in Ethiopia has ever seen the real one. . . ."

"They'll never know the difference. So, you want us to lie," Sam concluded. "But, this is all my fault. The priests trusted me!"

"It wasn't you. It was your old assistant, Marjorie," Mullins related sadly.

"Marjorie?" Sam asked, stunned.

"Yes, she also worked for the Archaeology Channel, for years, right?" Mullins said, a question intoning his voice as he read some notes from his folder. "Her story does not really add anything much, so it looks like she was just a pawn being used by the Australian. Seems that he persuaded her by promising her the world if she would help him to get the Ark, as he said, to its most rightful owners. He trumped up some big story to entice her, saying he owned a yacht that would sail the seven sees with her as his wife—he evidently turned on the womanizer act with her."

Sam let out a low whistle. "Wow!" he exclaimed. "I never felt completely comfortable with Marjorie. It was often like she had, well, more than one agenda. I could never quite put my finger on what was up with her."

Turning to Mullins, Kishor looked at him, his eyes steady, as he addressed him: "So, what you are telling us now is that this whole thing has to be reported differently. Well, there is one thing I need you to do for me if you want my help in pulling off your little fairy tale here." His voice indicated that he was deadly earnest.

"What exactly is it that you have in mind?" Mullins asked, a tone of reserve tincturing his voice. "I do have influence in the departments here, but it is not unlimited."

Kishor pulled out a picture of Adane he had taken in Nairobi before he had accompanied Sam back to the United States. "This boy is currently in compassionate custody for displaced orphans in Nairobi; I would like him here and his adoption approved within thirty days."

"I think I can make that happen, sir," Mullins assured.
"You'd better," Kishor glared.

-64-

The doorbell rang. "Sam!" Angela called out, "Our guests are here." As she opened the door, a relaxed-looking Kishor dressed casually in jeans and a tight-fitting black tee-shirt stood, his face smiling. In front of him on the stoop, Kishor's hands resting lightly on his shoulders, was Adane.

"Hey guys!" Angela affectionately rubbed the tight curls of Adane's head before he sprinted into the house and raced back to give her a warm hug. "It is so good to see you! There is no way I can ever thank you for bringing Sam home in one piece. You'll always be one of my heroes."

"It is good to see you, too," Kishor answered as he closed the door behind him. He gestured to Adane who was dashing around holding up a small helicopter: "He looks like he's grown a foot in just a month since our time in East Africa!"

She swished back her shoulder-length hair. "Hey, Kishor, you're doing great with him. He's totally coming out of his shell!" she continued.

From further inside the apartment, Sam entered the room and

embraced Kishor in a bear-hug. Tears welled up in Sam's eyes as he remained in the embrace. "Thank you," he whispered huskily. "Thank you again."

"Hey," Kishor broke away, "This guy on the card came to see me." He passed a business card over to Sam, his finger pointing to a gold-etched name inscribed on it. "They want to do a book and even make a movie about us, the shoot, the whole deal!"

"You're kidding," Sam said looking at Angela, whose smile had become even wider.

"I figure we will have to change some things in the storyline, 'cause no one will ever believe it," Kishor said in hushed voice.

"Yeah, you bet," Sam said. "Well, I had an idea too," Sam continued. "I'm anxious to get back into another dig; not anything like what's been going on the last year, but something much tamer."

"Great! Where are we headed this time? The site of the Red Sea crossing? Goliath's sword? The copper scroll?" Kishor rolled these names off with confidence.

"My, my, someone has been studying," Sam remarked.

Angela entered the room again, bringing iced lemonade from the kitchen on a large tray for them all. The ice clinked invitingly in the glasses.

"No, just watching this smart dude on the Archaeology Channel," Kishor grinned. "I recorded a weekend marathon of your shows while all the paperwork has been going on for getting Adane over here. That's quite remarkable how quickly and smoothly the adoption process has gone, isn't it?" Kishor grinned. "And all fees were even waived."

"So after I almost get you killed, you want another mission?" Sam asked.

"I've got Adane now. So, I cannot be a real commando or body-guard anymore. But I can still go with you, if you can use me if the Lord gives you another expedition," Kishor assured him.

"Kishor," Angela bubbled over, "you sound like you are a believer now."

"Yes ma'am," Kishor smiled and stroked Adane's head. He had come to sit next to him. "We both are." Adane smiled and put his arms affectionately around Kishor's waist.

"I thought I was just taking him to church, but I guess he was taking me. You know, those words that Dar spoke while we were traveling in his taxi did actually guide me and help me come to faith. And the influence of that preacher man, Dr. Adrian Rogers, certainly hit me. I've listened to a lot of his recordings since I have been back stateside."

"Wonderful," Angela beamed. "I love the way he could so clearly explain the Bible and its teaching."

"Adane means 'he rescues, he saves,'" Sam grinned. "He sure is living up to his name."

"So, where is it that we are going, Sam?" Kishor pressed.

"To church," Angela said, interrupting his gaze. Leaning down to Adane, she said, "Do you know what a ring bearer is?"

Sam stood up, opening his arms wide as he drew Angela to himself in a warm embrace, "And I am going to need a best man, Kishor, if you are available?"

-65-

Sam waited at the front of the massive sanctuary, with Kishor steadying him a bit. Brad stood with the groomsmen, his hair less spiky-looking and neater than it had been for several months. The music from the organ reached them, its tones rich, its melody stirring. The smell of roses and chrysanthemums wafted through the building, and light etched the colored glass windows in elegant patterns.

Dressed in a cream-colored suit, Adane walked slowly and with as much importance as a nine-year-old can muster, step by step, down the long aisle. As the bridal march began, the congregation stood up and Angela began her walk down the aisle.

As the music played, Sam smiled broadly. Kishor whispered something to him, and he nodded knowingly, replying, "Okay, but we can't tell her about our next trip, until after we get back from the honeymoon."

"She already knows, Sam," Kishor whispered back. "I think she wants to come, too!"

THE END

About the Author

David Peel is an attorney at law in the Memphis, Tennessee, area. He is a fisherman, author, artist, photographer, Bible teacher, missionary, woodworker, and a family man who loves to travel. *The Treasure of Solomon*, an action-packed faith novel, is his first fiction book, and he plans to write several more. His first non-fiction book, *Two Feet or Ten: What You Don't See When You Drive*, was an Amazon best seller.

Look out for David's next book in this series—it's to be titled *The Treasure of Constantine*.

You will usually find David at his law office with his office mascot,CrashtheLawDog, his English cream golden doodle that seldom leaves his side except when he's in trial. Crash has his own Instagram account and is potentially more famous than his owner.

A recent empty Nester, David has turned his car collection into a side business of www.memphistimemachines.com. Boasting of an accurate cannonball run Lamborghini Countach and a movie-quality, back to the future DeLorean Time Machine, his wife says there are worse things he could get involved in!

David also proudly reports that he is now a grandfather, and known as Papa. He very much enjoys spending time with his grandson or he maybe in his grandfather's vintage 1977 Ford pickup.

www.treasureofsolomon.com